Red Moon & High Summer

Red Moon & High Summer

HERBERT KAUFMANN

Translated by
STELLA HUMPHRIES
Afterword by
ROBIN HANBURY-TENISON

ELAND
LONDON

This edition published by Eland Publishing Limited
61 Exmouth Market, London EC1R 4QL in 2006

First published by Verlag Styria, Köln-Graz in 1960

Text copyright © Margot Kaufmann
Afterword © Robin Hanbury-Tenison

ISBN 0 907871 34 8

Cover designed by Robert Dalrymple
Cover Image: Man Cooking by Camp Fire/Niger
©Michael S Lewis/CORBIS
Map © Dr Heinrich Schiffers

Text set by Katy Kedward
Printed in Navarra, Spain by GraphyCems

Contents

For Judith and Michael Kaufmann,
who so much wanted to come with
us to the Iforas Mountains

Editor's Note

This story of Red Moon and High Summer is complete in itself, but the factual background of the tale, the way of living of the 'People of the Veil', has a fascination of its own. Because this information is not readily available elsewhere to most English readers, we have included a brief note on the Tamashek People, which is, for the most part, based on the lengthier essay appended to the original version in German.

There is also a glossary and some information on the pronunciation of Tamashek words that have been left untranslated.

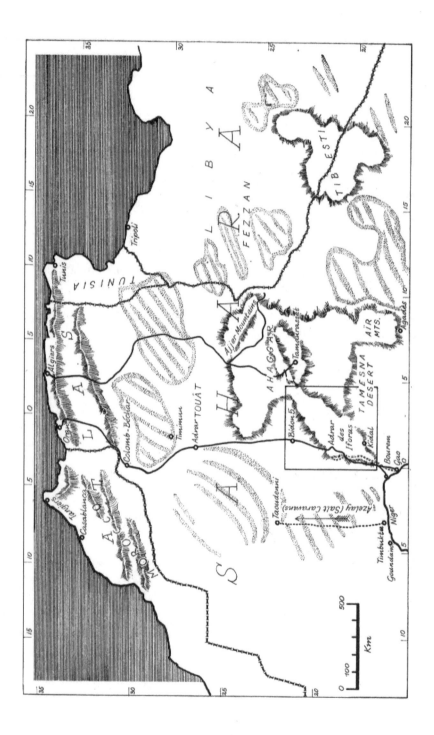

CHAPTER ONE

In Search of a Lost Donkey

MID-E-MID SANG in the North. There the mountains are black and purple and the plains are yellow with *alemos.**
But his songs travelled far and wide from mouth to mouth and from tent to tent. They hummed round the camp fires in the evening, while the millet cooked in its soot-blackened cauldron. They soared from the lips of sun-burnt shepherds, as they tarried with their flocks during the heat of the day in the meagre shade of the acacia trees. The women sang them as they pounded the brittle grey salt in wooden mortars, and it crumbled into fragments beneath the blows of their pestles.

Mid-e-Mid sang in the North. And the wind itself seemed to carry his songs into the green South, to the clans of the Kel Effele, to the Idnan on the borders of the *Oued* of Tilemsi, and to the great tribe of the Ibottenaten, whose camels grazed in the Tamesna Desert.

'Sing us a song, Mid-e-Mid,' said the men when they met the lad with his slanting green eyes, and his tousled hair sticking up on end like a hedgehog's spikes. Mid-e-Mid scratched his snub nose, grinned from ear to ear, and asked for some tobacco first. The men bent down, and groped among the blankets spread out on the sand. They brought out little red pouches, and sprinkled tiny heaps of tobacco in Mid-e-Mid's dirty hands. The boy smelt it and it made him sneeze. Then he stuffed the bone-dry wisps hastily into his mouth. He chewed and spat and coughed and felt very happy. Tobacco is scarce in the Iforas Mountains and much too dear for poor herdsmen to buy. But the Tamashek all love it,

* There is a glossary on page 231

11

men, women, and children too. They chew it until the brown shreds are moist with saliva, and then gratefully spit a jet of pungent juice before the donor's feet.

'I will sing something for you,' said Mid-e-Mid, 'but it will have to be a little song, for I am thirsty. It is days since I had any tea to drink.'

The men looked at each other significantly. This lad, Mid-e-Mid, was a devil of a boy. He conjured presents out of people's pockets as if they grew on thorn bushes in the nearest *oued*. But Mid-e-Mid took not the slightest notice of their reaction. Unconcerned he produced a knife and started carving his wooden staff, and he kept his mouth firmly closed, until someone wavered and fetched a leather bag from his saddle. It contained green tea, a piece of sugar-loaf, thumb-high glasses and a tin can. Someone else brought out charcoal, tinder and flint, and a third ran to fetch the water-carrier, which was made of hairy goatskin.

Mid-e-Mid was in no hurry. He gazed contentedly at the flames which had been kindled with dry grass and withered twigs, and watched closely to see exactly how much tea the men were prepared to sacrifice for a song.

'I like my tea strong,' he explained, 'and with plenty of sugar.'

'You will like what you get,' muttered one man, who wore a magnificent blue robe, but had ugly, prominent teeth.

'All right. But if the tea is so weak, I shall sing the song in a very weak voice, so that you can hardly hear it.'

'You should be ashamed of yourself for being so greedy!' retorted the man.

'I do not see why I should be ashamed of being thirsty. After all, you were not ashamed to ask me to sing.'

The man could not think of a quick answer and said nothing. He wrinkled his forehead, as he watched the other man measuring a glass and a half of tea-leaves into the can. One glass was the usual amount.

'How did you get your name, Mid-e-Mid?' asked one of the shepherds as he put the kettle on the charcoal, which had begun to glow.

'I do not know,' the boy replied. 'It is just my name.'

'I can tell you,' said an older man, who had not said a word so far. 'I knew his father, Agassum, before he was sent to prison, and I was there at the feast when the boy was named Ahmed. Agassum had slaughtered a goat, for many people had been invited. But many more arrived. So Agassum had to kill a second goat. Yes, he proved expensive when he was only a week old.'

'And now he is proving expensive to us too,' interrupted the man with the prominent teeth. 'I should not be surprised if he spends the rest of his life living at the expense of other people...'

They all laughed. But Mid-e-Mid was offended and carved away silently at his shepherd's staff.

'When he grew older,' the old man continued, 'Agassum's womenfolk used to call him 'Mid!' They found 'Ahmed!' too long. But he seldom paid attention when they called the first time, so they had to call him twice 'Mid, Mid!' And the name stuck, didn't it, Mid-e-Mid?'

The boy nodded, bored. He cared nothing about it. The water boiled. One of the men used the bottom of the glass to hammer the sugar-loaf and he mixed the broken pieces with the tea-leaves.

'Why was Agassum sent to prison?' someone asked.

'Ah, that is the fault of a man with whom he did business,' said the old man, hesitating, and glancing at the well-dressed man. Then he continued in a deliberate voice, 'Agassum had bought some guns, which he sold in the North for a good price. He used the money to buy camels. A certain man accompanied him on his journey. Afterwards they quarrelled. The man said that Agassum had not dealt fairly with him, and had given him two young camels less than they had agreed.'

The old man coughed. Water was poured over the tea-leaves, and the brew was left to draw a little on the hot charcoal.

'That was a lie!' exclaimed Mid-e-Mid excitedly. 'My father gave him half.'

'I happen to know that it was not half,' contradicted the man who had tried to serve the tea too weak.

13

Mid-e-Mid spat contemptuously into the sand, and determined to have his own back on the man at the first opportunity.

The old man tried to smooth things over. 'Perhaps he did not give him quite half. But it was Agassum who had had all the trouble getting the guns and selling them, and he had led the caravan. The other man had only travelled with him.'

A thin stream of amber tea was poured into a glass. The old man tasted it and poured it back again.

'Well, they argued so long that Agassum drew his sword from its sheath and challenged the man to a duel. But the other man would not fight. You know how strong Agassum is, and his is no ordinary sword. It is a noble Toledo blade, a splendid sword to be handed down from father to son, when a boy is old enough.'

'One day it will belong to me,' said Mid-e-Mid vehemently, and tossed his head. 'And then I shall take it and split that man's skull right down to his neck!'

The men laughed aloud. And the one with the buck teeth taunted him. 'A little lad who has not yet lived through fourteen rainy seasons should not speak such big words.'

'I am fifteen,' replied Mid-e-Mid, 'and I shall keep my word.'

'Yes, the man rode away, and Agassum kept all the camels for himself. But not for long.' The old man nodded and coughed again for the smoke worried his throat. 'The man went straight to the French authorities, to the Beylik, and said that Agassum had smuggled the weapons to the North. And he said that he could prove it. Then the Beylik sent his soldiers to look for Agassum, and he has been in prison ever since. And the other man got the camels as a reward, for betraying this boy's father,' and he pointed to Mid-e-Mid.

'I shall kill him,' repeated Mid-e-Mid, gritting his teeth, and grasping his knife, as if he were going to attack his enemy there and then.

As their guest, he was handed the first glass of tea. He gulped it down with relish, and calmed down a little.

'He should not have traded in guns,' said the well-dressed man. 'The Beylik had forbidden it.'

'We do not take orders from him!' shouted Mid-e-Mid. 'We are free men!' And his eyes seemed to slant more than ever in his brown face.

'Who are?' asked the other.

'My father and I,' replied Mid-e-Mid proudly.

The men held their blue veils higher to hide their smiles. For they liked Mid-e-Mid, and they did not want to hurt his feelings. Only the quarrelsome fellow laughed openly. 'It is time you learnt obedience, my lad!'

'Will you sing for us now?' said the others, trying to change the subject.

'Yes, when I have drunk my third glass.' They did not hurry over their tea. The sun moved slowly over the acacia tree in whose shade they had camped. The camels lay not far away in the glaring brightness of noon, and stretched their heads into the wind. There was a feeling of well-being, for the breeze was fresh. Far away to the north, rain had fallen in the Ahaggar Mountains and it had cooled the air. There were even a few silvery clouds sailing over the blue sky, like the vanguard of a fleet going into battle.

Then Mid-e-Mid started to sing, and the shepherds bent their heads, drinking in every note. And after the first words of the song, they beat time with their hands. Only one man did not beat time, but listened with obvious signs of impatience.

> At the foot of the mountain a motherless calf
> Wandered alone in its search for the well,
> Searching alone for the yellow *alemos.*
> Soon he was spied by the spotted hyena,
> The spotted hyena, the friend of the weak.

He paused a moment. Then he went down on all fours and mimicked the ungainly walk of the hyena and the way it bares its teeth. The shepherds laughed. But one man did not laugh.

> Follow me, calf, said the spotted hyena.
> I will take care of you if you obey.
> Come to my den, I shall teach you obedience,

> While you sing songs to me, playing your lute.
> So said the hyena and lowered its eyes.

Then the boy changed roles. He put his hands to his temples to indicate a calf's horns. The man who refused to beat time was now the hyena. Mid-e-Mid turned his back to him, stuck an imaginary tail in the air and pawed the ground with one naked foot. And as he sang the last verse, the shepherds shook with laughter.

> Go grind your teeth, oh you spotted hyena!
> Balek! Look out! And take care of yourself.
> You want me to sing for you? Here is my answer –
> How would you relish my hoof in your face?
> That is the song I shall sing, and the angels
> Waiting in Heaven, shall join the refrain.

The man with the prominent teeth gathered up his robes. 'I must see to my goats,' he said.

The others wiped away their tears of laughter. Mid-e-Mid's mimicry had gone straight home. How could anyone fail to notice that the man looked like a hyena, and behaved like one too! Then they grew serious. It occurred to them that if you make fun of people, they may take revenge.

'You should not have sung that, Mid-e-Mid,' they said.

'He insulted my father. But even young calves have hoofs. I shall sing that song again and again, whenever I can, so that everyone in the land hears it.'

'Don't do that, Mid-e-Mid,' they said. 'Sing us *Amenehaya* instead. Please sing us *Amenehaya*.'

And so Mid-e-Mid sang his song *Amenehaya*, with his own words, and the tune he had composed himself. All the Tamashek in the Iforas Mountains knew it. And whenever they sang it, they said, 'That is Mid-e-Mid's song.' But no one sang it like Mid-e-Mid himself.

> Inalaren, lance-bearer, and the son of Intebram,
> Come when the cattle graze in salt pastures,
> Come to the Well of In Tirgasal.

> Bring the proud stallion, Intedigagen,
> Stately and swift, for the grey-haired Magidi,
> Lead him to the Well of In Tirgasal.
>
> Look at the wind as it ripples the grass
> At the foot of the mountains, Adrar and Tigim
> Hard by the Well of In Tirgasal.
>
> Inalaran and Intebram's son,
> Can you see the maiden,
> Milkfed and comely and smelling of spices,
> There at the Well of In Tirgasal?

There were several verses. But the last was the most beautiful and all the herdsmen joined in. Their voices were soft and dark. But Mid-e-Mid's voice rang out like birdsong by the banks of the Niger, when it is time for the first morning prayer. This is how it went.

> Even Magidi, the grey-haired Magidi,
> Dances his stallion in time to the drum-beats.
> At night the warriors sing round the fire,
> Inalaran and Intebram's son,
> Singing the song of the men who are free
> By the ancient Well of In Tirgasal.

When the song was over, the shepherds asked, 'Where are you going, Mid-e-Mid?'

Mid-e-Mid pointed eastwards. 'I am going that way. I am looking for a donkey. It ran away from my mother yesterday.'

The old man nodded. 'I have seen a donkey's tracks. Its right fore-foot turns inwards.'

'That is the one,' said Mid-e-Mid. 'It broke its foot a year ago.'

'I think it was going towards the Well of Timea'uin.'

'Then I should be able to find it,' said Mid-e-Mid.

'It is three days' ride from here,' they told him. 'You will lose your way. There is no water-hole between here and Timea'uin.'

'I have a water-carrier, and my donkey to carry us both. What more do I need?'

'Then you had better be setting off,' said the old man, pointing the direction to the boy. 'Your ass is fresh and if the water-skin is a stout one, it will hold enough for three days. I will show you which are the *oueds* through which you must ride.'

He drew a line in the sand with his finger.

'These are the mountains without a name. They run from sunset to sunrise. You must ride through them for two hours. There is only one path.'

He drew two further parallel lines. 'You must cut across the next *oued*. It is called Tin Bojeriten and acacia trees grow there. There is a steep stony hill at the end of the *oued*, and if you climb to the top, you will see another *oued* before you. That is the *Oued* Timea-'uin. You must ride along it for two days. It will lead you to the well.'

'I can remember all that,' said Mid-e-Mid. 'Tell me one thing, though. Will I find any people on the way?'

'Yes,' said the old man in his kindly way. 'You will find three camps between here and the well.'

'Good,' said Mid-e-Mid. 'I shall ask the people for food.'

'Yes, do,' nodded the shepherds. 'And if at first they only offer you millet, just sing for them, and they will give you meat.'

'I do not sing for food. I sing because I must.'

'Ayé! Listen to him!' they laughed. 'You extorted tea and tobacco from us only a moment ago.'

Mid-e-Mid frowned. 'I should have sung anyway. But I saw that the man with the ugly teeth wanted to make me sing. That is why I asked.'

'Yes, he is a thorn in the flesh,' they agreed. 'But you have made an enemy of him.'

'I do not care,' retorted Mid-e-Mid. 'I shall sing my Hyena song everywhere, from Tadjujamet to Kidal.'

He sprang to his feet and slung the water-skin under the belly of his ass, humming as he did so,

> Balek! Look out! And take care of yourself!
> You want me to sing for you? Here is my answer!
> How would you relish my hoof in your face?

With the word '*balek*', he poked his knee hard into the little grey donkey's ribs, as if he had his enemy at his mercy. The donkey brayed. Mid-e-Mid untied the hobble rope, swung himself on to the ass's back, his thin brown legs clinging to its body, and struck it lightly about the ears with a short stick. 'Forward march!' he ordered, and turning to the shepherds, he called, 'Farewell!'

'*Inchallah* – please God!' they replied.

The old man with the weather-beaten features laid a hand on the donkey's head and barred his way.

'I have something to say to you,' he said slowly.

'What do you mean?' asked Mid-e-Mid.

'It is about the man you mocked,' said the man.

'I do not like him,' said Mid-e-Mid.

'You are quite right. That is Tuhaya.'

'Good,' said Mid-e-Mid. 'I shall remember his name.'

'That is not all,' said the old man and spat. 'He is the man who betrayed your father...'

Mid-e-Mid's face turned ashen. The old man put his hand on the boy's shoulder. 'Think of it night and day,' he said solemnly, 'but this is not the time to do your duty. Wait until you are strong and carry a sword.'

'I am strong now,' said Mid-e-Mid impatiently.

'Not strong enough. And do not forget that Tuhaya is the friend of the Prince, Intallah. Do not forget that.'

Mid-e-Mid wavered. But he realized that the old man's advice was sound. He could never have overtaken Tuhaya riding a donkey. Tuhaya rode a stately camel of noble breed, which took immense strides. Then he said, 'I thank you, old man. I shall wait.'

So they parted.

And Mid-e-Mid rode on to find the lost ass. His blue tunic fluttered in the wind. His heels drummed the donkey's sides. Its small splayed hoofs trotted over the gravel. The sun was high overhead, and the shadow of the rider and his mount was so fore-shortened that it looked as if a jackal astride the shell of a tortoise were making its way towards the mountains.

The shepherds watched him for a long time, shading their eyes with their hands. Yes, it was quite true. From Tadjujamet in the north to the town of Kidal in the south, all the Tamashek knew Mid-e-Mid's songs. And many people knew him personally, a skinny, ugly boy with green eyes, a snub nose, and hair like a hedge-hog's spikes. The herdsmen loved the lad, although they did not show it. But the women showed it openly. They gave him milk and dates and dried meat. And they called him affectionately *Eliselus*. That means happy-go-lucky, or blithe spirit. But they did not call him Eliselus to his face.

And Mid-e-Mid sang and rode, and rode and sang. And when he was tired, he laid his head on the donkey's neck, crossed his feet under its belly and fell asleep.

And the thorny branches of the *talha* tree and the yellow blossoms of the *tamat* acacia, the grey rocks and the sand, the sun and the wind all smiled to see him pass, sleeping as he rode. Only the donkey's head nodded gravely as it trotted eastward, as if it understood perfectly well that it had to make for the *Oued* of Timea'uin.

CHAPTER TWO

In the Marabut's Tent

TOWARDS EVENING, Mid-e-Mid reached the first encampment which the old man had described. From far away he could hear the bleating of goats and a woman's voice.

The woman clicked her tongue, calling '*Dak! dak!*' That was the noise the women used to call the goats in to be milked. So he knew that there would be fresh milk there. And he hurried, for he was very thirsty. He could have opened his water-skin, but the water would be warm, and would hardly quench his thirst. He could not see the woman yet. She was hidden by tall affasso bushes.

Some camel foals were tethered to a tree. They squealed nervously as he passed them and strained at their ropes. Presently he saw the copper-red roofs of the leather tents. A cauldron with a rounded rim hung from an iron tripod over a wood fire. He slid to the ground backwards over the donkey's tail. It was not considered polite to ride straight up to a camp-fire.

He looked round for the woman, and there she was behind him. She was tall and well built and probably about forty years of age.

'*Salam aleikum,*' he greeted her.

'*Aleik essalam.*'

'How are you?'

'I am well,' replied the woman, arranging her headcloth.

She looked at him.

'Are you not Mid-e-Mid ag Agassum?'

'Yes, I am.'

'You are welcome here. I will make you some tea. Unsaddle your donkey and sit down by the fire. The Marabut is milking the camels. He will be here presently.'

Mid-e-Mid liked the woman. She seemed sincere and did not ask questions. So many women would have expected him to relate all the events of the past year before they asked him to sit down by the fire. And there were others who only wanted to hear his songs, and quite forgot that a fellow gets hungry riding.

As he sat down, he thought that he could detect a movement from the tent behind him. But it might have been the wind, for the side of the tent nearest to him was closed with mats.

Mid-e-Mid took a pair of tweezers from his leather scrip which contained his possessions, an enamel mug with a broken handle, and the hobble rope to secure his donkey at night. He started taking a thorn out of his heel. It had been worrying him while he was talking to the woman. But it was not a job one could do in public.

The thorn lay deep and hurt him when he moved it. He pulled a face. As he did so he fancied he heard someone giggling, and he put the tweezers away quickly and sat up straight and serious. And again it seemed that the wind gently lifted the mats in front of the tent.

A man's footsteps approached. Mid-e-Mid heard them distinctly. The dry grass rustled beneath his feet. It must be the Marabut. He did not turn round to face him, for that would have been considered inquisitive and bad manners. He behaved as if he had heard nothing.

The Marabut was broad-shouldered and thick-set. A strong, bold nose curved between high, arched brows. A white muslin head cloth covered his head and concealed his ears, chin and lips. The veiling forced attention to his eyes. They were oval, very big and deep black. They rested on Mid-e-Mid, but showed no surprise. The fingers of his left hand played idly with the wooden beads of the Mohammedan rosary he wore. He stretched out his right hand to Mid-e-Mid, who had risen and pressed his own lightly against the Marabut's. Then each withdrew his hand and placed his fingertips on his breast.

The greeting was long and courteous, according to custom. It served several purposes. It was an interrogation, a cross-examination, and a means of getting to know one another.

'Are you keeping well?'

'*Hamdullillah.*'

'Are your animals in good health, Mid-e-Mid?'

'They are in excellent health, *hamdullillah.*'

'And your family, Mid-e-Mid, are they well too?'

'*Elhamdullillah.*' Here he sighed audibly, as if he had been released from a heavy burden. Now it was his turn to ask questions. He leaned on his stick, his right foot pressed behind his left knee.

'Have your camels found good pasture?'

'Yes, the pasture is very good, Mid-e-Mid. Their humps are firm and their udders are streaming with milk. *Hamdullillah.*'

'Have you many foals?'

'Two, and perhaps another one in a few weeks, *inchallah.*'

'Is your family well?'

'They are well.'

They sat down with their backs to the wind, so that the smoke from the fire should not blow in their eyes. The Marabut handed him tobacco and took a pinch himself.

'Your tobacco tastes good,' smiled Mid-e-Mid.

Both chewed and spat in silence. The woman put some water on the fire to heat. She did not speak. Women seldom take part in the men's conversation unless they are invited to do so. Mid-e-Mid gave her some tobacco and she thanked him and withdrew.

'I know your father well,' said the Marabut. 'Has he been released yet?'

'He has to wait two more rainy seasons,' replied Mid-e-Mid.

'So you are the man of the family?' asked the Marabut and an almost imperceptible smile played about his nostrils.

'I look after the cattle. My older brother tends the camels.'

'How many have you?'

'We have four mares and two for riding. My mother has a baggage-camel. It is very strong.'

'That is good. When your father was imprisoned, there were none left.'

'Oh yes there were!' laughed Mid-e-Mid. 'I had hidden them.'

The Marabut looked at the boy with respect. 'You are a man already, Mid-e-Mid. It is not too soon to give you your veil and sword.'

For the Tamashek, the veil and the sword are the first symbols of manhood, when a boy is old enough to carry arms and his beard begins to sprout.

Mid-e-Mid shrugged his shoulders. 'We are poor.'

'Yes, but with Allah's help, you will have many camels and they will find good grazing.' The Marabut thought for a moment. Then he continued, 'I have a pupil, Ajor Chageran...'

'Ajor Chageran?' asked Mid-e-Mid. 'Intallah's son? He is three years older than I. I have heard it said that my father wanted to call me *Ajor Chageran*, for the moon was red when I was born. But my mother would not allow it. She said that Red Moon was a name for the sons of the nobles. So they called me Ahmed ag Agassum.'

'Your mother was right,' said the Marabut emphatically. 'What would we have done with two moons in the land?'

Mid-e-Mid was silent. He envied Ajor Chageran his name. And for the first time the thought crossed his mind: why must the princes who are so rich in camels and herds also appropriate the most romantic names for their sons? And in spite of himself, he could not help blurting out, 'The moon belongs to everyone, like the sun and the water from the well. Why not names? I am a Tamashek and as good as he is.' He passed a hand over his hair and there was anger in his heart.

'Unhappy the man who is discontented with his lot and chafes at the will of Allah! Are you not strong and healthy with an ass to ride and water to quench your thirst? Have you not found a fire, and a place to lay your head? You are an ungrateful lad!'

'Mid-e-Mid is a cheerful name,' said a light clear voice. 'I like it.'

They turned their heads. The Marabut frowned. Mid-e-Mid was taken by surprise.

The tent mats had been pushed back and a girl was sitting on the ground, her head and body draped in blue. Only her eyes were visible. They were shining brown, and the lids were painted blue with antimony.

'Yes, I like it very much,' repeated the girl, before her father could reprove her. 'But I like the name Ajor too. His name suits him, and yours suits you, Mid-e-Mid.'

Mid-e-Mid's eyes opened wide in astonishment. He had never heard a girl talk like that before. His sisters would not have dared to open their mouths when a guest was sitting by the fire.

'Go and help your mother, Tiu'elen!' the Marabut ordered his daughter.

But she had already jumped to her feet and disappeared, alarmed at her own audacity.

'Please excuse her,' said the Marabut, embarrassed. 'She is still very young. And we seldom have guests by our fire.'

'*Tiu'elen*... High Summer...' repeated Mid-e-Mid.

'She was born before the rains came, that is why... But I wanted to show you these tablets.' The Marabut reached for two small tablets made of wood.

'What are they?' asked Mid-e-Mid.

'They are chapters from the Koran. My pupils learn to read them, and they can repeat them by heart.'

'Ajor is your pupil, is he not?'

'Yes, but he is leaving me now. Intallah wants his son near him.'

'Oh! And have you no other pupils?'

The Marabut shook his head thoughtfully. 'There is a vacant place in the tent,' he said.

The woman came to see if the water was boiling yet. She remained crouching near the fire, and looked at Mid-e-Mid attentively.

'When Ajor goes...' said the woman, and she looked at Mid-e-Mid as if she expected him to answer.

Mid-e-Mid felt his heart pound. The Marabut was a deeply respected man. If anyone in the tents fell ill, he came and prayed near the sick bed. Some patients recovered quickly. To others he gave a little leather amulet shaped like a purse, and painted black or brown or red or yellow. It was worn round the neck next to the skin and brought health, and protection against the evil eye. Sewn inside was a strip of paper with a few verses from the Koran. But very few people knew that, for the Marabut told no one but his pupils.

In return for his prayers and the amulet, the family of the sick man would give the Marabut a sheep or a goat. If it were a very serious illness, they gave him a cow. They never gave him a camel.

Mid-e-Mid thought, if I could fill this place in his tent... He thought, if I learn to draw these curious signs on wooden tablets and even to understand them... He also thought, Tiu'elen likes my name. And I like hers... High Summer.

'You must ask your father,' said the Marabut.

'No. I do as I please,' replied Mid-e-Mid, sticking out his chest.

'But you must ask your mother,' said the woman. 'Perhaps she needs you badly.'

'His brother is there,' said the Marabut. 'You will learn a lot here. You will be able to read the Koran. You will be able to recite prayers by heart. With the help of Allah, you will be able to heal the sick...'

The little can of water was now boiling rapidly. The Marabut became wholly absorbed in making the tea.

Mid-e-Mid spat out his quid of tobacco. 'My mother would not stop me. My mother forbids me nothing,' he said. But he knew that his mother would not like him to go away. She loved him more than his brother. Long ago he had observed that she took much more trouble over him, asked him questions, watched over him – this was sometimes trying – and she had taught him to sing and to write. His brother had been packed off to look after the livestock.

'You must ask your mother,' repeated the woman seriously.

The Marabut did not agree. 'Riding three days through the *oued* to look for a donkey is work for a man. Mid-e-Mid is old enough to decide for himself.'

Then his wife held her peace. Mid-e-Mid said, 'I can do all kinds of work. I can ride and I can guard the camels. I can follow tracks. And I am not afraid of the hyena.'

'That is good,' said the Marabut. He filled the glasses and handed Mid-e-Mid the first one. 'A hyena stole one of our calves.'

'Give me a good sword,' interrupted Mid-e-Mid quickly, 'and I will kill the hyena. I will go to its lair...'

'It is a big hyena,' said a clear voice.

It had grown dark by now, and there was High Summer standing near her mother. The red glow of the fire shone on her bare feet, and her face was deep in shadow. Mid-e-Mid did not pay any attention to her openly. But he stole a glance at her from the corner of his eye. She resembled her mother, but her face was lighter and fresher and the mouth was softer. Her hair was combed smoothly back from a centre parting. She wore golden earrings. Her robe was as tattered as his own. She was a little taller than he, and perhaps she was a little older.

'Yes, it is a big hyena,' agreed Marabut. 'I will go with you.'

'Ajor was not brave enough to tackle the hyena,' said Tiu'elen.

'I have no sword. That is why.' Red Moon had approached them so noiselessly that no one had seen him come. Or perhaps High Summer had seen him, and had said the wounding words deliberately. Girls often say hard things, but their hearts are tender.

Ajor gave Mid-e-Mid his hand. He did it with the dignity of a grown man and the condescension of a Prince's son. No one could doubt that Red Moon was one of the sons of the nobles. He was so tall at eighteen that he overtopped the Marabut by a head and a half. Even in the fire-light, his skin could be seen to be much lighter than Mid-e-Mid's. The fine straight nose, the narrow lips, the deliberation of his movements all revealed the son of Intallah. And Intallah was the greatest tribal Prince among the Tamashek. There was no mightier chieftain in the Iforas Mountains. And it was not only his own clan, the Kel Effele, who called him *Amenokal*. That means King.

'My father will lend you a sword,' replied Tiu'elen.

27

'Go to your tent,' the Marabut ordered her, flashing his great searching eyes.

High Summer withdrew. Only a faint scent of attar of roses remained. And even this was soon lost in the smoke of the fire. But Mid-e-Mid was aware of it, and Ajor breathed its fragrance, gratified. The flask had been his parting gift, and he had asked her mother to give it to Tiu'elen. His present had been accepted. The Marabut had praised his generosity.

They drank their tea. Ajor sat down by the side of the Marabut, and said, 'I met a man riding a four-year-old camel. He came from Timea'uin. He rode in great haste.'

The woman unhooked the cooking-pot from the tripod and put it to one side to let the food cool, for the millet was cooked.

'Why did he not come to my tent?' asked the Marabut.

'He was on his way to his clan. He was an Idnan. Some of their tents are pitched by the Well of Telabit. It was bad news. Abu Bakr has arrived at Timea'uin. The people are fleeing and driving their cattle before them.'

The Marabut placed one hand on Ajor's knee. 'Are you sure the man spoke the truth?'

'Quite sure,' replied Ajor quietly. He drank a second glass of tea.

'That is bad news indeed,' said the Marabut.

'I have hobbled the camels with a triple rope. You can hear them now. They are grazing near the two *teborak* trees.'

'If Abu Bakr has camped at Timea'uin,' suggested the woman, 'perhaps he will make for the north-east and the Ahaggar Mountains.'

'I do not think so,' said Red Moon. He spoke very slowly weighing every word. But his voice was soft and husky and one had to get used to it. 'The man was convinced that Abu Bakr is on his way to attack a date caravan, which is due to arrive any day from the North. Their route leads through this *oued* as you know. It is ideal for holding up a caravan.'

'That is true,' said the Marabut. He had still not drunk his first glass of tea. 'But I am afraid that Abu Bakr is coming here for a different reason, not the date caravan.'

'The man knew that some herds belonging to his people were grazing towards the west,' Red Moon went on. 'He wanted to warn them.'

'He did not think of warning us,' said the woman indignantly.

'He was not one of our tribe,' said Ajor. 'The Idnan are not like us.'

A jackal whimpered. It sounded like a tiny child who has cried in vain for its mother for so long that it has not much strength left.

'Abu Bakr is armed,' said the Marabut, and shook his head.

'Yes,' said Ajor. 'The man told me that Abu Bakr wears two ammunition belts crossed over his breast, and a third belt round his body. He also said that Abu Bakr has a gun with a strange tube along the barrel. When he looks through this tube, he can hit the eye of a gazelle at five hundred paces. I do not know if it is true. But that is what the man said.'

'It is quite true,' said the Marabut sombrely. 'I knew the man to whom it belonged originally. No one knew what became of him. The Beylik had a search made. But he was never found.'

'Why doesn't the Beylik arrest Abu Bakr?' asked Mid-e-Mid. 'Everyone knows that he is the most terrible brigand in the land. He has stolen many camels, and they say that he has killed men too. My father never killed a man, but the Beylik...'

Red Moon turned full face to the boy. It was a long, clever face, with a high, straight forehead, the forehead of a thinker, and sharp eyes, eyes which could command.

'My father Intallah told me that Abu Bakr lives in the mountains between the Well of Tin Ramir and the Adrar Hassene Mountains. The soldiers dare not penetrate into that territory. They do not know where to find water. Abu Bakr knows. He knows all the hiding places too.'

'I have seen the Beylik's trucks driving through the desert,' retorted Mid-e-Mid. 'Why does he not use them?'

'Trucks are all right in the open desert. But only if there is a track. There is no road for cars in the mountains. Only camels can climb the mountain paths. That is what my father said.'

Mid-e-Mid would not be put off. 'The Beylik has many camels... '

The Marabut nodded. 'The Beylik has camels, but Abu Bakr's are better. He has stolen them whenever he could. And so he travels faster than this pursuers. And then, as Ajor told you, only he knows where to find water.'

'The Beylik has aeroplanes, too,' said Mid-e-Mid. He said it more to provoke Red Moon than from conviction. He had heard aeroplanes often enough and had seen them too, but he knew nothing about them. He had no idea if it would be possible to catch Abu Bakr that way.

Nor did Ajor know if it was possible to capture a bandit with an aeroplane. He thought for a moment. 'No,' he decided. 'Aeroplanes are too fast and too high. They could not see Abu Bakr. As soon as he heard one in the sky, he would hide beneath an overhanging rock. No, the Beylik's aeroplanes are not a serious danger to Abu Bakr.'

The Marabut gulped his cold tea and poured out another glass all round. He coughed. The night air was growing chilly. The woman placed the pot of unsalted millet in front of the men and went away. She and her daughter would eat when the men had finished.

'People say that Abu Bakr carries information about the Beylik's enemies to Kidal,' continued Ajor. 'And the Beylik has many enemies, more than there used to be.'

'Do they want to steal the Beylik's fine camels?'

Red Moon smiled. 'No. They want to overthrow the Beylik and hound him from the country and make themselves rulers.'

'Ayé!' said Mid-e-Mid eagerly. 'That is good. Then I, too, am the enemy of the Beylik. If we get a new Beylik, my father will be released from prison, will he not?'

'Possibly. But then it may be someone else's turn to be locked up.'

'Why must there be a prison? There are no flocks there. And there is no milk, fresh from the camel. There is not even sheep's milk. It is very hard for a Tamashek to be imprisoned. He is better off with his herds. Prisons are no good for anyone. People have died there, simply because they could no longer ride over the desert nor sleep in a tent. My mother says so. It is true.'

The Marabut reached for the cauldron and took a handful of millet. '*Bismillah*,' he said briefly.

Then Red Moon helped himself. Only Mid-e-Mid stared at the pot and ate nothing.

'Eat!' said the Marabut kindly. 'Or are you not hungry?'

'Yes, I am hungry, but... but... tell me, Ajor, if Abu Bakr renders services to the Beylik, is he not my enemy too?'

Ajor smiled again. But there was no warmth in his smile. It came from his head, not his heart.

'Of course he is your enemy. Abu Bakr is every man's enemy. For him there is no Beylik. He steals and kills, and when he needs more ammunition, he simply sells the camels he has stolen in the faraway markets of the South, where no one knows the brand marks on their necks.'

'Yes, Ajor. But what about your father? He is the Amenokal. Surely he knows that they are our camels, the property of the Kel Effele people. He knows that, doesn't he? Yet he does nothing to capture Abu Bakr.'

'If Allah wills, Intallah will capture him,' said the Marabut.

Mid-e-Mid was not satisfied. He thought, the Amenokal must protect his tribe. If he fails to guard his people...

Then he started to eat hungrily and crammed the food so hurriedly into his mouth, that he burnt his tongue. But the thought of Abu Bakr worried him still.

'I shall keep watch tonight,' he announced abruptly in a loud voice.

'And when Abu Bakr comes, you will run away,' jeered Ajor. 'Lie down and go to sleep. Abu Bakr does not steal donkeys. If he comes, we shall protect ourselves. My father has shown me how to throw a spear...'

The woman reappeared and poured rancid butter over the millet. They set to with renewed appetite as if they had eaten nothing so far. Soon the pot was empty. They groped in the sand for thorns to pick their teeth.

High Summer brought a calabash with water. They drank in turn. Each man took a mouthful, spat it into his hands, rubbed his face with it, then took another mouthful and spat it into the sand.

The girl watched them.

'I shall keep watch all the same. I have no lance like you. But I know how to use my stick. I once killed a jackal that tried to steal a kid...'

Red Moon was about to reply. But Tiu'elen spoke first.

'Will you sing something for us, Mid-e-Mid? People say that you have a lovely voice.'

'They exaggerate,' replied Mid-e-Mid. As it was dark, no one saw the blood mount to this cheeks.

'Do sing for us. Please.' She brought him a mat and sat down close by him. He felt her knee against his, and the fragrance of the rose perfume was intoxicating.

'If you sit so close, I cannot sing,' he said in torment.

So High Summer went and sat near Ajor Chageran. That was just as bad, if not worse. But he had to sing all the same.

The Marabut's wife was scouring the cooking-pot with sand. When she saw that Mid-e-Mid was going to sing, she stopped, although she had not quite finished. The Marabut threw a branch on the fire. It smoked a little before it burst into flame. The ants beneath the bark had no time to escape. They could hear them sizzling to death.

'What shall I sing?' asked Mid-e-Mid.

'Your song!' said High Summer eagerly.

'Which one do you mean? I have made up quite a lot.'

'The Song of the White Camel – I like that best. Please sing that one.'

Mid-e-Mid replied, 'It is too long. I shall only sing the first verse.'

'Yes,' they said, 'just sing.'

And Mid-e-Mid sang the Song of the White Camel. Or rather, the tune was the same, but the words seemed to change of their own accord, so that Tiu'elen came into the song. Mid-e-Mid himself did not know exactly how it happened. But this is what he sang.

> Tell me, O shepherds, have you seen Tiu'elen?
> The blue of antimony darkens her eyelids.
> Fairer is she than the swift gazelle
> Soaring in flight from the spear of the hunter
> Over the sunlit dunes...

Here he broke off. Without meaning to, he had composed a new song. And it had nothing whatever to do with the White Camel.

High Summer pulled her headcloth over her forehead. Her face was hidden as she said, 'Thank you, Mid-e-Mid. No one can sing like you.' She got up and ran into the tent. She did not come out again that evening, although Mid-e-Mid sang many more songs.

At last they were all tired. The Marabut stretched out both his hands to Mid-e-Mid. 'I shall keep Ajor's place free for you...'

'Let me think it over,' said Mid-e-Mid.

Then he took his stick and went out into the night. He had to be alone with his thoughts.

Ajor and the Marabut turned to the East and recited the evening prayer. They made sure that the camels were safely hobbled, and they decided to put out the fire, so as not to draw attention to their presence if Abu Bakr chanced to pass that way. But Abu Bakr did not come that night.

CHAPTER THREE

The Raid

A BU BAKR CAME next morning. Mid-e-Mid had held a watch far into the night. He lay close to his donkey and felt the warmth of its fur against his back. He could hear the snapping and crackling of twigs, for the camels were grazing not far away. He felt the light breath of the bat fluttering uneasily round his head. His feet grew cold, but his head was still afire. Poems flashed like shooting stars from his lips, a moment's glory, then quickly extinguished.

He could still see before him the sharp cut features of the Marabut as he said, 'There is a vacant place in the tent.' He could see Ajor's high-spirited and intelligent face. And ever and again he could see the lovely face of Tiu'elen. 'She is beautiful, very beautiful,' he murmured to himself. Then he remembered that he was poor, and that Red Moon was very rich, and could offer her father camels and goats as bridal gifts.

One day, he thought, when I have the sword that my elder brother never wears, one day when I have killed Tuhaya, one day, I shall ask her to be my wife. And I shall sing for her as I have never sung before. I shall sing of the tents, of the cool waters of Tin Azeraf, and the green *oued* close by Kidal. I shall sing of High Summer. Yes, I shall sing of Tiu'elen.

High Summer shall decide between you and Ajor, said the voice of the Marabut. Yes, said Ajor. She shall decide. But Mid-e-Mid drew his blade from its sheath of red leather. Let the swords decide! And in his angry determination to stake his very life, the tears started from his tight-shut eyes. His hands gripped the hilt of the sword. Then the donkey brayed. Mid-e-Mid was clutching its fur.

The braying woke him up. It was very cold. His arms and legs were covered with goose-flesh. He crept practically underneath the donkey to get warm. Tomorrow, I shall tell the Marabut that I will be his pupil. I shall find the donkey at the Well of Timea'uin, and take it home to my mother. And then I shall return. Yes, that is what I will do.

The thought of Abu Bakr flashed through his mind. He cocked an ear and listened. The night was still. The stars winked like eyes of silver in the sky. A jumping mouse rustled in the grass. The Marabut's camels were lying down. He could hear the placid grinding of their big flat teeth. They would go on chewing until the first red light of dawn.

There seemed no point in keeping watch any longer. Nestling closer to the donkey he fell asleep and snored with open mouth. He did not feel the ants crawling over his face. He slept the deep sleep which comes as a reaction to great excitement.

Abu Bakr arrived with the grey of dawn.

He was not a man to move softly, unless he wanted to. 'Ho there!' he called 'Marabut! Ho there!' and as there was no immediate reply, he chopped at the two front tent-poles with his sword. Part of the leather roof fell on the sleepers.

Red Moon was the first to crawl out from under the tent. Abu Bakr did not wait for him to get up. He struck him across the side of his head with his fist. Ajor lay there like a felled tree, without uttering a sound.

'Marabut! Ho there!' called Abu Bakr. And there was a brutal cheerfulness about his voice.

'I can hear you,' called the Marabut from under the tent.

'Come out then! We must talk!'

The Marabut emerged, clutching his rosary in his left hand and gripping his sword in his right. But as he lifted the leather folds and tried to stand upright, he stumbled over the sword. Abu Bakr stamped on the blade and roared with laughter.

'Each man to his trade,' he shouted as he tore the beads out of the man's hand and flung them in his face. 'A Marabut should not tamper with the sword, and a brigand should not meddle with the rosary. You can pray later, you good-for-nothing priest... How many camels have you?'

'What harm have I ever done you?' asked the Marabut bitterly.

'Listen,' said Abu Bakr and in the grey half-light, his figure in its flowing *burnouse* stood out like a jagged rock, dark, threatening, implacable. 'I have little time, and less patience. How many camels have you?'

The Marabut saw the ammunition belts like a crude black cross on Abu Bakr's breast. He could not see the barrel of a gun, but he knew that the brigand never travelled without his long-range rifle.

'I have two mares with foals, one in foal and two riding-camels.'

'The young ones and the one in foal you can keep. I shall come for them next year. Who is there in your tent?'

The Marabut felt his heart race. He did not know if his wife was still inside the tent or not. Tiu'elen had quietly lifted the mats at the other side and crept into hiding. He had seen her as he was struggling to get out himself.

As he did not answer, Abu Bakr slashed at the tent with his sword. The blade went through the leather like water. He stabbed the walls twice more. Then he hacked at the six remaining tent poles. The roof lay like a coarse shroud over all the Marabut's worldly goods.

'Take me to your camels,' thundered the robber's voice.

The first red light of day suffused the landscape, the dry thorn bushes, the *teborak* and the *talha* trees, the soft carpet of *alemos* and the tough *affasso* bushes. Pink and yellow tufts of clouds floated in the blue-grey of the sky. At last the sun rose like a pale streak above the horizon, too weak to give out any heat. The Marabut could feel the chilliness of the pebbles and the gritty sand beneath his naked feet. Behind him came the brigand's heavy tread, the creaking of his leather belt, the dragging of his sandals.

'*Allahu akbar*,' he murmured. 'God is great.' And he sighed.

The camels lay where Red Moon had left them the previous evening, under the *teborak* trees. They turned their long necks uneasily towards the men and got up nervously as they approached.

'Unhobble them,' Abu Bakr ordered, sword in hand.

The camels bellowed as they always do, when they think that someone is going to make demands on them.

Mid-e-Mid awoke. A fist was hammering on his breast.

'Listen, Mid-e-Mid, listen!' whispered a voice.

He looked up. High Summer knelt before him and her eyes were like dull coals. There was a scent of roses. Her hair was loose and fell over her shoulders.

'He is here,' she gasped.

'Who is here?' asked Mid-e-Mid. He could not make out what she wanted.

'Abu Bakr! And you were fast asleep!'

'I... I...' stammered Mid-e-Mid.

'Quietly – if he hears you... Mother and I ran away... now...'

'And Ajor?' asked Mid-e-Mid. 'Where is he?'

'I think he is dead,' said the girl. 'Abu Bakr knocked him down.'

'What about your father?'

'He is alive, but Abu Bakr is going to steal our camels. He has made my father show him where they are.'

'I shall kill Abu Bakr,' said Mid-e-Mid and was about to spring to his feet.

'No,' said High Summer and pressed against his shoulders to try to stop him from getting up. 'He is much stronger than you are and he is armed.'

But Mid-e-Mid pushed her aside. 'Leave me alone,' he said. 'Women can run away and hide. Men fight.'

He seized his stick and jumped to his feet. He could hear Abu Bakr's voice and Tiu'elen's pleading call, 'Mid-e-Mid!' But he ran on. He saw the Marabut bending down to unhobble the camels. He saw the robber's powerful back and his round head. He saw the milky gleam of the sword and he heard the animals snarling. He did not stop to consider that he was a mere slip of a shepherd boy and that his opponent was a strong man in the prime of life. Blind with rage, he darted like an arrow from the bow and sprang at Abu Bakr like a wild cat attacking a mountain sheep.

The first blow caught Abu Bakr on the back of the neck. The second fell on his arm. Then the stick broke and Abu Bakr ducked and spun round. He grabbed Mid-e-Mid by the arms. His hands gripped the lean flesh like bands of steel. Mid-e-Mid felt himself lifted high into the air and dashed to the ground. He did not feel the kick that followed. He was unconscious.

Abu Bakr looked at him inquisitively. 'A young lion,' he said feelingly, as he rubbed his neck. 'Is he one of your brood, Marabut?'

'He is Mid-e-Mid, Agassum's son,' answered the Marabut.

'That accounts for it,' growled Abu Bakr. He prodded the boy with his foot. But Mid-e-Mid did not stir. 'He has the face of a hedgehog, but the heart of a stallion,' he went on 'Take a rope and bind him fast – hands behind him'.

The Marabut obeyed. The brigand dangled his sword. He watched to make sure that the cord was tightly fastened.

'Who was the man I knocked down in front of the tent?'

'Ajor Chageran, Intallah's son,' said the Marabut and rose to his feet.

'Tell Intallah not to send his cattle and donkeys so far to the north. These are my feeding grounds. His are further south.'

The Marabut said nothing.

'Go over there,' ordered Abu Bakr, 'there, by the two rocks. Do not turn round, or I will shoot. Stay there until the sun begins to grow warm. Then you can go back.' He pointed to the ruined tent.

The Marabut clenched his teeth and stumbled away over the stones. The tiny hooks of the *cram-cram* grass lodged in the cracks between the horny skin at the ball of the foot, but he did not feel them. His eyes were wet, for even men have tears. But they were not tears of pain. They were tears of anger. He did not see Abu Bakr roping the camels together and securing them with a leading string to his own mount. He did not see Mid-e-Mid slung over the crupper of one of the camels and firmly tied in position. He did not hear the beasts howl as Abu Bakr swung to the saddle, prodded his camel's neck with his toes and trotted off. He thought that Ajor was dead and feared the worst for his wife. When he reached the rocks, the sun was so bright that it dazzled him. He bent down and cleansed his arms, hands and face with sand. Then he bowed towards Mecca, recited the morning prayer in a loud voice, and found the comfort of Allah in the repetition of the call.

For nearly two hours, Abu Bakr rode through the *oued* in the direction of Timea'uin. Towards eight o'clock, he made a halt between two leafy thorn trees.

He did not make his camel kneel to dismount. He swung his legs over the cross on the pommel of the saddle, then slid down the camel's neck to the ground. The tree on the right had green thorns and tiny white blossoms. The lower branches had been eaten bare by the goats. But the higher branches cast deep shadows, and hundreds of flies and bees, attracted by the scent, buzzed among the foliage. Only the highest tip of the tree was shorn of its blossoms and leaves, for grasshoppers had stripped its crowning glory.

Abu Bakr went up to the tree and broke off seven thorns. He threw them down on the sand and trod them in with his foot. That was to propitiate the spirits who live in these trees, who would otherwise torment him. Then he made the camels lie down. He tugged at the leading-rope of plaited goat's hair and leather.

'*Sho!*' he cried. '*Sho! Sho!*'

Slowly, reluctantly, the great beasts bent their fore-legs. Laboriously, the rump followed. Abu Bakr untied the blackened, greasy rope which held the saddle in position, and removed the vivid blanket with its pattern of red and black and white and green, and spread it in the shade.

When the camels had been unsaddled and had risen again, he hobbled them and removed their bridles. They looked about them timorously, and slouched off hesitatingly towards the trees, for the *oued* was unfamiliar. It was quite some time before they stretched out their necks and ventured to tear off a few leaves and thorns.

Abu Bakr turned to Mid-e-Mid who lay where he had dumped him, still tightly bound.

'Well?' he asked curiously.

Mid-e-Mid gave him a look, then shut his eyes to indicate his abhorrence.

Abu Bakr knelt down and loosened the cords which had cut deep into the boy's skin. He untied the string of the water-skin and filled a beaker with cold brown water.

'Drink,' he ordered. 'It is cool. The water-skin was hanging on the shady side of my camel.'

Mid-e-Mid screwed up his eyes and emptied the beaker at one draught. The water refreshed him. But his arms and legs were stiff with cramp.

Abu Bakr brought him a second beaker. Then he stretched himself out on the blanket, one arm resting on the saddle, and gazed thoughtfully at his human booty.

Mid-e-Mid drank the water in little gulps. He did not know if he could count on a third cupful. Abu Bakr's face was absolutely expressionless. He had taken off his veil. His black hair fell in tangled locks round the nape of his neck. His forehead was shaven. A thick, strong nose stopped short above full lips. The thin growth of hair which covered his cheeks became heavier towards the chin. His sleeveless blue tunic was new. Heavy grey bracelets of stone cut into the flesh of his upper arms. A brown woollen *burnouse*, such as the Arabs wear in North Africa, lay in a careless bundle at his feet. His whole bearing spelt toughness, and at the same time, a kind of coarse humour, a wild beast of prey, who would laugh sardonically, if his victim tried to scratch.

But the strangest feature about the man was his eyes. They were slanting like Mid-e-Mid's. But there was not a trace of the boy's impishness and love of mischief. They were melancholy, even gloomy, a pale green in colour, like rain-water which has lain too long in some ravine, rejected by the sun. The round head set on its short neck added to the impression of massive strength, which the powerful body indicated.

'Well?' asked Abu Bakr again.

Mid-e-Mid rubbed his legs. The blood in his veins, constricted for several hours, had started to flow freely again, but it pricked and tickled painfully. He sat in the sun. He did not dare sit on the blanket.

But I am not afraid of this man, he thought. What about High Summer? Had Abu Bakr knocked her down too? He thought, I shall run away when he is asleep. The idea obsessed him. He looked hard to see how the camels were hobbled and where Abu Bakr's gun lay.

The brigand followed his glances unmoved. 'You will not run away, Mid-e-Mid,' he said in his deep voice. He drew a dagger from the girdle which secured his voluminous black trousers. 'Do you see what this is?'

'*Bussaadi* – a dagger,' said Mid-e-Mid, and although he had not felt frightened before, his heart missed a beat. It bodes evil to show a man a dagger. It usually means that he has not long to live.

'Yes, a dagger,' repeated Abu Bakr, pleased. 'I have another one in my saddle-bag. I might make you a present of it.'

'Me?'

'I can see that you have courage. There are not many people who would dare to attack Abu Bakr with a stick.' He cleared his throat. 'And of those few who tried it, not one has lived to tell the tale.' He stuck out his lower lip. 'Yes, I might give you that dagger if you will stay with me. I would make a man of you...'

'I only want to find my mother's donkey,' replied Mid-e-Mid.

'Donkeys? Let beggars worry about donkeys. Abu Bakr and his friends ride camels, the noblest beasts between the Adrar of the Iforas and the Ahaggar Mountains. Forget about your donkey.'

He pulled the saddle-bag towards him, and felt inside for a dagger in a red leather sheath. He balanced it in his hand, then threw it over to Mid-e-Mid.

'It is yours.' Abu Bakr's sad eyes fastened on the boy.

'I do not want it,' he said, and laid it in the sand near by.

'I thought that Agassum's son would be a man, like his father, but...'

The robber's eyelids drooped and he played with an amulet which hung on a black cord round his neck.

'Do you know my father?' asked Mid-e-Mid surprised.

'We are friends. We are also kinsfolk. The father of your grandmother and the mother of my mother were brother and sister.'

In sheer amazement, Mid-e-Mid opened his mouth and passed his tongue over his lips.

'So you see, you struck your uncle,' said Abu Bakr. His laugh boomed ominously.

'I did not know,' Mid-e-Mid apologized, and looked uncertainly at the ground.

'You know now. Have you not noticed that we have the same slanting eyes? And the same fearlessness?'

'The eyes, yes.' But Mid-e-Mid's mistrust was not allayed. There was something sinister and terrible about this man. His nose appeared to thicken when he laughed, his body became more massive and threatening.

'And we have the same enemies, Mid-e-Mid.'

Mid-e-Mid listened.

'Come and sit near me,' said Abu Bakr. 'I will tell you.'

Mid-e-Mid sat down on the soft blanket, but remained at a safe distance from the brigand.

'You know who sent your father to prison?'

'The Beylik.'

'But the Beylik would never have caught him if he had not been betrayed.'

'Oh! You mean Tuhaya! When I find him, I shall kill him.'

Abu Bakr sat up with a jerk. 'That is what I like to hear, Agassum's son.'

'But I am not a brigand,' said Mid-e-Mid firmly and pursed his lips.

'No. I am the brigand,' and Abu Bakr's laugh boomed out once more. 'And there will never be another like me. But you are my nephew and I like you. We are of one blood, and that is why I shall help you to find Tuhaya.'

'Why is Tuhaya your enemy, Abu Bakr?'

'Tuhaya is a jackal. He eats what the lion has slain and the hyena spurns. I steal camels, that is my trade and a good trade too. I shall teach it you. You have had your first lesson today.' He scratched the stubble under his chin.

'I did not like it,' protested Mid-e-Mid.

'Think things over before you decide. Well then, to get back to Tuhaya, I said that he was a cowardly jackal. Now and then I get him to sell the camels I have captured. It is I who steal them, not he. It is I who brave the tents, not he. But now I know that he will betray me as he betrayed your father. I know that the Beylik has given him money to reveal where I pitch my tents.'

'Does he know the place?'

'He is the only one who does. And now he is preparing to betray me. But I have friends in the land too. I shall not wait for the soldiers to come and get me.'

He leapt to his feet with one bound, remarkably agile for a man of such heavy build. He poked Mid-e-Mid with his foot.

'Mid-e-Mid – I mean you well. Here, take this.' He put his hand to his girdle and held out his sword to the boy. At first, Mid-e-Mid hardly dared to touch it. It was one of the best swords in the land, and it was so famous that it bore its own name. It was called Telchenjert. It commanded the same respect as a pedigree camel, a beautiful woman or a noble thoroughbred horse. Abu Bakr was giving him Telchenjert! He fingered the finely worked leather, the inlaid hilt with its copper head.

The bandit drew the sword from its sheath. The supple blade sparkled in the sun. He took the point and bent it back to the hilt. Then he let it spring back again.

'You will not find another sword to compare with Telchenjert,' said Abu Bakr. 'It is yours, until Tuhaya has tested its edge.'

Mid-e-Mid passed his fingers over the bright steel, the dark notches in the metal, and the ancient inscriptions, for the sword was centuries old. It was the Portuguese who brought these swords to the coast of Africa. And the caravans had sold them to the Tamashek. It had been passed down from father to son. And much blood had stained it. But the blade was as keen as ever.

No, there was not a sword like it in the Mountains of the Iforas. There was not a single Tamashek who would not have given much to possess it.

'What must I do for it?' asked Mid-e-Mid, looking up at the brigand's head, like a rugged globe outlined against the blue of the sky.

'Avenge your father,' answered Abu Bakr. 'I will tell you a secret. Tuhaya is going to Timea'uin tomorrow. He has promised the Beylik to deliver me into his hands. That is why he has asked me to meet him five hours north of Timea'uin in the Soren Oued. But the Beylik has a troop of soldiers lying in wait. As you see, Tuhaya is a jackal. He does not fight himself. He would not fight your father. Do you know that he refused to fight with him?'

'Yes, I know,' said Mid-e-Mid.

'Now we are going to take a short cut. We shall surprise Tuhaya, and you will do your duty as a son, and I will help you.'

'Suppose the Beylik's soldiers find us?' said Mid-e-Mid.

'They will arrive too late,' replied Abu Bakr firmly. 'Do not worry about them.'

Mid-e-Mid held the sword in both hands.

'I shall do it,' he said gravely.

'Choose a camel for yourself,' said Abu Bakr.

Then Mid-e-Mid remembered that they were the Marabut's camels and that Abu Bakr was a brigand.

'I do not want one,' he said. 'I shall go on foot.'

Abu Bakr looked at him and understood the reason for his refusal.

'You will ride,' he ordered. 'If you wish, you may return the Marabut's camel afterwards. I do not need it. I shall take Tuhaya's instead.'

Then Mid-e-Mid went to get a camel. Abu Bakr gave him an old blanket and he folded it and placed it in front of the camel's hump, for there was no saddle for him. They set off, although it was already getting hot. The robber was in a hurry to confront Tuhaya before the meeting place they had agreed.

They rode at a trot and gave the camels no respite. The animals trotted in step, their ears laid back, their bridles held so tight that their heads were silhouetted against the sky. Up and down swayed the long necks. Up and down swayed the men in the rhythm of their riding. Mid-e-Mid found it difficult to keep up with Abu Bakr. His was the better camel. It flew over the stony *reg* and the soft powdery sand with equal indifference and ease.

They crossed cattle tracks, skirted rocky boulders and grey heaps of crumbling granite. They met no one. The land was parched and gave no grazing for livestock. Not even a goat could have survived here. A soft steady breeze blew sand in their eyes. They fastened their veils high over mouth and nose, so that only a slit was left for the eyes. They rode on a long way. They saw the shadows to the left of the camel dwindle, vanish and reappear on the right. Their direction was north-north-east and their goal was the head of the Soren Oued.

In spite of their pace, they made hardly any sound. The soft soles of the camels rose and fell noiselessly. Occasionally a stone rolled or a dried twig snapped under the powerful hoofs. Only the camels' heads stretched stiffer and stiffer. They snorted, and damp spray from their nostrils was blown towards the riders. The sky was a pitiless blue. In the distance rose the Mountains of Samak, a violet ridge on the horizon.

It would be difficult to say what was going on in Abu Bakr's mind. His face was expressionless behind the veil, his dull eyes fixed attentively on some point in the distance. He felt so sure of his companion that he did not once glance back. Mid-e-Mid pressed his feet hard against the camel's neck and he was conscious of the muscles rippling between his thighs, and the weight of the sword on his left hip.

Only yesterday, he had set out in search of a donkey, and today, he was hunting down his man, the man who was to blame for his father's long imprisonment. Yesterday he was still a boy, a carefree singer of songs. Today, he carried a robber's sword, and wore his veil like a man.

Tuhaya, he thought, I am coming. Tuhaya, I have Telchenjert by my side. He thought, if High Summer could see me now... If she could see that I am not just a singer of songs... If she saw me avenge my father... If only she were here...

And in his mind's eye, he saw himself leap from his camel, and pluck Telchenjert from the scabbard. He heard the clash of blade against blade, and felt the point pierce the heart of his enemy. He recalled how, as a child, he used to take his father's sword from the tent, and play at fighting a tree, slicing away at its thorny branches, and uttering shrill war cries, until his mother called, 'Mid-e-Mid, go and milk the cows. It is getting dark...' Now Telchenjert hung by his side, and the unsuspecting Tuhaya was on his way to meet him in the Soren Oued.

When I have killed him, he thought, I shall take back the Marabut's camel, and I shall ask High Summer... I shall ask her...

'Tiu'elen!' he said aloud. And he fitted the syllables to the rhythm of his riding. But only the wind heard her name. And the sound trembled on the breeze, like the cry of a cheetah calling to its mate.

And so they rode to Soren. And whenever they came to the top of a hill, they could see the Mountains of Samak. But they disappeared from view as they descended into the hollow valleys. On the evening of the second day, they called a halt among the rocks at the western approach to the Soren Oued. And Abu Bakr said, 'Be prepared to kill your man.'

'*Inchallah* — God willing,' replied Mid-e-Mid.

And for the first time since he had made up his mind to challenge Tuhaya, he felt a twinge of fear.

CHAPTER FOUR

Plot and Counterplot

THE SOREN OUED is bounded north, west and south by low hills. Towards the east, the *oued* extends further than eye can see. Behind the hills on the southern flank, a rocky range is visible. It stretches away into the distance, lengthening into a long black massif and enclosing the approach to the Well of Timea'uin to a tortuous camel track which winds along hard up against the cliffs. Close by the path, meanders a narrow river bed with numerous dried-up water-holes and dark green bushes. The place seems made for a surprise attack.

Abu Bakr guessed that this was where the *goumiers*, the Beylik's soldiers, would lie in wait for him. That was why he had made a great detour to the north to spend the night on the western flank of the *oued*. His only precaution for the evening was to light a fire of pressed camel dung, not of wood. It gave out very little heat, but burned with a paler flame.

The sun had already set and left behind a sky covered with blood red clouds. Dead acacias stood out against the blue-grey dusk like charred and mutilated skeletons. The rough voices of shepherds called to their cattle and camels, and the whimpering of sheep, the braying of asses and the curious bleating of goats filled the plains. Dust rose in tired clouds, driven along towards the south-west by the evening breeze.

As night fell, the *oued* seemed to come to life. Twinkling eyes of red indicated campfires. The tents squatted black like humped beasts, from whose unseen throats rose the cries of women and children. From far and wide, year after year, the tribes of the Tamashek drove their herds over the endless steppe to and from the Soren Oued, and sometimes, too, there could be seen the dark, closed tents of the Moorish Kounta, a powerful tribe, who were not Tamashek, but disputed water and grazing rights with them.

There was so much coming and going that no one took any notice of new arrivals or departures. All the same, Abu Bakr was careful not to send his camels out to graze before it was dark. His famous stallion, Inhelumé, was far too striking, and could have given away his master's presence. Inhelumé was a salt grey beast, with a thin elongated head and liquid brown eyes. A strikingly strong, arched breast bone, stronger even than that of a plump baggage camel, indicated great powers of endurance. And indeed, he was a tireless runner. There were faster camels than Inhelumé, but none which could be ridden so long and so steadily at a sharp trot. That was how Abu Bakr managed to leave all his pursuers behind him.

Then again, Inhelumé was completely confident on mountain tracks. He knew how to set his feet so surely on a mountain path, that the sharp flints did not hurt the soft pads of his soles. If need be, he could even be ridden at night over the mountains. The rider could leave him to find the windings of a path for himself without hesitation. Only where the way forked, might he need a gentle pull at the bridle to show him the direction.

Inhelumé was not a particularly big animal. He might have been taken for a youngster. But he was eight years old and had already half his camel's life behind him. He owed his name to the peculiar black stripes on his coat. These stripes ran from the hump to the thighs of his hind legs and they looked like the ropes with which the Tamashek secure their blankets and light packs. These cords are made of black goat's hair, and they are called *inhelumé*.

Abu Bakr had a secret way of calling the stallion to his side, which the animal obeyed on the instant. Nevertheless, there was a tacit understanding between them that this call would only be used in case of emergency. Usually, Abu Bakr went to find his animal like any of the shepherds. Despite the hobble, the camel could wander off during the night as much as eight miles in his search for fresh twigs or thorns which are rich in water. During times of danger, the brigand would keep him within ear-shot and could summon him with a hissing noise.

That evening, Abu Bakr did not let Inhelumé out to graze. He secured him with double hobbles and told Mid-e-Mid to do the same with his camel. Then he climbed a hill and listened. But the wind was blowing from the wrong quarter. He could hear plainly the voices of the herdsmen and the women calling in the goats. But he waited in vain for the unmistakable sounds which a troop of soldiers makes. In the parched air of the desert they could be heard from far away. There was nothing he could do until it was really dark, and he returned reluctantly to the camp. There Mid-e-Mid had prepared some tea.

For a time they sat silent by the dull fire, each with his own thoughts. The biting smoke crept into their clothes and worried their throats.

Mid-e-Mid thought, why did my father never tell me that Abu Bakr was one of our kin?

There was no dishonour in being a brigand in the eyes of the Tamashek. And among camel and horse thieves, Abu Bakr was respected for his outstanding courage and intrepidity. Others stole in the dark of night. Abu Bakr was not afraid to show himself by day at the well, and demand a sheep. He would simply seize one from the flock, cut its throat as it struggled and let it bleed to death. Then he would hang it from a tree by its hind legs, and through a slit in the body he would draw out the heart, liver, kidneys and the fatty intestines. Lastly he would skin it and throw the hide to the owner and bellow, 'Here is a present for you!'

If the man to whom the sheep belonged thought that he would at least be invited to share the meal, he was very much mistaken. Abu Bakr would roast the ram on a wooden spit over the fire, and would eat the whole carcase, including the head. The intestines, and especially the eyes, were considered delicacies, and he would eat them first. What remained when he had eaten his fill was hardly enough to tempt a jackal.

Abu Bakr would rise from his meal fortified, mount his camel and drive his herds peaceably towards the mountains. There amid all but impassable ravines, lay his feeding grounds. No one dared to follow him. The rifle across his back spoke a language which had no words, but no one could misunderstand.

Mid-e-Mid thought, we have neither meat nor grain. We must surely go hungry this evening. He had not tasted food for twenty-four hours. He felt in his pocket for some tobacco and found a little. He pushed it into his mouth and chewed.

Abu Bakr said, 'Tuhaya has some food with him. Tomorrow we will eat our fill.'

A camel called after her foal. It was a dull protracted boom, deeper in pitch than the short howl a camel usually makes when its rider mounts or dismounts.

A sickle moon arose. It was growing cool. Mid-e-Mid could feel a great weariness creeping over his limbs. He rolled himself up in his robes, laid his head on his arm and fell asleep at once. But Abu Bakr did nothing of the kind. On the contrary, he got up to test the hobbles once more. But as he was returning to the fire, which had burnt down to a faint glow and could hardly be seen even a short distance away, he stopped abruptly.

Among the dry noises of the night, the rustling of beetles, the chirp of crickets, and the crunch of the sand beneath his feet, a strange sound froze him in his tracks. He thought he heard someone slip a safety-catch. He turned suspiciously to Mid-e-Mid. But he could make out the curled-up figure of the boy, lying still like a dark clod of earth in the bluish light of the moon. When the night wind dropped for a moment, he could hear his light breathing. Abu Bakr dropped flat on his face. Like a sand viper, he crawled between the *affasso* bushes, circled the camp site and crouched behind a rock. He saw that his gun lay undisturbed by the fire.

I must have made a mistake, he thought. But suspicion was second nature to him. He possessed an instinct that told him when there was something unusual afoot. And he trusted this instinct completely, like an animal.

For the best part of an hour he remained crouching behind the rock without moving. If anyone had been watching, they would have taken his round head for a boulder, ground and polished by the restless sand to the shape of a skittle. Such shapes are quite common among the rocks. They look as if human hands have formed them, but they are capricious toys of nature.

Just as he thought it would be safe to get up, he heard whispering. At first, he could only hear the soft murmur of human voices. But as they came nearer, he could distinguish the words.

Someone said, 'You are mistaken, Mohammed.'

The person addressed as Mohammed replied, 'No, I am not. I know Inhelumé's tracks as well as my own camel's.'

'It is too dark now,' said the first voice. 'Let us turn back.'

'He cannot be far away,' said Mohammed. 'I can smell the smoke of his fire. It is made of camel dung. That can only be his fire. The shepherds burn acacia wood. That smells quite different.'

Abu Bakr had recognized one of the speakers, Mohammed Tuhaya. The other must be one of the *goumiers*. Possibly there were more of them behind. It was senseless to take on an unknown number of adversaries in the dark. He must use his advantage to get away. Light as a feather, he made his way to Mid-e-Mid, shook him awake, and hissed in his ear, still heavy with dreams, 'Follow me. Tuhaya is here.'

He seized his gun, but left the blanket on the ground, so as to make no sound.

He made a detour away from the fire. Mid-e-Mid followed hard on his heels. They crawled along in the shadow of the bushes, keeping their heads well down, and their eyes fixed on the ground. The breaking of a twig, even a rolling pebble could have betrayed them. Thorns hooked themselves into their feet, but they took no notice. Abu Bakr paused to sniff the wind. They had covered almost three-quarters of circle. He calculated that they would be behind the troop by now and he was about to rise when he heard a familiar sound. Someone was trying, unsuccessfully, to suppress a belch. Abu Bakr realized that he must have strayed into a line of men, widely spaced to comb the whole area. They were working their way stealthily along the ground, one after the other, like automata obeying some remote control.

It would be madness to fight against such superiority of numbers. He would be lucky if he could save his skin. Softly he touched Mid-e-Mid's hand and pointed to the place where Inhelumé was grazing. Apparently the *goumiers* had paid no attention to the camels. The *oued* was full of animals and only by daylight was it possible to distinguish the spoor and the characteristics of the famous Inhelumé.

Abu Bakr brought his mouth close to Mid-e-Mid's ear. 'You will have to sit behind the hump,' he whispered. Mid-e-Mid nodded. His skin tingled with the imminence of danger. He no longer thought of running away from Abu Bakr. The strength, the animal sureness of the robber's personality drew him like a fire to which a wanderer stretches out his hands in the chill of the night.

This was hardly a time for contemplation, but he would have been surprised to learn that it was not his impending duel with Tuhaya that suffused him with a profound feeling of well-being. It was the joy of the hunt. He did not know if he were the hunter or the hunted. He could not see where his enemy lurked. But the overpowering breath of the hunt filled the air. He could smell the sweat which fear exudes. And he could not have said if it came from his own body or someone else's. Waves of danger, of unspoken threats surged round him and he shivered. Is it fear? he wondered.

Why should I be afraid? he answered himself silently. I have Telchenjert by my side. And he was suddenly aware that his fist had been clutching the hilt of the sword all the time. It felt warm and moist.

Abu Bakr made a hissing noise, like a snake when danger threatens.

Inhelumé stopped nibbling. He cocked his head in the direction from which the sound had come. Abu Bakr hissed again. He heard a whisper, 'There is a viper about,' and then two or three steps like men scurrying out of harm's way.

The camel moved towards them. His feet were hobbled and he could not run. He jumped with his forefeet together, then drew his hind legs after, step by step. The hobble dragged behind. But it was a sound that is heard a thousand times in the night, wherever there are camels grazing. It aroused no suspicion.

Inhelumé stopped when he reached Abu Bakr. He unfastened the hobbles. That was easy, for they consisted of a short loop with a thick knot. His fingers groped high along the animal's neck until he could feel the mouth. With his left hand he gripped the nose-ring, while the right stroked the soft upper lip of the camel. Slowly Inhelumé bent his head.

'*Sho!*' whispered Abu Bakr in the camel's ear.

Obediently the great beast knelt down. He did not bend his hind legs, however, for his master had flung himself on to his back with one powerful spring. Mid-e-Mid was astounded. He had never in his life seen a camel mounted without a single grunt. Camels invariably protest, either by uttering their hideous complaint, or even by trying to bite.

Abu Bakr had folded his *burnouse* beneath him for a cushion and now he threw a noose round the camel's mouth with a skilful throw. There was no time to secure the cord to the nose-ring. He reached a hand to Mid-e-Mid and lifted up the slightly built lad like a fish on a hook. Mid-e-Mid sat behind the hump and held on tightly with both hands to Abu Bakr's belt. He felt the animal's coat warm between his thighs. He gripped its body with his legs. Then he saw Abu Bakr take his rifle and fire.

The shot whipped through the air and whined aimlessly, as bullets do when they meet no resistance. Missed, thought Mid-e-Mid. But he did not know what Abu Bakr had tried to hit.

The brigand jerked the camel sharply to the left and kicked him so ferociously in the neck that the animal reared and in spite of the darkness, set off at a gallop which made the wind bite round the heads of the riders.

'Look out, Tuhaya!' shouted Abu Bakr. 'I'll have your head yet, you jackal!'

The answer came in a shower of bullets. But they sang harmlessly through the air. They heard the excited voices of the *goumiers*. Fragments of sound reached their ears, calls for lights and for the camels. Then the night swallowed them and, for the moment, they were out of danger.

Abu Bakr slowed down a little and after a time Inhelumé fell into a steady trot.

'Did you see how it was done?' he asked, pleased with himself.

'Yes,' said Mid-e-Mid. 'Your camel is incomparable.'

'You are right,' agreed Abu Bakr. 'There is no camel in the land like Inhelumé.'

'What were you shooting at?' asked Mid-e-Mid and tried to find cover behind the older man's thick body, for the night wind pierced his thin garments.

'Nothing in particular. I only wanted to show them that I had out-witted them. They almost got us. You were fast asleep.'

'Indeed, I was tired and hungry.'

'Tomorrow we will shoot a gazelle,' said Abu Bakr. 'Now we have to ride and gain time.'

The pale moon gave only poor visibility. Abu Bakr was heading for Samak. He had no water with him and he had to reach the well before his pursuers and get hold of a water-skin somehow. Without it, he could not travel any long distance.

It was hard going without a saddle. After an hour, the boy's limbs began to ache. But Mid-e-Mid said nothing. He tried to make himself more comfortable by sitting on his hand, but it went to sleep and he had to take it away again.

At the northern edge of the Soren Oued stood great cairns, like the petrified figures of giant watchmen. Their black shadows fell across the track. Pebbles rumbled into the gullies whenever the camel's feet trod too near to the edge of the chasm. One false step was enough to send them plunging headlong to their death. Or a hole, only a foot or two in depth, could break a camel's leg and send the riders over its ears on to the rocks below.

Eventually they reached the far side of the range and rode over gravelled sand which rattled like grains of corn beneath the camel's broad hoofs. Clouds blew up and settled like still white flocks around the moon. A jackal screamed and a chorus of other jackals joined in, whining. Once a hyena howled. Then Abu Bakr's laugh boomed out. 'Do you know what he says?'

'No,' replied the boy.

'It says 'Tuhaaaya's flesh'. Listen when it calls again.'

And the hyena howled a second time and Mid-e-Mid seemed to hear that it really cried 'Tuhaaaya's flesh'.

'That is so,' he said.

'Soon... soon it will crack his bones... Are you tired?'

'No,' answered Mid-e-Mid, but he was so tired that he could have cried.

'We are nearly at Samak,' said Abu Bakr. They had been on the way for about five hours and had kept to a trot when the going was good.

The moon had set. Only the stars showed them their direction.

When at last they halted, the water-hole at Samak lay in a hollow before them.

'We can sleep until sunrise,' said Abu Bakr. 'Then we shall get water and eat and ride on.'

Mid-e-Mid did not ask how they would carry water, nor did he ask what they would eat. He lay down where he had dismounted. Abu Bakr covered him with his *burnouse* and then settled down himself near the camel, still holding the leading rope in his hand. He had tied the animal's feet so that it could not get up.

When the sun rose yellow and red over the Samak Oued, neither of the sleepers had moved an inch.

CHAPTER FIVE

In the Samek Oued

T HE WATERING-PLACE of Samak is simply a shallow hole in the sand of the *oued*. Although the water is a light-grey in colour, it is good to drink. But it sometimes happens that the animals taint the water. Then it tastes bitter and the shepherds dig a new hole with their hands, and they cover the old one over with thorny twigs to stop the young animals from falling in.

As Mid-e-Mid and Abu Bakr approached from the southern slope, only two men and a few women were there with their herds of goats and little mouse-grey donkeys. By their dress, it looked as if they came from the Ahaggar Mountains. And indeed, they told them that they were Kel Ahenet, and had made the tedious trek to Samak to find water and undisturbed grazing for their flocks.

They were poor, timid people. They recognized Abu Bakr, and feared for their scanty possessions. Mid-e-Mid was a stranger to them, for they had no contact with the Tamashek of the Iforas Mountains.

'Are you alone in the *oued*?' asked Abu Bakr, reining in his camel.

'No – some other families will come at noon.'

'Are they Kel Ahenet, like you?'

'Yes – that is so.'

'Why are they coming later? Is there not enough water here?'

They shook their heads. 'There is water enough, good water,' they replied. But there was no grazing in the *oued* itself, they explained. *Alemos* for the cattle, juicy *djir-djir* and yellow blossomed acacia for the camels grew only two hours away.

Abu Bakr stroked his chin. 'Water my camel,' he ordered.

The Kel Ahenet pointed to the water-hole, which was carefully covered over with thorn branches. 'The goats have fouled the water,' they said. 'Wait until noon. We shall have dug a new hole by then.'

'I am in a hurry. Water my camel,' he barked.

Without a word, the men and women began to tug at the branches and drag them away from the water. But their faces betrayed their fear and anger. Only a little naked boy went up to Mid-e-Mid in a friendly way and touched his hand.

'Give me some tobacco,' he said.

'I have none,' growled Mid-e-Mid. He would have liked some tobacco himself, but his pocket was as empty as his belly.

The boy looked at him dubiously. 'Is that the truth?' he asked.

'The truth before Allah,' said Mid-e-Mid.

'Then give me tea,' demanded the boy, his hand outstretched.

'I have nothing, no tea, no sugar, and no rice either,' said Mid-e-Mid angrily.

The boy stepped back a pace. 'You are hungry, aren't you?'

'Yes, I am.'

'Come,' said the boy, 'eat.'

He led him to a tall tree, where caravans used to halt with their herds. The ground beneath was littered with camel dung. It was a tree of great antiquity, blackened with the smoke of countless fires, and its twisted branches were covered with dark red resin.

The boy pointed to a wood fire. Close by was a heap of wet tea leaves, the remains of the morning brew.

'There is a lot of sugar with the tea,' said the boy. 'Eat.'

Mid-e-Mid bent down and grabbed the leaves. He crammed them into his mouth, chewing avidly. They were bitter and moist, with here and there a lump of undissolved sugar. He devoured them very quickly. Meanwhile the boy went back and watched the men and women drawing water in the goatskin bucket.

They had dug a small trench in the sand and placed a calf's skin over it. Into this they poured the water and Inhelumé drank it in huge draughts. If the skin was empty before the dipper had been refilled, he threw back his head and shook it vigorously. This movement uncovered the bit and allowed him to suck in the cooling air, which he blew out again in a fine spray.

Time and again, the bucket was lowered into the hole. There was no quenching the camel's thirst. His body swelled visibly until it was tight and round and still he gulped the muddy water, mixed with earth. When at last he looked away, no longer interested in the calf skin before him, he had drunk over twenty-six gallons. The shepherds' muscles ached, and their horny hands were hot from handling the primitive dipper.

Abu Bakr kept his eyes fixed on the southern bank of the *oued*. On that side, one conspicuous tree stump had been levelled and encircled with walls of dressed stone. These were high enough to give a man cover from bullets if he kept his head down, and stout enough to withstand a prolonged attack. Flying buttresses strengthened the fortification, which commanded the narrow entrance to the *oued* and the water-hole itself.

The Beylik's soldiers had occupied this position for some years by the time the Second World War came to an end. They had protected harmless shepherds and their livestock from marauding bands who made the countryside dangerous. Now that things had settled down again, the soldiers had been withdrawn. The ramparts lay silent in the sun. The air grew hot and shimmered against the blue of the sky and the whole landscape of lifeless stone seemed to vibrate.

The Fort of Samak had vivid associations for Abu Bakr, good ones and bad. He was one of those who had lain in wait by the watering place, day after day, to demand tribute from the herdsmen. He had fired at those very walls and bullets had been fired at him in reply. There was a deep scar in Abu Bakr's body, and from time to time it broke down and festered. The bullet that lay buried there had come from the Fort of Samak. He did not know who had fired it.

The thought of those days did not usually worry him. But with something like the sensitivity of a hunted animal, he had an apparently irrational horror of revisiting places where his life had been in danger. He had never been near Samak since he was wounded. Only the direst necessity had forced him to overcome his reluctance now. And even so, his misgivings were so great that he hardly supervised the watering of his camel, but watched the fortification with mounting anxiety.

His pursuers could not possibly have caught up with him yet. He had over an hour's lead, according to his calculation. And he had not lost even half that time so far. But he was uneasy and vague premonitions spurred him on to leave as soon as possible. He drew his veil high over mouth and nose, right up to his eyes, as if he wanted to protect his face from impending evil.

'What have you to eat?' he demanded of the Kel Ahenet.

Frightened as they were, they thought that they had done enough by watering the camel. They plucked up courage and said, 'We have nothing, for our tents lie far from here.'

But the little boy who had shown Mid-e-Mid where the tea leaves were, said, 'We have some millet.'

One of the women made a sign to him to hold his tongue. But it was too late. The boy was terrified at his blunder and ran away to hide behind the rocks. He could not understand why no one had invited the strangers to share their food, as was the custom.

The women went reluctantly and fetched the pot of millet.

'You seem to have forgotten the laws of hospitality,' said Abu Bakr.

They apologized. 'We did not want to offer it to you. It is not done yet.'

Abu Bakr plunged his right hand into the cauldron, rolled the grain into a ball with his fingers, lifted his veil with his left hand and pushed the food into his mouth. The millet was only half-cooked.

'Butter,' he ordered.

They poured rancid butter over the mash and watched while Abu Bakr and Mid-e-Mid wolfed it down, hot and raw as it was.

These men are very hungry, they thought, and suddenly they realized that they must be on the run. Their self-confidence returned.

With his mouth still full, Abu Bakr pointed to a donkey under whose belly hung a water-skin. 'Tie that on to Inhelumé's saddle,' he said. No one moved. The Kel Ahenet behaved as if they had not heard. Mid-e-Mid did not dare to look at them. In spite of his hunger he could hardly swallow the millet. It choked him. Abu Bakr got up, rubbed his hands clean with sand and turning to the man nearest him, he struck him a ringing blow on the side of his head. The man clutched his ear. The other man ran to get the water-skin and slung it on the camel. The women fled, shrieking.

Mid-e-Mid was disgusted at Abu Bakr's brutality. He wished that he had run away from him and could not understand why he had stayed. Could he not have paid for what he took? His mother had always taught him that if you want a sheep, you must give a goat. If you want a camel, give an ox. If you have nothing to give and want to eat and drink and be received as a son in a strange tent, then be pleasant and sing them a song...

It was a long time since he had given his mother a thought. Now her words burned him. He untied the thongs and cords which bound his iron knife to his arm. It was not a good knife. Its wooden handle was worn, and the blade was jagged. He threw it to the man whom the robber had struck. 'For the water-skin,' he said softly.

The knife fell in the sand. The man did not stoop to get it.

Abu Bakr growled, 'Keep your knife, you will need it.'

Mid-e-Mid shook his head. Even the common fight against Tuhaya and their distant kinship could not bridge the gulf between them, between the singer and poet and the brigand who not only robbed when he was hungry, or when he saw something he wanted, but simply to show that he was still a power in the land.

Yes, Mid-e-Mid and Abu Bakr were as different as soft skin and tough leather, as are the scent and the thorns of the *tamat* tree, as are love and callousness in the hearts of men.

The brigand kicked over the cauldron with his toe. The millet broth poured out into the sand. He looked around. 'Have you no camels?' he asked.

60

The man replied, 'You can see there are none. Otherwise we would have given you one for your son.'

'I am not his son,' said Mid-e-Mid.

'We have no camels,' replied the man. 'I speak the truth.'

With a sharp movement, Abu Bakr took his gun from his shoulder. The Kel Ahenet threw himself to the ground screaming, 'It is the truth, by God, I swear it!' But the weapon was pointed at the stone wall, or rather at the path which led down from the fort to the *oued*. The man's screams stopped and he looked towards the path. And Mid-e-Mid saw a man on a camel. He was riding fast towards them, but his figure was still nothing more than a blue blur on the camel's back.

Abu Bakr did not wait for him to get nearer. He did not hail him and he expected no greeting. He fired and hit. The man fell. The camel trotted on a few paces further, and then stood still indifferently, as if nothing out of the way had happened and his master would soon come to fetch him.

When Abu Bakr had made quite sure that there was no movement behind the stone walls, he mounted Inhelumé and rode over to the man. Mid-e-Mid came running behind him with huge strides. The two Kel Ahenet came too. Only the women did not move, but peeped furtively from their hiding places.

The man was not dead, but it was plain to see that he was mortally wounded. Abu Bakr looked at him from the height of the saddle. He did not know him. He was not a *goumier*. He was old and poorly dressed. He had shot an innocent man. 'Who are you?' Abu Bakr asked.

The old man's face was the colour of wax. His mouth was open, and there were big gaps between the teeth. His breathing was hardly perceptible. His eyes were already shadowed with the inevitable end. But as Mid-e-Mid hurried up, the old man stared at him and his lips trembled. But he did not speak, and turning his head to one side, he died.

Mid-e-Mid stood as if rooted to the spot. The man before his bare feet was the one who had told him about Tuhaya, and had described the way to Timea'uin, when Mid-e-Mid was still looking for his donkey. Yes, it was the same friendly old man who had listened to his songs with the other shepherds.

Abu Bakr watched him. 'You know him?' he said.

'I spoke to him once. He was very kind.'

'I took him for Tuhaya,' said Abu Bakr. 'He arrived at the wrong moment in the wrong place. I have to save my skin. I cannot wait for the other man to shoot first.'

'He did you no harm,' said Mid-e-Mid dully.

'He will never harm me now,' replied Abu Bakr coldly. 'You cannot tell if a man is your friend or your enemy until he is dead. Over there...' he pointed to the fortress, 'there were soldiers quartered. They did not know me, but still they fired. Here,' and he lifted his robe high, so that the broad pink weal was visible in the brown flesh above his hip, 'they did that to me, although they did not know me either.'

'But he was an old man,' protested Mid-e-Mid.

'He would have died soon anyway,' said Abu Bakr and gave a bitter laugh. 'Death comes for every man – for me too.'

He turned to the Kel Ahenet who had stood there in silence. 'Bury him,' he told them.

He pointed to the dead man's camel. 'Take the camel, Mid-e-Mid. This is no time for talking. We must be off.'

'I shall stay here,' said Mid-e-Mid defiantly.

'If it is the will of Allah, the innocent must suffer. That is something you must learn in life,' said Abu Bakr. 'If Allah wanted to take him to Paradise, who are you to say it is wrong?'

Mid-e-Mid did not reply. His sadness overwhelmed him and he could not think clearly.

'You think that just because you are an honest lad, there is justice in the world. Look at me, Mid-e-Mid. When I was your age, I wanted to be a good man too. See what I am now. Do you think I have any regrets? No. Allah willed it so. Allah is great.'

Mid-e-Mid looked hard at the brigand. The boy stood, legs wide apart, and lifted his head to him. Then he said, 'I only want to do what is right, Abu Bakr. That is all.'

'*Elhamdullillah.*'

'If people cannot trust each other, how can they be friends?'

'There are no friends, Mid-e-Mid. Think of your father. Think of Tuhaya.'

The Kel Ahenet were digging a hole with their hands.

'Come on now,' Abu Bakr urged him. 'We have no time to lose. Let us be off.'

'I am staying here.' Mid-e-Mid was stubborn. 'I have never injured anyone. I want to...'

Abu Bakr's patience was at an end. 'Have the ants you trample underfoot ever hurt you? All right then! Stay here and lick the dust from Tuhaya's sandals.'

He clicked his tongue, dug his spread toes into Inhelumé's neck and turned away to leave the *oued*.

Mid-e-Mid watched him uncertainly. He swallowed hard.

Without warning, bullets spurted round him in the sand, and the echo of the salvo resounded fourfold from the rocks.

Abu Bakr forced Inhelumé into a gallop. His *burnouse* fluttered behind him like a brown flag, and thin clouds of yellow dust rose behind the camel's hoofs and were torn to shreds by the wind.

The second burst of fire could not reach him. He had swerved to one side, and disappeared among the underwood and brush.

Mid-e-Mid did not wait for the second burst either. When he thought about it afterwards, he did not know how he had sprung on to the back of the riderless camel. Crouched in the saddle, he followed in Abu Bakr's wake, blind to everything except the fear of death.

Shots were fired behind him. He kept his head well down to the cross on the pommel of the saddle, and his bare heels urged the beast to such speed, that foam welled up round the bit. As soon as he reached the cover of the trees, he turned round. But the *goumiers* were not following. *Hamdullillah*, he thought. They have ridden through the night to overtake us. They are tired.

He had no idea that it was the dead man who had saved his life. When the *goumiers* reached the body, they jumped down and spoke to the Kel Ahenet. They asked them many questions, which they could not answer. They wanted to know about Mid-e-Mid.

'Who is the man on the second camel?' they asked.

'He is a young lad,' they replied.

'Why did he run away?'

'You fired at him.'

'We were firing at Abu Bakr,' they protested loudly.

Then they asked, 'What is his name?'

'Mid-e-Mid,' said the Kel Ahenet. 'That was what Abu Bakr called him.'

The goumiers cried out in astonishment. 'Mid-e-Mid?' they kept asking. 'Do you mean Mid-e-Mid who sings so beautifully? The son of Agassum? Has he slanting eyes? Is his mouth as wide as a frog's? Are you sure you heard aright?'

One man pressed to the fore. He was not a *goumier*. He wore the blue robe of the Tamashek and was older than the soldiers. His upper teeth were ugly and widely spaced. He was the last to ride into the *oued*, and by then, Abu Bakr was out of sight and the men had already slung their rifles on their backs again.

The man laughed maliciously and said, 'Agassum is the Beylik's enemy and Mid-e-Mid takes after him.'

'Mid-e-Mid is very young,' said the *goumiers*. 'It is news to us that he has thrown in his lot with Abu Bakr. We thought that he lived with his mother, and we know that he goes from tent to tent among the Tamashek singing his songs...'

Tuhaya said, 'Did you not know that Abu Bakr and Agassum were kinsmen?'

'No – we did not know that,' replied the *goumiers*.

'You know it now,' said Tuhaya. 'You can catch two jackals in one trap.'

The leader of the *goumiers* answered. 'Our orders are to arrest Abu Bakr. We know nothing of Mid-e-Mid.'

'Why do you not pursue them?' asked Tuhaya.

'We must water our camels first. Then we shall follow them.'

The Kel Ahenet said, 'He has stolen one of our water-skins.'

The women came up and begged for tobacco. The *goumiers* gave them some. Then they saw to their camels. There were eleven *goumiers* and eleven camels to be watered, as well as Tuhaya's mount. They forgot about the murdered man. Only the naked little boy ran up to the corpse and looked at it for a long time. Then he threw handfuls of sand over it. When it was lightly covered over, he ran back and begged for tobacco. The soldiers were generous with it, for they were good-natured fellows, and had only just received their pay. And it amused them to watch the child spit.

When they eventually set off from Samak, the fugitives had a considerable start. But their tracks in the sand were so clear that the *goumiers* had no difficulty in picking them up.

The tracks pointed towards Tirek.

CHAPTER SIX

The Life of a Brigand

IT WAS THREE DAYS' ride to the Well of Tirek. This was the only path of escape open to Abu Bakr, the way to the North, the way to the arid heart of the desert. He knew that the *goumiers* would hunt him in groups as the Tamashek hunt lion, day and night without tiring. They were men of his people who followed him, even if they wore the Beylik's uniform.

He would reach Tirek first. But they would follow him still. He would penetrate further into the desert, perhaps into the Ahaggar Mountains, if they did not bar his way. But that is just what they would try to do, for they knew as well as he that there was no grazing for a camel northwards from Tirek. He must make for the oases of Algeria, provided Inhelumé could hold out so far.

Yes, Inhelumé would hold out for a long time, longer than the best of the Beylik's camels. But even the strongest animal reaches the limit of its endurance if it is overtaxed. Abu Bakr knew what happens then. He had seen it more than once in his lifetime. The camels goes on literally until its last breath. Then it simply collapses under its rider and dies. And once his camel is dead in the heart of the desert, the man... the man is as good as dead too, unless he can get hold of another camel.

Thus ran Abu Bakr's thoughts as he spurred on Inhelumé with his feet.

By noon, he had thought of a way out. He turned round to Mid-e-Mid, who was having some difficulty in keeping up with Inhelumé's pace. His camel was too young, and had certainly never been pressed so hard before.

'Can you go on?' he called to Mid-e-Mid.

'I can,' Mid-e-Mid shouted back, 'but the camel is not strong. It is sweating. I can smell it.' It is a peculiar sweetish, oily smell which rises from the animal's coat when it is being over-strained.

'We must rest it then,' said Abu Bakr.

They found a place to stop where the dry *had* plant was growing. Inhelumé began to nibble it greedily. This salty plant is devoured eagerly by camels when it is fresh. Once it has dried out, they will only eat it if they have been well watered beforehand. Mid-e-Mid's camel rolled over in the sand, straining its head towards its hump, as if it wanted a different view of the world for once, and there it lay, gazing at the landscape.

'It was not watered in Samak,' said Abu Bakr. 'That is why it will not eat such dry stuff.'

Mid-e-Mid nodded, ill at ease. He got up to find some wood.

They made a big fire, for they had several hours' lead. They had ridden hard and they knew that the *goumiers* would have to spend some time getting water in Samak.

Abu Bakr shot a gazelle, a powerful buck. There was even some fat on it. They skinned it and cut the meat into broad strips, some of which they roasted in the fire. The rest they hung on a branch to dry.

'Which part do you prefer?' asked Abu Bakr. 'The leg or the stomach and guts?'

'The guts,' said Mid-e-Mid. 'I should like to make an *abatal*.'

'Yes, do,' said Abu Bakr, 'and forget the hard words between us.'

'I have forgotten them already. You were quite right. They fired at me, although I had never done them any harm. Yes, you were right, Abu Bakr.'

'I am always right,' said the bandit and threw him the full entrails and the stomach. He had cut them out with his knife and his robe was spattered with dark blood. The beautiful head of the gazelle he flung into the fire. The stench of its blackening horns filled the air. A few ravens settled within a stone's throw.

Mid-e-Mid squeezed the intestines until they were empty and placed them inside the stomach. He pulled hot stones from the glowing fire and pressed them in among the entrails, skewered the stomach lining together with thorns and laid it among the ash. As it sizzled and hissed he turned it backwards and forwards to brown it evenly.

Abu Bakr held a leg of meat in the open flame for a few minutes and ate with great relish, although it was still raw. He had already finished it before the *abatal* was ready and Mid-e-Mid opened it and removed the stones.

'Would you like some?' he asked politely.

'I have enough here,' said Abu Bakr, helping himself to a second leg.

So Mid-e-Mid ate the *abatal* by himself and felt replete and tired. He took a thorn and picked the bits of meat from his teeth and watched Abu Bakr, methodically gnawing the bones.

The sun sank below the line where sky and desert meet. Inhelumé stretched himself out on the ground, and Mid-e-Mid's camel picked listlessly at the dry *had*. The heat of the day could still be felt.

They slept for some hours. When they awoke, the moon was shining. They drank water and talked. They planned to set off about midnight and would reach Tirek the following evening.

Abu Bakr stirred the glowing embers and put some more wood on the fire.

There is plenty of wood in the desert. Trees grow in the thin layer of earth, firmly rooted in the subsoil which hoards the precious rainwater, until a year comes when the tornadoes fail to break. Not a drop of rain falls, not a shower refreshes the earth. The roots of the trees thrust deeper and deeper, but can find no moisture. Gradually they lose their strength and the tree dies. The desert is strewn with these dead trees, and shepherds seldom have to worry about fuel for their fires.

Abu Bakr said, 'They cannot be here before midnight. Once the moon has set, they cannot see our tracks.'

Mid-e-Mid nodded. 'They had no sleep last night.'

Abu Bakr laughed. 'When I was young, I could hold out for four nights without sleep. I could ride a camel to death before I would drop from my saddle.'

He moved Mid-e-Mid's saddle behind his back to make himself more comfortable. 'Yes, I used to hold out longer than any of the others – and I can still do it today.' He drew his feet up, for the wind was against him and tongues of flame licked the soles of his feet.

'Have you always been a brigand?' asked Mid-e-Mid thoughtfully.

'No,' said Abu Bakr, 'only since I left the Beylik's service.'

'Do you mean you were one of the Beylik's soldiers?' Mid-e-Mid could not imagine him in the ranks.

'I did not know then as much as I do now.' The robber turned his narrow watery green eyes to the lad, as if he guessed his thoughts. 'I was as slim and wiry as a gazelle in the desert, but stupid and inexperienced.' He scratched his black, shaven forehead.

'When I was your age, I decided to give my services to the Beylik. My father's tents stood in the Oued Arli Mennen. And the Beylik was in Tamanrasset in the Ahaggar Mountains. I took a donkey and set out for Tamanrasset. On the way, the donkey died. I found another at the Well of Tin Rerho. That carried me to Tamanrasset. In Tamanrasset, they said I was too weak. But I was only weak because I had had nothing to eat for three days. They could not understand my dialect properly and I went back to the Oued Arli Mennen.

'Two years later I set out once more for Tamanrasset. This time I needed only thirteen days to get there. When I told them that I had come from Arli in thirteen days, they would not believe me.'

Inhelumé had risen and stood outlined against the moon, so that a shadow fell on Abu Bakr and Mid-e-Mid could not see his face. But he heard his deep voice, and it seemed to come from the heart of the night.

'They still thought that I was too young. But in the end, they gave me a camel. It was not a good camel, I swear it. Its hump was flabby and its soles had been hurt on sharp flints and the cuts had not healed properly.'

He spat into the fire. A little white scorpion found the smouldering wood too hot for it and ran out across the sand.

Mid-e-Mid took a stick and killed it with one blow. He was going to throw it in the fire, when Abu Bakr stopped him.

'You must not burn a scorpion,' he said.

'But it is dead,' said Mid-e-Mid, puzzled.

'All the same, if you throw it in the fire, all its friends will come to mourn it and they will sting us. That is the truth.'

He picked up the scorpion carefully by its poison sting and dropped it into a hole. Then he covered it over with sand.

'Listen,' he said. 'In Tamanrasset, they said to me, 'Here is a camel, and here is a bag. In the bag are letters for the Beylik in Kidal. Ride to Kidal and come back. If you can do it in less than twenty-two days, you can stay with us and we will give you a rifle and ammunition.' That is what they said.

'It takes twenty-two days on a good camel, you know that.'

'Yes, I know,' said Mid-e-Mid. 'My father once...'

'Let me finish,' growled Abu Bakr's voice. 'I took the camel, half-dead as it was, and set out for Kidal. By the fifth day, I knew it was impossible with that beast.

'That evening, I saw a fire ahead of me and rode towards it. Then I saw that they were *Ulliminden*, people to avoid in those parts.'

'Ayé,' said Mid-e-Mid. 'They must have been men of the tribe of the *Imochar*...'

'By Allah, so they were!' said Abu Bakr. The camel moved away and the brigand's face lay once more round and coarse in the pale moonlight. 'They were *Imochar* and they had just made a raid and captured a fine string of camels. I crept over to their fire and listened to their talk. I knew that this was the moment for me to act. I unbuckled my saddle and placed it on one of their camels. I hung my bag with letters on the saddle cross, and fastened the bridle. I crawled back to the fire and took one of their guns. But they heard me. I shot one of them in the belly. They stopped and I got away.'

'And did they not pursue you?'

'I do not know,' said Abu Bakr, and shrugged his shoulders. 'I had taken their best camel. It took me thirteen days to get to Kidal, although I had never seen the trail before, and I gave the Beylik the mail. The Beylik would not believe that I had ridden so fast. But I think it said in the letters when I had left.'

'Did the Beylik accept you then?'

'Wait a moment. In Kidal, they gave me a sack of millet and two sugar loaves and a kilogram of tobacco and a blanket. I did not need to pay for them. They were a present from the Beylik. And I rode back in thirteen days.'

'How did you find the way, Abu Bakr?' The wind was rising and rustled the grass. White clouds trailed before the moon and dimmed its light.

'By day I steered by the sun and the mountain peaks, and at night I took my bearings from the stars...'

'That is what I do,' said Mid-e-Mid eagerly.

'Well, in Tamanrasset, they gave me two more sugar loaves, but no more tea and no millet... And they said that I had ridden well, and I could keep the camel.' He laughed scornfully. 'That is the kind of people they are! I had taken a camel from under the very noses of the *Imochar* and killed a man, and they kindly allowed me to keep the beast. Does a man need the Beylik's permission to keep the camel he has fought for and won? By the beard of the Prophet, no! But I was too young to realize their impudence. They gave me ammunition and an ammunition belt and I had to put my thumb on a moist cloth and press it on a sheet of paper. My thumb mark remained on the paper. It was blue. Then I was a *goumier*. And a *goumier* I remained for six years. I fought for the Beylik in the mountains, and against the Aïr Tamashek and the *Ulliminden* by the River. Do you think I was a coward?'

'Never,' said Mid-e-Mid.

'Do you think I can shoot?'

'I know you can,' replied the boy.

'I have shot more men than any other soldier of the Beylik's. That is the truth.' He took a deep breath. Despite the years that had passed, he still felt the burning indignation of a man who has been bitterly wronged.

'I was their best *goumier*, and no one knew the desert like I did. Then one day I shot a gazelle which was with young, and I ate it because I was hungry. The Beylik heard of it, and said I must be punished.'

'But why?' asked Mid-e-Mid in astonishment.

'There, you see. Everyone asks 'Why?' The Beylik said because it was with young. But none of us could understand why that should make a difference. There are plenty of gazelles in the desert. More than the Beylik can ever eat. Was he afraid that he might starve, if I went on shooting two gazelles with one bullet? If he thought that, he does not know the desert. There are gazelles enough...'

The wind was mounting, and they wrapped themselves closer in their robes and moved nearer to the fire.

'But the Beylik insisted on having me punished. I think an evil spirit had taken possession of him, for I had done no wrong.'

'That must have been it,' said Mid-e-Mid. 'How can it be a crime for a man to shoot a gazelle when he is hungry? It must have been an evil spirit.'

'They led me to a house which had no windows and they left me there.'

'I know what that is,' said Mid-e-Mid. 'My father lies in such a house. It has no roof. Only high walls. They call it a prison.'

'Yes, they build prisons like that these days, without a roof, so that a man can at least see the sky and the stars and the sun, and breathe the air. My prison house was closed in. I could not see the sky. They left me there for two days. At least people told me afterwards that it was two days. For there is no time in that house. I did not know if it was time to wake or time to sleep.' Abu Bakr shook his heavy head on its short thick neck. The night wind lifted his tousled hair and the strands waved like black tongues.

'A man came and brought me some water. I lifted the pail to my mouth and drank it at one draught. I was thirsty. Then I saw that this man had the keys in his hand. I rammed the empty bucket over his head, locked him in the house and walked out. I saddled my camel, and took my gun and rode back to the Oued Arli Mennen, back to my father's tents.'

'And then you were no longer one of the Beylik's men?'

'No, never again,' said Abu Bakr in a very loud voice. 'I decided to be a herdsman like everyone else and tend my cattle.'

'Did the Beylik try to find you?'

'Yes, but he did not find me, for I was in hiding. He must have seen that he had done me an injustice about the gazelle, for he sent a *goumier* to bring me my pay. They had deducted the money for the keys and for the gun which I had taken, so there was not much left. But I knew that the Beylik wanted to put things right with me. Otherwise he would not have sent me my pay, would he?'

'No,' agreed Mid-e-Mid, 'but you never can tell what the Beylik is really thinking. My father...'

'Let me finish,' said Abu Bakr. 'I have not told you everything yet. You must hear the whole story. It is good for you to know it all. I have never told anyone before... The Beylik did not look for me any more, and I did not go back to him. But one day – it was a year after my father's death – Intallah came to me...'

'The Amenokal? Ajor Chageran's father?'

'Yes, of course. What of it? He came demanding tribute. You know that Intallah belongs to the nobles, and from time to time they come to us vassals, to people like your father and my father, and ask us for presents. That has always been the custom with us Tamashek. I gave Intallah a fat sheep and a sturdy calf. That is a lot, is it not?'

'Yes indeed,' confirmed Mid-e-Mid. 'We need only give a sheep.'

'I gave him a sheep and a strong calf as well. But Intallah was not satisfied. He demanded a cow. I said, "Intallah, what do you do for me? Why should I give you a cow?" and Intallah replied, "If you have a quarrel with the Beylik, I am the man to help you." And I answered, "When I had a quarrel with the Beylik before, I settled it myself. But perhaps I will need your help one day. I will give you a cow."'

Abu Bakr licked his lips and listened into the wind. His pursuers must still be far away. The wind carried none of the noises a troop of armed soldiers would be bound to make as they rode through the night.

'Intallah took my cow and went back to his tent. I have never thought much of the nobles. They are rich because they rob us of our herds. But when it comes to doing things for us, they can only talk.'

'From my father, I had inherited two negro slaves. They were well looked after in my tent, I can tell you. My herds were not large and they had only to drive them to the well and milk them morning and evening. They ate their fill and were seldom beaten. But with negroes, it is the same as with the Beylik. You never know what is going on in their heads.

'The slaves stole two of my best camels and ran away. I was told, 'Your slaves are riding towards the River. We have seen them.'

'I rode after them. They had not fled to the Niger after all, but to Kidal, and they had told the Beylik that they had run away.'

'So the Beylik punished them?' asked Mid-e-Mid.

'That is what I thought he would do, but I was wrong. The Beylik said that it is illegal to own slaves and they need not return to me and I might not punish them. "They are as free as you are," he said. "Yes, they are free as the nobles themselves." That is what he said.'

'But I do not understand,' said Mid-e-Mid. 'They were black and had been born slaves.'

'The Beylik said that it was forbidden to keep slaves at all and that I had committed a crime. He returned my stolen camels. But he would not give me back my slaves. I remembered that Intallah had promised me his help against the Beylik and I went to see him. I said, "Intallah, my slaves have run away and the Beylik refuses to give them back to me. What shall I do?"

'Intallah said, "Perhaps the Beylik needs your slaves and will give them back to you later." I said, "You do not understand. I may not take them back by force, and I may not beat them."

74

'Intallah sent a message to the Beylik in Kidal and asked if what I had told him was true. The Beylik replied that it was true and that the negroes had now reached the River and would never come back.

'Then Intallah said, "I can do nothing for you." I reminded him of the cow which he had taken from me. But he only said, "Against the Beylik I am helpless."

'I said, "Then you lied to me." At that, he had me thrown out of his tent by his slaves.'

A night bird pierced the darkness with its screech. The fire spluttered in a sudden gust of wind. Mid-e-Mid's lips were parted and his eyes did not leave the storyteller's face.

'I went back in the night and I killed Intallah's slaves. It was not difficult. They were cowards like all slaves. I thought that Intallah would report what I had done to the Beylik. But he came himself to take revenge. He burned down my tent, and took away all my flocks, camels, cattle, goats, sheep, even the donkeys.'

'Was there nothing left?'

'Nothing. I was not there when it happened. I had ridden to the River to find my slaves, but...'

'You have seen the River?' Mid-e-Mid burst in. 'Tell me, is it true that there is water there all the year round? And that people can sail on the water? And that all the people there are as black as our negroes?'

'Yes, that is so,' said Abu Bakr, 'but that is another story. I will tell you about it another time. I looked for my slaves but there were too many black people and I could not tell one from the other. Afterwards many other slaves fled. They ran away from all the tribes and settled by the River. But Allah will punish them. It is not His will that a slave should be a free man like the Tamashek. People say that many of them starved there. And Intallah's servants, the ones I did not kill, ran away later. Only two ugly old women stayed with him. Now you see why I am against all princes who have no real power, and against Intallah, who burned my tent to the ground.

'Tell me, what else could I do then, but take to the mountains? From that day to this, I have seized what I needed. And I shall go on doing so, *inchallah*.'

'Why did you attack the Marabut's tents?' asked Mid-e-Mid.

'I heard that Intallah's son was there and I said to myself, it is time to show Intallah that his writ does not run in the North. And I had to show the Marabut that he could not receive Intallah's son with impunity as long as I lived.'

Mid-e-Mid said, 'The Marabut has never done you any harm.'

'And I, you master of wisdom,' bellowed Abu Bakr, 'what harm had I done? What wrong had I done the Beylik, that he should keep my slaves from me? What harm did I do to Intallah that he should take my cow and break his promise, and have me, a free-born man, thrown out of his tent by slaves? What is wrong and what is right? Think of your father! Did he harm Tuhaya?' He snorted with anger and excitement.

'You have talked a great deal this evening,' said Mid-e-Mid. 'My head cannot take it all in.'

Abu Bakr looked hard at him. And his slanting eyes had the pathetic look of an animal in distress. 'You must understand,' he said in a worried voice. 'It is vital for you to understand.'

He looked at the moon.

'The moon will be setting presently,' he said. 'We had better be on our way. I am giving you Inhelumé. I shall take the other camel.'

'No,' replied Mid-e-Mid. 'If they pursue us, you can save yourself on Inhelumé. The other one...'

'I intend to save us both,' said Abu Bakr. 'We must separate. I shall ride to Tirek on the young camel and you will go to Tin Za'uzaten on Inhelumé. That is where my tents are pitched, in the mountains not far from there. Look after my herds for me until I come back. Until then, Inhelumé is yours.'

'But when they see our tracks part,' objected Mid-e-Mid, 'they will follow Inhelumé's.'

'That is what I intend,' said Abu Bakr thoughtfully. 'They will follow you, but they will have to turn back. There is no water between here and Tin Za'uzaten. The wells at In Uzzal, Debnat and Tin Elha'ua are all dry. On Inhelumé you can follow the track. Inhelumé can hold out for ten days without water. But the Beylik's camels cannot survive that long. With your water-skin, you will manage until you get to Tin Za'uzaten.'

'And how shall I find the trail?'

'I shall draw it for you in the sand.'

And in the waning light of the moon, Abu Bakr drew the track in the sand, and showed him which were the landmarks to watch for. And he told him the stars to guide him, and how long each stage would take by camel.

'I shall remember it all,' said Mid-e-Mid. 'Now tell me, when will you come back?'

'I shall come when Tuhaya and the *goumiers* have returned south. And they will do that if they do not catch me by Tirek. You see, I have thought of everything.'

'Yes,' agreed Mid-e-Mid. 'You have thought of everything.'

They took down the dried gazelle meat from the thorn bushes, loaded the camels and mounted.

'*Bismillah*,' said Mid-e-Mid.

'*Bismillah*,' replied Abu Bakr.

Then they went their separate ways.

When the *goumiers* reached the fire, the ashes were already cool. They went on northwards, and only at dawn did they discover that they had lost Inhelumé's tracks. They divided the party. The leader of the *goumiers* and three of his men went on towards Tirek. Tuhaya and the other seven turned back.

'If you want to find Abu Bakr, you must follow Inhelumé,' said Tuhaya. They rode back for three hours. They found that Inhelumé's tracks went first due east and then south-east.

Tuhaya said, 'I know Abu Bakr. He has gone to In Uzzal, in the mountains. From In Uzzal, he will make for Debnat. We must take a short cut and surprise him at Debnat.'

So they abandoned Inhelumé's tracks and set out for Debnat in the cool of the morning.

CHAPTER SEVEN

The Vulture

ACCORDING TO HIS RECKONING at sunrise, Abu Bakr was eight hours ride south of Tirek. He rode to the top of a sand dune and from there he could already make out in the half-light the high cliffs behind which the well lay hidden among white boulders. Between him and his destination lay an arid waste of gravel and sand, the *reg*.

Lifeless dunes, black stone overlaid with orange, forced him to swerve from his northerly direction. He recalled the last time he had had to face this wilderness, fourteen years before. People who live in the desert seem to develop a special faculty for conserving their recollections of places, and it was as if he pulled out a series of photographs to compare them with the actual landscape before his eyes.

The curved dunes had not changed. There were still the same fantastic pillars of sand, myriads of whirling grains, rubbed and scoured and polished and carved by the wind into towering mushrooms. Stone tumuli, graves many thousands of years old, sprawled like massive cartwheels, half astraddle the forgotten cattle tracks, or crowned the bleak summits of barren chains of hills.

But his memory showed him clearly that there had been changes too. Instead of tall green bushes of *djir-djirs* and plentiful tufts of the salty *had* plant, there now lay nothing but yellow sand, mingled with pebbles of red, green, black and white. The desert had marched on. It had scorched and strangled all forms of life. Nothing was left but the peeling wood of derelict trees.

As he passed one rock, Abu Bakr saw a dead hedgehog. The animal bore no signs of injury. It had died of hunger. Even the insects had fled and the long-legged jumping desert mouse had forsaken this waste land. No track of gazelle or ostrich crossed his path. Once he saw in the sand the zig-zag trail of a viper, and the hollow shell of a black beetle. Yet once the tornado had lashed the land with its scourge of rain, life would revive and there would even be pasture.

Abu Bakr let the reins lie loose in his hand. There was no sense in driving the young camel too hard. Earlier he had beaten it with his ox-leather whip and, with a shrill cry of protest, it had broken into a gallop. But very soon it relapsed into the slow swaying step of the animal used to the pace of a caravan, and there was nothing he could do about it.

Shimmering lakes appeared in the distance and then dissolved into nothing as he approached. Devils water, he muttered and clutched the leather amulet on his breast. The air grew hotter and a trembling haze rose high into the air, hiding the Tirek massif from view. White splinters of salt dazzled him, so that he drew his veil high, leaving a mere slit for his eyes.

He did not turn round to see if his pursuers were in sight. He had had a big advantage. In any case, he had no doubt at all that the *goumiers* had followed Inhelumés track. Even if they had divided their party, and this had occurred to him, he would still be in Tirek before them, and could find a hiding place in the rocks above the well, from which it would be easy to prevent access to the water.

They are all stupid, he thought. They will never believe that I have given Inhelumé to Mid-e-Mid. He thought, if the boy follows the trail I showed him, he will get away safely. They will have to turn back and it will be hard enough to reach Samak again. Ah! and the disgrace for Tuhaya...

He thought, Tuhaya, you have hounded me into the desert and you would like to seize my herds as you stole those of Agassum. But you are not the man to capture me, Tuhaya. I promised you I would wring your neck. And so I will, if Mid-e-Mid does not do it before I find you... He is a fine lad, the son of my friend and brother Agassum. But he is not like me. He has not the stuff of a brigand in him. His heart is not hard enough. Mid-e-Mid, if you knew mankind as I do... But you must learn that for yourself. Experience, Mid-e-Mid, is something no man can pass on to another. People can tell you this and that, and you can think things over as you ride through the day or sit by the campfire at night, but no one can actually live through another mans experience...

He thought, if I had had a son like Mid-e-Mid... His eyes closed and he tried to imagine how it would have been if he had had a wife and a son. But women did not care for Abu Bakr. He was too coarse, too rough, and perhaps too unstable, even for the Tamashek women who are used to a nomads life. Twice he had wooed women and had been repulsed. He had never made a third attempt. His vanity was hurt, and he had lived his life proof against hate or love. Yes, he was free. There was no one in the Iforas Mountains as free as Abu Bakr. But no one had paid so dearly for his freedom. All the same, he thought, I have made a name for myself between Kidal and Tamanrasset. I am more feared than the Amenokal, and not less than the Beylik himself.

A white vulture sailed out of the blue. Abu Bakr looked at it, perturbed. A vulture means a carcase. Not far away there must be a dead camel, or even a man, or it could be a caravan. But the vulture did not alight. It circled round in great sweeps. Its prey is not yet quite dead, thought Abu Bakr. Otherwise it would attack it. But I wish I knew what it is waiting for.

With scarcely a movement of its outstretched wings, the bird floated in leisurely fashion, coming lower and lower. Then it settled on a heap of stones. It did not fold its wings, but held them curved like feathery white arms against the sun.

You are hungry, you eater of carrion, said Abu Bakr, laughing. And I fear that you must go on starving. In this land, even the mice have died, and the hedgehog rots behind a stone.

The vulture did not stir. Its eyes never left the robber.

Do not be afraid, said Abu Bakr. Even if it meant dying of hunger, I would not shoot you for meat.

The vulture scratched its breast feathers with its hooked beak.

Friend vulture, said Abu Bakr, over there in the east, Tuhaya is following Inhelumés tracks. He will turn back, and he will die of thirst. How would it be, my friend, if you took an interest in his affairs instead of mine?

The vulture seemed to understand his words. It beat its wings a few times, and rose swiftly and squarely into the air. Then it circled once round the lone figure and flew off eastwards, a tiny black dot which soon disappeared behind the haze.

That is a good omen, thought Abu Bakr. It is still four hours to Tirek.

The time of the greatest heat of the day had arrived. The camel moved above its own shadow. Abu Bakr felt thirsty. But he had to hold out to Tirek. He had given the water-skin to Mid-e-Mid.

The landscape was changing gradually. The vast plains of gritty sand and gravel were giving way to black rocks and rugged table land. The towering turning columns of brown sand, which had whirled along the *reg* like living vortices, were ripped to pieces by powerful gusts of wind. Naked stones, black and grey and purple, crumbled beneath the camels feet. Abu Bakr had to pilot it over hands breadth paths which straggled over the backs of the mountains like clumsy spiders webs. The camels hoofs no longer left any impression behind. Abu Bakr was relieved to see how surely the animal placed its feet with the leathery skin creasing into folds above its heels. He could feel the strain of the hind legs going uphill, and he held his breath when it slithered over the curved smoothness of the stones on a downhill stretch.

The heat shimmered in the ravines. Up on the ridges, the north-east wind sprang up and blew fiercely against the man and his camel. From the depths of the Sahara came blasts of hot sand, which pricked the rider from head to foot with needle-sharp arrows. The camels eyes were almost closed. The hairy, heavily-lashed eyelids winced under the painful stinging grains. The sky dissolved into grey and brown, and visibility dropped to a few paces.

This is good, thought Abu Bakr. I shall find my way to Tirek. It is only two hours away. But the *goumiers* will perish in the sand. They will lose their way, and then they will despair. They are all Iforas people. They have never dared to penetrate the heart of the desert before.

He had to leave the camel to find the mountain paths for itself. The storm itself gave him the right direction, but from the height of the saddle, he could not see the ground through the driving sand. Shrouded beneath his heavy robes, he could feel the sweat running down his beard. Relentlessly his foot pressed against the camels neck. The animal needed some tangible proof of his masters presence. That was the only way to overcome its instinctive timidity and blind fear.

The more the wind raged and the gusts buffeted him, the more his spirits rose. Here in the mountains, the ravines gave occasional protection and breathing space. Out on the *reg*, one was helpless against the fury of the whirling sand-laden wind, which could go on for hours at a time without respite. Out on the *reg* were his pursuers.

There was a little hill ahead of them. The rage of the sand-storm seemed to mount even higher. Abu Bakr crouched low in the saddle to keep his balance. But the camel could not reach the summit. It gave a yelp and stopped. The robber slid to the ground and took hold of the bridle and pulled. It was in vain. He dealt it a blow with his leather whip and kicked it in the ham. It dropped to the ground and stretched out its long neck as far as it could.

Abu Bakr knew that if a camel lies down in such circumstances, one must go warily. It might become obstinate, and bite and kick and endanger its life, to say nothing of the man's, by mad leaps and uncontrollable contortions.

He wound the reins several times round his left arm and curled up against the animal's body away from the wind. He covered his face with his veil and, like the camel, bowed his head to the earth. Thus they remained for several hours. Then the force of the storm abated a little. *Hamdullillah*, he said thankfully. He could feel the sand crunching between his teeth.

His lips felt brittle, like crusted earth. The skin on the back of his hand, when he touched it accidentally with his lips, tasted of salt.

Abu Bakr rose to his knees and despite the continuing storm, he began to recite the afternoon prayer.

Abu Bakr was not a pious Moslem. He did not pray at the appointed times of day, nor observe the decreed fasts. He had a hearty contempt for all scholarship and religious observances, and if he revered the Koran as a holy book, it was simply because the Marabut could heal sickness by means of verses from the Koran.

Still there were times when he remembered to say the appropriate prayers. When God gave him something, he gave God a prayer in return. He hated to be under an obligation to anyone.

The prayer was a short one. He stood up and peered through the continously driving sand, to make out which was the path he should strike to cross the ridge.

He decided on a track among the loose scree, and tugged in sharp jerks at the bridle. The camel bayed, and all but dislocated its neck in its struggle to resist the pull on the nose-ring. But it did not get up.

You devil, cursed Abu Bakr bitterly. I'll break your bones for this!

He beat it brutally and kicked it in the soft parts. The animal tried to bite him, but it actually got up, screaming in protest, and stood still on three legs. The left forefoot hung limply, just off the ground.

Abu Bakr thought that he had found the answer. It must have a thorn in its foot, or perhaps it had cut it on a sharp edge of rock. He bent down to examine it. He could not see any injury. But the beast yelped every time he touched its leg. Then Abu Bakr tried to grasp the foreleg with both hands and force it to the ground, but the camel bit him in the shoulder.

The bite did not go through the *burnouse* and robes. Perplexed, Abu Bakr stepped back a pace. You prefer to stay here, is that it? But I want to go on. And I am master here. Just wait a minute, and he fumbled in his wallet and shook out some tobacco dust from the seams. You need freshening up a bit, he said. The camel looked at him, its upper lip drawn back.

Here you are! He rubbed tobacco dust in both its eyes, gripping the nostrils with one hand so that the animal should not break away.

It started to blink, and big bluish tears dropped from its eyes. Abu Bakr was certain that this traditional remedy would have the desired effect.

But even the tobacco failed. Nothing could shift it, neither tugging at the nose-ring, nor beating with a whip, nor even friendly and encouraging words.

The brigand screwed up his eyes and looked down at the foot again. It hung limp, as if it did not belong to the leg. It was broken.

Beads of sweat broke out on Abu Bakrs brow. You dog of Satan's brood! His voice was savage. You good-for-nothing brute!

He loaded his gun and took aim. There was a dull sound and the bullet tore a great hole in the camels flesh. It shuddered, started and slithered a little way down the slope. Its mouth gaped, showing the flat yellow teeth. Its legs crumpled. The saddle girth ripped in two.

With bitterness in his heart, Abu Bakr watched the blood stream out and trickle in red rivulets over the sand. Accursed be the mare that suckled you! he roared. But the camel was dead.

His fury was so great that he picked up stones and hurled them at the carcase. Then he realized the futility of his anger and turned away. He slung his gun on his back and with shoulders braced against the wind, he set off up the hill.

I shall reach Tirek on foot, he thought. And there we shall see. An armed man is not lost.

He wished that the *goumiers* were at his heels. Then, he thought, he would fire at the first one and he would topple from his saddle. The others would turn and flee at his fire, and he would seize the riderless camel. But then, was there anyone actually following him? Were they not pursuing Inhelumé still?

The sky cleared. Patches of blue quivered between the whirling dust. I am in luck, he thought. The sand-storm is over.

A tiny black speck appeared, grew visibly larger and circled round, coming lower and lower.

You knew what would happen, Brother Vulture, you foresaw it all, he muttered to himself. Off with you! Your meat is there, behind the hill!

The white bird was now so low that Abu Bakr recognized the powerful span of its wings. In smoothly gliding flight, it rapidly cleared the ridge and disappeared behind the height.

From the top of a hillock, Abu Bakr confirmed that he had kept the right direction. The black massif of the mountains before Tirek was just visible through the haze. He might have been looking at it through grimy windows. He even thought that he could make out the whitish dunes which surrounded the well itself.

His mind at rest, he went confidently down the hill.

Then the sand-storm started again. Grey whirls of dust and wild gusts of wind roared through the valleys, and hurled themselves against the lonely fugitive, battering him with volleys of sand. The sky grew livid.

Abu Bakr struggled on. The sand blinded him. He put his arms in front of his face and stumbled forward as if bowed by a heavy burden.

I must wait, he thought. There is no help for it. I must wait. The storm is too strong.

He dropped to the ground and covered his head with his robes and crouched with hands and elbows pressed firmly against the earth. He could feel the pricking of the sand against his naked loins, and the tearing of the wind in his flowing black trousers. Tuhaya will never live through this, he thought. I wish I could see him die.

Water would be good, he thought. A little water. I should feel better if I had some water. But Tirek is not far away. I have seen the dunes. And the well is there, just between the dunes.

A handful of water would be enough. I would roll it round my mouth, and spit it into my hands. Then I would rub my face with it. I would not drink it. I do not need to drink it. Or perhaps I would. I would take one pull. A mouthful would be enough.

Once he freed his head, and thought he saw the vulture perched near by. He was very frightened. He fired at it. But even as he pulled the trigger, he knew that there was no vulture there. He covered his head again.

The *goumiers* found his body three days later on the way back from Tirek. A vulture had devoured his flesh. They recognized him by the head which was still intact, by the shaven forehead, the thick nose and the slightly receding chin. The mouth was open.

They searched a wide area for his camel, but they did not find it. They puzzled for a long time on how he had met his death. They simply could not believe it possible that a man like Abu Bakr had lain down in a sand-storm.

They placed the head in a saddlebag, quarrelled over his gun and rode south, still wondering and arguing.

In spite of the proof they brought with them, it was several years before the Tamashek would believe that Abu Bakr had died of thirst.

CHAPTER EIGHT

Mid-e-Mid and the Fool

MEANWHILE TUHAYA and his men had made a bee-line for the Well of Debnat. But they found no trace of Inhelumé either on their way, nor when they arrived. But Mid-e-Mid had followed Abu Bakr's directions and ridden by a more southerly track. He had avoided all the water holes and made straight for Tin Za'uzaten.

Debnat was dry.

Tuhaya said, 'We must wait here. Abu Bakr hopes that he will lure us to In Uzzal. But I am sure that he will come here.'

The *goumiers* said, 'Abu Bakr is in league with the Devil, and so is Inhelumé. Suppose he has taken another track which does not touch Debnat?'

But nothing would persuade Tuhaya that he might be wrong.

There was no fodder at Debnat, no acacia trees and no flowering grasses. The only plant was the *tagilit*. It bears big globular fruits, rather like ostrich eggs to look at, and they are heavy with juice. But only the asses dare to eat them. All the other animals avoid them, for they are more bitter than quinine.

On the second day, the camels began to show by their bellowing and biting that they were hungry. Camels can stand thirst extremely well, but to remain strong they must have a certain quantity of fodder, grass, or leaves and twigs.

The goumiers said, 'Tuhaya, we must turn back. We do not believe that Abu Bakr will come now.'

Tuhaya insisted on waiting at least one day longer.

'Very well,' said the *goumiers*, 'the camels can hold out one more day.'

In the afternoon, the sky was covered with cloud. The wind dropped. The sun, still shining behind the thick clouds, cast a diffused light which hurt one's eyes. There was no dazzle, but neither was there any shade. The heat bore down on man and beast. The Mountains of Adrar in Uzzal were shrouded in heavy mist, rising from the sand.

At sundown, a dispute arose. 'We do not take our orders from you,' said the *goumiers* menacingly. 'You were supposed to show us the way to Abu Bakr's tents. What are we doing here?'

'How could I have known that Abu Bakr would keep us waiting so long?' replied Tuhaya. 'It is your own fault. You should have kept your eyes open in the Soren Oued, when I led you right up to his campfire and you let him get away.'

'That was your fault,' said the *goumiers* indignantly. 'You led us badly.'

'I am absolutely certain that he will come to Debnat.'

'By the time he comes, we shall all be dead and the camels too,' scoffed the soldiers.

One of them said, 'We should have followed Inhelumé's track instead of cutting across the desert. How are we going to feed the camels? Tell us that! Or show us a gazelle, so that we shall have meat.'

Tuhaya did not answer.

'You can all stay here if you like,' said another man. 'I am going to saddle my camel and go back.'

'You cannot ride through this mist,' objected a third.

But the man would not be deterred.

Some of them sided with the man saddling his camel. Others wanted to make for Tirek to join the smaller group. Some again preferred to stay with Tuhaya. The firm hand of a leader was badly needed.

They could not agree.

Under cover of darkness, the ones who wanted to turn back, made off, taking all the water-skins with them.

The ones who remained behind only discovered the theft next morning. In their fury they beat Tuhaya with camel whips. Only by promising on solemn oath to lead them straight back to Samak without any delay, did he save his life. But for weeks afterwards, his skin carried the green and blue marks of his beating.

By the tracks in the sand, they could tell that the men who had stolen the water-skins had ridden due south. They tried to force Tuhaya to follow them. It needed all his oratory to convince them that they would not strike water in that direction until the Iforas Mountains.

By means of forced marches, he got the panic-stricken men back to Samak, but the pace cost him his own camel.

No one heard anything more of the other band, which consisted of three men. They must have met their death on the way south. They were never seen alive again. Nor were their bodies ever found.

For a long time, Mid-e-Mid's fate remained a riddle.

There were shepherds who said that they had watched him drawing water at the Well of Timea'uin. Others thought that they had heard him singing. Some people believed that Abu Bakr had killed him after he had kidnapped him from the Marabut's tents.

The *goumiers* who had pursued him from Samak were pestered with questions. But their explanations and descriptions threw no light on the mystery. And the wilder the rumours, the more were Mid-e-Mid's songs treasured. The mocking song about Tuhaya went the rounds of the Tamashek, and the one praising High Summer's beauty spread all over the Adrar of the Iforas.

Tiu'elen believed that Mid-e-Mid was dead and mourned him deeply. She never spoke of him to anyone. But she became more serious and reserved, and she never left the tent except to carry out her daily tasks.

Only one woman firmly believed that Mid-e-Mid was still alive. That was his mother.

'He will come back, and bring me my donkey,' she said when people asked her about her younger son.

'If you say so...' nodded the herdsmen. But they did not really believe her.

89

Then the speculation about Abu Bakr and Mid-e-Mid was pushed into the background by events which touched the whole tribe. There were repeated bloody encounters with the Kounta people, and a battle was fought for the Well of Asselar. The Tamashek lost and found themselves barred from using the well. Everyone clamoured for Intallah to do something for his people, and it was in this connection that he had summoned his son, Red Moon, back from the North. But more of this later.

It was six days since Mid-e-Mid had parted from Abu Bakr. There was only a trace of muddy water left in his water-skin. At last, famished and exhausted, he saw before him the tall green tamarisk trees which marked the approach to the Oued of Tin Za'uzaten. He had no notion of what had happened to the brigand, nor where were Tuhaya and the *goumiers*.

As soon as it was dark, Mid-e-Mid drew near to the water-hole. Abu Bakr had told him that only one person guarded it. He was called Kalil, and he was an idiot.

Tin Za'uzaten was an important water hole with a copious supply, even in the years when no rain fell. But the grazing grew sparser year by year and the Tamashek gradually avoided this part of the country, preferring to wander further south.

Only the fool, Kalil, remained. The *oued* possessed everything he needed, which was little enough in other people's eyes. He had built a straw tent among the stones on the bank. He had even planted a small garden, in which he grew onions and beans. He kept a few goats, and whenever strangers came to the oued, he would cheerfully water their thirsty herds. Occasionally he was rewarded for these services with tobacco, tea and sugar, or dried tomatoes and rancid butter. But that did not happen often.

Mid-e-Mid avoided Kalil's fire, and led Inhelumé straight up to the water hole. He found the bottom of an old petrol can which the *goumiers* had once used for watering their camels. He filled it without any trouble, for the water stood high in the sand. He was so thirsty that he drank from the tin side by side with the camel. If anyone had watched them in the dark, they would have taken him for some small animal quenching its thirst cheek by jowl with the camel.

Then Mid-e-Mid hobbled Inhelumé's forefeet as usual and let him forage for himself through the night. He himself lay down in the sand beneath a huge tamarisk, whose dense foliage no shimmer of moonlight nor starlight could pierce.

That night, Mid-e-Mid dreamed of his mother, and as she took him by the hand, he awoke joyfully. But it was not his mother who touched his fingers. It was a man, small and very dirty, with matted hair and streaming blood-shot eyes.

Mid-e-Mid's hand flew to his sword. But the man shook his head and laughed soundlessly. He had brought a big calabash, hammered together with copper nails and he dipped his finger in it and licked it. Then he smacked his lips with gusto.

'Drink!' he said in an unnaturally high falsetto voice. 'Drink!'

Mid-e-Mid guessed that it was the idiot.

The calabash was full of milk, still warm from the goat. Mid-e-Mid drank it in great gulps. Kalil emptied the rest at one pull.

The fool asked, 'How are you? Have you had a good journey?'

'Yes, I am well,' answered Mid-e-Mid.

'Is your camel well?'

'It is well. It is grazing somewhere in the *oued*.'

'It is just over there,' said Kalil, picking his nose.

'Is there anybody here in the *oued*?'

'Yes, I Kalil, I am always here...What is your name?'

'Mid-e-Mid ag Agassum.'

'Mid-e-Mid ag Agassum.' He repeated the name slowly as if it ought to mean something to him. But the association eluded him for the moment and to Mid-e-Mid's astonishment, he started beating his head hard with his fists.

'It is coming!' he cried. 'It is coming! Wait!' He shook his head backwards and forwards and screwed up his eyes. 'Now!' he cried.

'I must be going on,' said Mid-e-Mid gently, for the Tamashek are always taught to be kind to fools.

'It is here!' cried Kalil. 'Sit down! Agassum was sent to prison by the Beylik, was he not?'

'That is so,' said Mid-e-Mid in surprise. 'How do you know that?'

91

The idiot whinnied with delight. 'Kalil knows! Three days ago a shepherd passed by. He told me...' He slapped his thigh with the flat of his hand and his torso rocked to and fro.

'Be off with you,' said Mid-e-Mid. 'My father has been locked up for years. That is not news.'

'He is no longer locked up,' said the idiot, beaming.

'He is free?' Mid-e-Mid's mouth fell open in astonishment.

'He is free... but he is dead.' Kalil could hardly speak for laughing.

'That is not true,' shouted Mid-e-Mid indignantly.

'He is free – he is dead,' tittered the fool. He took handfuls of sand and made a hole in the ground. 'Here,' he crooned, 'he is here. Kalil knows!'

'You idiot!' roared Mid-e-Mid, beside himself. He stamped his foot and it would not have taken much for him to have set upon the puny half-wit.

'Dead – free!' chortled the idiot. 'Dead – free,' and laughed.

Mid-e-Mid's eyes filled with tears. 'I do not believe you, Kalil. But if what you say is true, I shall send Tuhaya to Hell, as surely as I carry Abu Bakr's sword.'

'Abu Bakr?' cried the fool. 'Abu Bakr is dead. *Hamdullillah.*'

'Now I know that you are talking nonsense,' said Mid-e-Mid, relieved. 'I left him only a few days ago, in good health. And you cannot have seen him since.'

'Kalil knows,' giggled the fool and pulled a face. 'You have killed him... Mid-e-Mid has killed him... Ha!ha!ha!'

'I have something better to do than listen to your raving,' said Mid-e-Mid, getting up.

'Kalil knows. You have Abu Bakr's camel. Yes, Kalil knows everything.'

'He lent me his camel. Now talk sense.'

'Abu Bakr, dead, dead, dead... Abu Bakr, dead, dead, dead...' The fool's voice grew softer with each repetition and his head swayed on his shoulders. Suddenly he cupped his hands round his mouth, as if he wanted his voice to carry far into the distance. But it was only a high-pitched whisper which emerged.

'Kalil will tell you a secret, but you must tell no one. No one, do you hear?'

'Tell me,' said Mid-e-Mid, curious.

Kalil coughed violently, and pointed to Telchenjert at Mid-e-Mid's side. 'Abu Bakr was killed by his own sword. It pierced his heart... Kalil knows.' His coughing shook him so painfully that he groaned and his red-rimmed eyes filled with tears.

'Agassum is free,' he said abruptly. 'But Abu Bakr is only dead.' The shrill, penetrating laughter possessed him again. He clapped his hands like a child who is offered a piece of sugar.

'I have no time for your fooling,' said Mid-e-Mid.

'Try to understand poor Kalil a little... Poor Kalil... It is all up here,' the idiot pointed to his forehead with both hands, 'but it cannot get out. The sword, the sword...'

'Yes,' said Mid-e-Mid soothingly, 'you have a bad cough. You must drink milk with red pepper for it. It helps. *Bismillah*, Kalil. I cannot give you a present. I have nothing to give you. Do not forget the milk – with red pepper!'

'*Bismillah*,' murmured Kalil sadly and he did not look at Mid-e-Mid. He rubbed his thick, low forehead as if he were trying to erase a mark that no one could see.

Mid-e-Mid's feet sank into the soft sand of the oued as he went to find his camel.

'He is an idiot, just an idiot. It is only a fool's talk,' he kept telling himself. But deep down inside him, Kalil's strange words took root and would not be dislodged. What did he mean, that he had killed Abu Bakr? And what had the shepherd really told him about his father?

Only when he mounted Inhelumé and had to concentrate on the path before him did these disturbing emotions subside. He had one more task to discharge before he could return to his mother's tent. He had to look after the bandit's camp until he arrived. He had promised. Then he would look for his mother's donkey. Perhaps he would see the Marabut again too. But he did not know if the attraction that drew him thither was the wise man's learning or his very beautiful daughter.

CHAPTER NINE

In the Mountains

EAST OF TIN ZA'UZATEN, mighty cliffs of rock tower skyward. Their forbidding mass seems completely inaccessible. Steep chasms and gullies, ravines which no camel could negotiate, defy an intruder's curiosity. But Abu Bakr had given Mid-e-Mid detailed instructions about the one access to this wilderness of rock. So he rode forward towards the mountains without any misgiving. At first, he used the *oued* itself as his path. But soon, he saw an old trail that led steeply uphill, and disappeared behind the first grey stones.

This must be it, thought Mid-e-Mid, for Inhelumé seemed to climb the path with obvious alacrity. Usually, camels need the firmest persuasion to tackle a mountain track.

The day was clear without a breath of wind. It was early yet, and the chill of the night still clung to the ravines. Mid-e-Mid shivered and his bare legs were covered with gooseflesh. As he had no other means of warming himself, he started to sing. And the words sprang to his lips of their own accord.

Tell me, O shepherds, have you seen Tiu'elen?

He sang the verse, and made up others until the mountain track came out on to a broad plateau. As far as eye could see, there were smooth, shallow domes, and big square blocks of granite that reminded one of ruined houses, and jagged columns like the remains of ancient temples. Giant lizards patterned in red and blue, with basalt eyes and prickly tails, guarded the solitude like dragons. When they saw camel and rider enter their stony dominion, they raised and lowered their heads vigorously. It was a fantastic, pumping movement, and one half expected them to soar into the air when they were fully inflated, and fly away spitting fire and smoke.

Feathered hunters wheeled by, hot in pursuit of wild doves, which darted hither and thither like living arrows. Rock-badgers on sentry duty lurked close by their dens. And the prickly yellow heads of the *cram-cram* trembled on their stems in the breeze, alert for the slightest touch of foot or fur, so that they could strike home.

Up and down swung Inhelumé's head with that dancing rhythm which is the mark of the pedigree camel. Not a pebble was dislodged by his horny soles. He placed his feet as the ground permitted, sometimes one behind the other, sometimes crossed like a dancer's, but every step was as sure as if he were treading the flat surface of the *reg*.

And Mid-e-Mid rode, and Mid-e-Mid sang. And he made up a poem about the stallion Inhelumé.

> I drank the white waters of Telabit
> Of Sandeman and In Abutut
> But I found you not, Inhelumé.
>
> I followed your track to Sadidän
> From tent to tent where the campfires smoke,
> But I found you not, Inhelumé.
>
> I breathed your name to the whirling wind,
> I whispered it to the singing sand,
> I asked them both, where have you gone?
> But I found you not, Inhelumé.
>
> Only Tallit, the Lady Moon,
> Hears the stamp of your hoof
> As you drive the mares
> Turbulently across the dunes, Inhelumé.

He was so delighted with his song, that he cried aloud with pleasure, and stretched out his hands to stroke the camel's neck.

But Inhelumé was not used to such fondling. He shied away and pressed forward more eagerly than ever to the camp he knew so well.

And Mid-e-Mid forgot the misery of the past few days, the hunger, the thirst and fleeing for his life, and he forgot, too, the garbled words of the idiot, Kalil. His high spirits returned with his song. It seemed as if he could breathe more freely here in the scarred heart of the terrible, stony desert. Nothing could touch him here, neither Abu Bakr's ruthlessness, nor Tuhaya's malicious persecution; neither could his mother's goodness and the friendship of the herdsmen, nor Tiu'elen's affection surge to these heights, far above the sandy plains. He felt himself borne along a stream of unbroken boundless freedom. And from the fullness of his heart he poured out his songs.

He had ridden for nearly two hours, singing and daydreaming, when the path swerved away from the plateau and plunged abruptly downhill. Mid-e-Mid saw that they had come to a monstrous canyon with towering perpendicular walls, and sandhills as white as bleached bones piled up on the rock-strewn floor of the abyss. In many places rocks of crimson and grey had worked loose from the edge of the precipice and burst asunder as they fell. There they lay, like the missiles of some battle of the Titans, undying testimony to the never-ceasing travail of the earth.

With cautious steps, Inhelumé descended the precipitous trail. Mid-e-Mid had to lean well back against the hump, so as not to topple head over heels from his saddle, and he braced his feet firmly against the camel's skull.

At the foot of the ravine, there was a trampled dirt path which was still apparently used by men and herds. There were traces of cattle dung here and there. Beneath an overhanging rock, he noticed a drawing of two rearing horses scratched in the stone. These pictures had been carved with meticulous care by the unknown inhabitants of the land many thousands of years before. But the past meant nothing to Mid-e-Mid and the drawings had no significance for him.

He rode on until he reached the widest part of the gully. One half was suffused with sunlight. The other lay deep in shadow. At the edge of the shadowy side grew stunted green trees with bushes here and there. On the sunny side, the white sand dunes glittered. But here, even the dunes bore life. The long roots of a small prickly plant spread like wires criss-cross over the hummocks. Everywhere there were traces of sheep and cows, of camels with their young and of numerous asses.

Rounding a bend in the gorge, Mid-e-Mid saw the robber's tent before him, a tall copper-red tent, under the branches of an old thorn tree. He could hear the bleating of the goats and the dull lowing of the cattle, but he could see no one. Abu Bakr had told him that there were two servants in the tent, who would help him to draw water. They were called Amadou and Dangi. Mid-e-Mid knew that they must be negro slaves. No Tamashek had names like those.

He made Inhelumé kneel and jumped down to the ground.

'Ho there!' he called. 'Amadou! Dangi! Ho there!'

There was no answer. He turned inquisitively to the tent. Mats were spread on the ground and others hung from tent poles. A wooden mortar lay overturned at the entrance. A goatskin had been spread out to dry. In the corner stood two new spears with polished blades of iron. The fire had been left uncovered. That meant that the two negroes could not be far away.

Mid-e-Mid looked at the animals. The cows and calves grazed in the shadow of the cliff. The sheep huddled beneath the shade of the tree close behind the tent. Only the kids and goats had scrambled up among the rocks and looked down with great yellow eyes at the stranger. There were no camels to be seen.

I shall wait, thought Mid-e-Mid. He tied his water-skin securely and hung it in the branches of the tree, so that the water would stay cool. Then he lay down on a mat inside the tent.

He heard the voices of the two servants from far away. They came padding through the sand, carrying yellow calabashes on their heads. They steadied them with both hands.

When they saw Mid-e-Mid near the tent entrance, they stopped short, frightened, and did not know whether to run away or to come nearer.

'There is Inhelumé!' Mid-e-Mid called to them instead of a greeting, and pointed to the camel.

Still apprehensive, they edged a little closer. The milk slapped over the rims of the bowls and dripped down on to their bodies.

They were young boys, no older than Mid-e-Mid, as black as charcoal, with shaven heads and full red lips. They wore short sleeveless tunics of blue, and simple bracelets of stone.

'I am Mid-e-Mid,' he said. 'I shall stay here until Abu Bakr comes back.'

He gave them no other explanation, for even if he belonged to a vassal caste and came from a poor tent, he stood towering over the two negroes, whom Abu Bakr had probably kidnapped from some village.

They pushed the milk towards him, and watched him while he drank.

Amadou was the older of the two. He was the first to pluck up courage, for a slave does not address a Tamashek unless he has permission to do so. But Mid-e-Mid's friendly, ugly face and his jaunty spikes of hair waving in the breeze gave him confidence.

'Will you beat us much, Mid-e-Mid?' he asked.

Mid-e-Mid laughed and replied, 'Only a little!' No one had ever asked him that before. And he laughed so heartily that Amadou and Dangi began to laugh loudly too. You could not hear the bleating of the goats or the lowing of the cows for laughter.

Both of the lads were ready to pin their faith on Mid-e-Mid's laugh, his broad mouth and his mischievous slanting eyes.

Dangi said eagerly, 'Do you know, Abu Bakr beats us every day! Every morning when he wakes. He says it is good for us. It will make us as strong as lions. But I do not want to be as strong as a lion. Not if it hurts so much!'

At this, Mid-e-Mid laughed so much that he had to roll on the ground, clutching his sides. When he got up, he felt ashamed of himself. He remembered that a Tamashek should never show any emotion, neither joy nor grief, and especially in front of negroes. To hide his confusion, he declared that he was hungry, and demanded something to eat in a gruff voice. Soon they were all sitting round the fire listening to the millet hissing in the pot, while Amadou told him of their life with Abu Bakr.

There was a little pasture at the western approach where the rocks gave place to a broad *oued*. Every day, the boys led the herds there to graze. There was water there too. It oozed in during the night to form a shallow pool, which sufficed to water the cattle and goats, and the little grey donkeys too. But once a week, the camels had to be taken to the distant well of Tin Ramir. The donkeys went too, to carry the water-skins, for the pond water was bitter and not fit for human beings. Abu Bakr did not allow them to use the well by day for fear of meeting the *goumiers* there. As a result, Amadou and Dangi never saw another person face to face apart from the brigand, and they knew little of the world outside their rocky valley.

'We have to go to the well tomorrow,' said Amadou. 'Will you come with us, Mid-e-Mid?'

'Yes, I will,' he replied. 'How long does it take to get there?'

'A day and a half,' said Dangi, 'but the track is good going.'

They ate their millet and went to sleep. In the evening, all three went off to milk the camels, and the cows, too, for they yielded more than a quart of milk each. They did not drink it all, but put some aside for making butter. A leather bag was used for this purpose, and the milk was shaken by hand, until the butter formed. Mid-e-Mid left this work to the slaves.

Night fell very early in the ravine. It was quite dark down below, but the soaring cliffs still glowed like polished copper in the setting sun. The warmth of the day lingered in the valley until well past midnight.

In the morning they drove the cattle out to graze. They roped the camels one behind the other, so that they trotted along in single file, and only the donkeys with the water-skins and the camel foals ran untethered.

The donkeys knew the way and trotted in the lead, their heads nodding energetically as they went. The young foals ran whimpering near their mothers and tried to reach the udders. But Dangi and Amadou had covered the teats with little woven baskets, which were held on by leather straps over the camels' backs. Otherwise there would have been such constant stopping that the caravan could have made no real progress along the track. Last of all came Mid-e-Mid on Inhelumé. They travelled throughout the day over the plateau and at evening, they rested in a narrow *oued* for a few hours. At midnight, they set off again and reached their destination before sunrise on the second day.

The Well of Tin Ramir lies at the foot of a mountain in the middle of a dried-up water-course. It is not very deep. Indeed, it is not even a proper well, built of dressed stone. It is just a hole, dug in the hard ground. At one time the surface must have been at ground level and the shepherds had only to stoop and draw the water by hand. But now, over twenty feet of rope had to be paid out before the bucket reached water level. A beam of wood lay across the mouth of the well. It was deeply grooved, scored by the rope as the heavy leather dipper was hoisted brimming to the top.

Night still covered the *oued*. Only in the east was there a glimmer of grey. Day was not far off. They were in a hurry to get the animals watered before other herdsmen arrived on the same errand. For the well lay in a hollow, and no trees or bushes grew near by, so that the place was visible from a considerable distance.

They shared the work. Amadou and Dangi did the hauling, and Mid-e-Mid took the bucket from them and poured the water into a calf-skin. The camels crowded round greedily and jostled and bit each other trying to get there first.

It was a tedious job, for there were nine fully grown camels, including Inhelumé, and they could drink more than twenty-five gallons a head. Then there were four foals, and the donkeys clamoured for their share too. Finally, they needed fresh water to take back to the camp. In all, the boys had to lower and raise the leather bucket more than two hundred times before all their wants were satisfied.

Back and forth went Mid-e-Mid, using his stick whenever the stronger animals were too greedy at the expense of the weaker. Thirsty camels bite dangerously with their blunt molars, and these did not spare the foals, who ran squealing to their dams.

At last they had finished. They had just secured the water-skins and slung them under the donkeys, when an old woman came up, driving a large flock of sheep. The slaves were busy roping the camels together and checking all the cords, and they only saw the woman when she was quite close to Mid-e-Mid.

'*Salam aleikum,*' she called.

'*Aleik essalam,*' replied Mid-e-Mid.

The woman scrutinized his face. After the customary questions about health and camels and grazing she said, 'I have never seen you before. Is this the first time you have been to Tin Ramir?'

'Yes,' said Mid-e-Mid, half turning away. Abu Bakr had warned him not to give any information away to strangers. Everything you say – he had stressed this – can be reported back to the Beylik. And the Beylik will leave no stone unturned to capture me.

'Are those your herds?' the woman went on.

'Who else's would they be?' replied the boy. 'What news have you?' he added quickly, to change the subject.

'Ah!' sighed the woman. 'There is little good to report. The grazing is very poor this year. But in the south, near Kidal, they say it is better...'

'Yes,' said Mid-e-Mid, 'I have heard that too.'

'Have you heard that the man the Beylik put in prison for having too many guns has died?'

'Whom do you mean?' asked Mid-e-Mid and fear gripped him.

'I did not know him,' said the woman, 'but I have heard that he was a man called Agassum. Did you know him, or have you heard the name?'

Mid-e-Mid turned away his face and spat into the sand so that the woman would not see his tears. He wiped his face with his arm. Without looking at her, he answered, 'Yes, I have heard his name... I know whom you mean. Can you tell me how he died?'

The sheep thronged round the water hole and the woman had to drive them back with her stick, for in their stupidity, the ones behind would have pushed the ones in front down the well.

'Oh, he was not ill.' The woman turned back to him. 'The man who told me said that he died of homesickness. But he did not know exactly how it happened. So many people have died lately...'

Mid-e-Mid thought, must I hear from a strange woman that my father is dead?

He remembered the words of the idiot Kalil. Ah, Kalil, he thought, I did you an injustice. You told me the truth. For dead and free... for one man the prison-house, for another desert... dead and free... yes, it is all the same...

The woman babbled on, 'Yes, some of the *goumiers* who tried to capture Abu Bakr are dead too.'

'Did he kill them?'

'No one knows. They never returned.'

'And Abu Bakr? Do you know anything about him?'

'I know nothing. There is a rumour that he is dead, too, and the *goumiers* took his head to the Beylik. But I do not believe it. None of us believe it. If they brought a head, it must have been a stranger's head. We have suffered much wrong at Abu Bakr's hands.' She pointed to her flock. 'He took away my finest ram, a ram as big as a calf. And he stole a camel from my brother. Ah yes. He is a wicked man. But that they cut off his head... No, I do not believe it!'

'I do not believe it either,' said Mid-e-Mid.

'This is not good news. But I know of nothing better. Can you spare me a little tobacco?'

'No. I must ride to Kidal and buy some more. I have had none for a long time.'

'No one has any tobacco left,' said the woman. 'We must all wait until the tornadoes come and bring rain, and the herds can find rich pasture.'

'Yes,' said Mid-e-Mid. 'Have you heard anything else?'

'Oh, I hear lots of things. All the shepherds who come to the well have something to say. Have you heard that a war has broken out?'

'That is news indeed,' said Mid-e-Mid, concerned. 'Who is doing the fighting?'

'It is actually an old quarrel... But now blood has been shed. The *Kounta* have attacked our people and many are dead.'

'Where did it happen?'

'It was at the Well of Asselar. Twenty-one men were killed. No one dares to go there any more. And the cattle need the well so much. It is a salt well, you know, and that makes them very strong.'

'Yes, I know,' said Mid-e-Mid. 'But tell me, what will happen now?'

'Allah alone knows. I think that there have never been such troubled times as now... I hear that Intallah has called his son home.'

'Ajor Chageran?'

'Yes. He was summoned to his father. They say it is on account of Asselar. They say that he was called back to lead a war against the Kounta. Intallah is too old.'

'But Ajor is too young,' objected Mid-e-Mid.

'Ah, these days boys grow up so fast... There is a boy not much older than yourself, whose songs are sung all over the Mountains of the Iforas.'

'Tell me his name,' said Mid-e-Mid.

'Eliselus,' said the woman. 'That is not his real name. But people call him that.'

'Eliselus?' repeated Mid-e-Mid, taken aback. 'What a peculiar name.'

'Oh, his real name is odd too. He is called Mid-e-Mid.'

'Oh! And what do people say of him?' asked Mid-e-Mid, trying not to smile.

'They say he sings more beautifully than anyone else. But Abu Bakr is said to have kidnapped him.'

'I can give you better news than that, and perhaps you can spread it a little so that his mother hears it... she must be worried about him. I have heard from one who knows him well that he is in good health and suffers no want. He will soon return to his mother.'

'That is good news,' said the woman. 'I should love to hear him sing. But I have never chanced to be in the *oued* where his tent is pitched.'

'Perhaps he will pass this way one day,' smiled Mid-e-Mid.

'He must sing like the wind dancing over the rocks,' said the old woman.

'Surely you exaggerate!'

'No. It is the truth. All the world sings his songs.

> Tell me, O shepherds, have you seen Tiu'elen?
> The blue of antimony darkens her eyelids...

'I sing it badly, but I know it by heart.'

'Do you like it, then?'

'Who would not like it! And think of it! Young men spring to the saddle and ride off just to see Tiu'elen.'

'Oh!' said Mid-e-Mid, startled. 'Do they really do that?'

'Why, even from Tin Ramir a man set out and took sugar and tea and his best clothes... Just to see Tiu'elen.'

'They should not do that,' said Mid-e-Mid emphatically.

'Why not? If I were Tiu'elen, I should rejoice over every suitor who came, and I should take all their gifts and marry the one who brought the best presents.'

'And what do you think is the best present?' Mid-e-Mid gazed intently into her face, as though his life depended on her answer.

'That is a stupid question,' said the woman and tittered. 'Camels, of course, or even horses. The word has gone round that it is no use wooing Tiu'elen unless the suitor can ride six horses. You know what that means!'

'Yes,' said Mid-e-Mid and he turned away and hurried off towards Inhelumé. 'Only a Prince has six horses...'

'Are you in such a hurry?' the woman called after him.

'You can see that my herds are out of sight already. *Bismillah*, and thank you for the news. *Bismillah*!'

'Farewell!' shouted the woman. She watched him go and shook her head. Then she took the bucket and lowered it into the well. Ah, she said to herself, I have learnt one piece of news at least. Mid-e-Mid is well and suffers no want. Then she began to water her flock.

Mid-e-Mid kicked the camel so hard in the neck that it set off at a gallop along the trail, and in a few minutes he had caught up with the others.

Once again his heart was moved by all that he had learned – the death of his father, the war against the Kounta, the rumours about himself and the report of the suitors for High Summer.

And by turns he was radiant with joy and heavy with grief. He saw neither the landscape around him nor the camels ahead of him, neither the ever-nodding donkeys nor Amadou and Dangi who ran barefoot by their side. He followed his own thoughts. Sometimes, he wondered if he had ever had to think so hard in his life before.

I shall wait until Abu Bakr returns, he said to himself. But suppose he is dead? Bah! Kalil is only a fool. Still, he knew the truth about my father. And what if it is true about Abu Bakr? I must wait... wait...

He had no doubt that his mother would receive the news about him. News travels fast in those parts. I should have sent a message to High Summer too, he thought suddenly. But I could not confide it to that woman... Everything will turn out for the best, *inchallah*, he thought.

'Ho, there! Amadou! Dangi! Drive the beasts faster! We have no time to lose. We must be in the shade of the *oued* by noon. It is too hot on the plateau.'

The boys goaded the camels on. The donkeys ran faster of their own accord. The water lapped against the sides of the goatskin carriers and the mares called cries of warning to their foals.

They climbed into the mountains, the sun on their backs and the dazzling towers of rock ahead. Towards midday, they reached the resting place which they had left at midnight, and they completed their homeward journey without encounter or incident.

So it was that Mid-e-Mid began a new and uneventful life among the rocks of Tin Za'uzaten. Night after night, before he slept, he looked up at the Milky Way, waiting for the day when he could go back home, waiting for Abu Bakr's return. But he waited in vain.

CHAPTER TEN

The Wisdom of the Amenokal

AJOR CHAGERAN WAS the youngest son of the Amenokal. But Intallah had decided that he should succeed him. This was against the custom. Had he not been an outstanding personality, the old man could hardly have carried out his wishes. But he was greatly respected among the nobles both for his age and his piety. And among the princely chieftains of the seven Tamashek clans in the Adrar of the Iforas, he was the only one who bore the title of *Amenokal*. In matters which concerned the whole Tamashek tribe, the Beylik treated him as their spokesman. In disputes, his judgment was decisive.

In spite of it all, however, Intallah might still have been unable to get the consent of the other princes to his choice, Ajor Chageran, had he not secured his popularity by a dramatically bold decision.

One day, the Beylik himself had said to him, 'Your son, Red Moon, is growing up. Will you not send him to one of our schools?'

Intallah had replied very firmly, 'Red Moon will do as his father did before him.'

The Amenokal had never been to school, but he had been instructed in the wisdom of the Koran by a Marabut. He disliked the Beylik's schools. And all the Tamashek were with him to a man.

It needed great courage to give the Beylik such a reply. He was much more powerful than an *Amenokal*. Many decades before, the Beylik's soldiers had fought against the Tamashek and conquered them. And he could make short work of deposing a Prince who defied him.

Everyone waited for the Beylik to take sharp action against Intallah. But nothing happened. Many people believed that this was due to Tuhaya's intervention. It was known that Tuhaya was a friend of the Beylik, and it so happened that from that time, he had free access to Intallah's tent. No one knew for certain. Tuhaya was a great talker, but where the Beylik's affairs were concerned, he knew how to hold his tongue. He understood the responsibilities of a man who carried on his two shoulders the fate of a nation.

The tornadoes had not yet set in when Ajor returned to his father's tents. His young stepmother was the first to greet him.

'How strong you have grown, Ajor! Four years ago, when you went away to learn wisdom, you were a mere boy. Now you are a man.'

'People do not generally grow younger with the years,' he observed drily.

'It is good. You will need all your manhood and all your wisdom. Heavy times are upon us.'

'I see no famine. The cattle are fat and there is plenty of water in the wells.'

'You see only what the others see. As *Amenokal*, you will have to look further than other people and see into the future.' She played with the silver pendant on her breast. 'What if strangers drink the milk from our camels, and our herds are driven away from the feeding grounds of the Iforas Mountains?'

Red Moon looked at his stepmother's face thoughtfully. She was hardly more than thirty. Her features were clear and regular and her mouth and chin revealed great determination. She was not one of the Kel Effele, but came from a noble family of the Ibottenaten. Her girth was impressive. After the custom of her tribe, she had been more or less forcibly fed on milk as a young girl. She had to drink a gallon and a half or more every day, until she was so fat that she could hardly move without support. That was considered the height of beauty among the Ibottenaten. From far and wide, men came to sing her praises and to bring her presents. When Ajor Chageran's mother, Intallah's second wife,

107

died, Tadast was betrothed to the Amenokal of the Kel Effele. No one asked her consent to the marriage. But then, she would never have expected to be consulted.

Their marriage had been a happy one, and they were delighted when she gave birth to a daughter who was now seven years old. Since then, she had lost much weight and was barely sixteen stone. Apart from her relations, no one deplored the loss.

Her influence with Intallah was enormous and Red Moon had been devoted to her before he went away. For she was not only a charming person. She was uncommonly shrewd too.

'You speak of hard times,' said Ajor. 'What do you mean?'

'Your father is sick,' she said. 'His cares are great. And his advisers are evil.'

'Who advises him?' asked Ajor tensely.

'A man named Tuhaya. You must know him.'

'Yes, I know him,' said Ajor.

'But not well enough. He is more the Beylik's lackey than the son of his people. If he had not advised your father badly, we would have driven the Kounta away from Asselar.'

'The Kounta are strong,' replied Ajor.

'They are not stronger than we, the Tamashek, my son. But Tuhaya told your father that the Beylik would send his soldiers if we resorted to arms.'

'Perhaps it is true,' said Ajor.

'Did the Beylik send his soldiers when twenty-one of our men were murdered by the water-holes of Asselar? He said, "Everything will be investigated." '

'And was it?'

'I do not know. All I know is that our people may no longer use the well. Need I say more?'

Red Moon said, 'Thank you for telling me all this.'

'In the old days, you would have asked, 'What shall I do?' And I would have given you advice,' she said angrily.

'I shall always be glad to have your advice. But you know that I have not yet spoken to my father... How is my little sister Takammart?' he asked, changing the subject.

'She is playing there by the tent,' she said, offended. She realized that she could no longer twist him round her little finger.

Takammart was playing with her dolls. An old slave of Intallah's had made them for her, little straw puppets draped with bits of blue rag, to represent men and women riding camels. *Takammart* is a common name among the Ibottenaten. It means 'cheese from fresh milk'. The child's skin was very light in colour, only faintly tinged with brown. The Tamashek consider this ivory pallor to be a sign of great beauty, and when they compare it with goat's milk cheese, it is a compliment.

But Ajor was not able to greet Takammart after all. A man appeared to summon him to his father in the straw tent.

It was pleasantly cool under the thatch. Intallah sat on a leather cushion, over which a pale blue rug had been spread. His back was bowed and he leaned against one of the tent poles. He wore on his feet broad sandals of coloured leather which had come from Agadès.

Red Moon would tell at a glance that his father had aged very much. His tall frame – he was over six feet six inches in height – had shrunk. His eyes were sunken and his face was scored with wrinkles and furrows. His veil was wound untidily round his head and covered neither chin nor mouth. His beard was silver, although when Ajor had left his father's tents a few years previously, there was not a white thread to be seen there.

Ajor took in the contents of the half-dark tent with one quick glance. There was the old munition chest to his right with presents from foreign visitors; the brown box with a horn sticking up, which sometimes played Arab music; and the cuckoo clock with its gilt pendulum which had called the hour but a few times. It had been a present from a young geologist, who had given it to the Amenokal in exchange for a fat sheep. But the cuckoo got sand in its throat and there it remained, shut in behind the closed doors of its little Black Forest cottage, for ever silent.

All these were old familiar objects. And yet, Ajor could sense that something new, something strange was present. He could feel it distinctly, although he could not say what it was.

'Welcome, my son,' said Intallah and stretched out both hands towards him. 'I have waited a long time for you.'

Ajor embraced his father in the Arab fashion, as he had learned at the Marabut's. 'I heard that you were sick, Father...'

'My time is approaching,' said Intallah with a sigh. 'Soon I shall taste the joys of Paradise, *inchallah*...'

'You must not leave us yet,' said Ajor with deep emotion. 'Who will rule the people and dispense justice?'

'My hopes rest on you, my son,' replied the Amenokal reflectively. His hands, which rested on his knees were too weary to brush away the flies from his mouth. 'I sent you to the Marabut to learn the great truths of the Koran.'

'I have taken great pains to learn all that he could teach me, Father.'

'Yes, I know. That is why I am entrusting the rule of the tribes to you.'

'I shall observe the law, Father. And I shall practise justice and deliver judgment according to the Koran as I have learnt it.'

'That is not enough,' said the Prince. 'Mohammed the Prophet, praised be His name, wrote the Koran to make mankind happier. His law is for the good of men, not against it.' He offered his son a red pouch, which contained tobacco.

They both helped themselves and chewed. Red Moon saw how the skin of his father's cheeks hung in leathery folds. He saw the aquiline nose sharp as a blade, and the parted lips, and for the first time he realized to the full that his father had survived seventy rainy seasons, and had borne the honour and the burden of dominion for forty years.

'I am listening,' he said in a choked voice.

'Whenever I have had to give judgment, I have always tried to make people happier, to award satisfaction, to soften anger, to reconcile opponents. The honour of an *Amenokal*, my son, lies not in his sword, but in the happiness and well-being of his tribe.'

He spat out the quid of tobacco. 'I cannot even enjoy tobacco these days,' he said and tried to smile. But it was only the skin of his face which moved. 'I did not always know this. For many years,

I relentlessly extorted tribute from the people, because I thought that it was my right as Amenokal, that it would make people admit my power and that I should be feared. But in doing so, I drove away one man, who should have stood in the forefront as one of the great ones of the tribe...' He sighed and cleared his throat.

'Whom do you mean?' asked Ajor puzzled.

'Abu Bakr,' said Intallah. 'I took away his cattle and made him promises I could not keep. We became enemies. We should have been friends...'

'Abu Bakr!' cried Ajor. 'But he is the man who attacked me in the Marabut's tent! He dealt me such a savage blow that my head was swollen for several days and I could not return to you...'

'If he struck you, he did it on account of the old enmity between us... But now he is dead...'

'Is that true?' said Ajor. 'I heard a rumour on my way here... But I cannot believe it.'

'It is quite true,' said Intallah. 'I have seen his head. Tuhaya hunted him to his death.'

'Tuhaya?'

'Yes, I spurred on the *goumiers* and put them on his scent,' said a voice from the darkest corner of the tent.

Ajor spun round as if he had been stung. Now he knew why he had felt some strange presence in the tent.

'Who else is here?' he called out and his hand flew to his sword.

'It is only my friend Tuhaya,' said the Prince. 'You did not notice him when you entered the tent and he did not wish to disturb our conversation. Greet him as a friend, my son. He has been a devoted servant.'

'My services have been very slight,' said Tuhaya. He came forward and stretched out his hand to Ajor.

But Ajor did not take his hand. 'This conversation is not for you. Leave the tent quickly before I get angry. Get out! Now!'

'Ajor!' pleaded his father.

'Forgive me, Father, I respect your friends. But these are words between you and me alone. They concern no one else.'

Tuhaya hesitated. But as the Amenokal did not press him to remain, he said, 'Your arrival took me by surprise, Ajor Chageran. I ask your pardon.'

When he had gone, Red Moon said quietly, 'If he does not learn to do my bidding, I shall have to do his. I shall call him when I consider it necessary.'

'Now I see myself in you, my son,' said Intallah. 'That is why I did not contradict you. But do not be too hasty with your tongue and be slow in your deeds, or you may have cause for regret. It is easier to lose friends than to win them.'

'People say that I have a hot head, but cool blood.'

'They speak the truth of you, then,' replied the Amenokal. 'But it is not the whole truth.'

'What do you mean, Father?' He felt embarrassed, like a man who overhears strangers talking about himself.

'They forget to say that a man does not consist only of head and blood. The heart must be taken into account, too. And your heart, my son, is the thing that troubles me.'

Red Moon said nothing, but gritted his teeth. The wind rustled the straw of the tent. The voices of servants drifted through the air and the pounding of millet in a mortar shattered the peace of the afternoon.

'You have your father's heart, Ajor. But my heart – I did not know this when I was young, but I realize it now – my heart is not very sensitive. It does not betray any secrets, but it receives none either. Allah made it so...'

'Father,' said Ajor, 'I...'

'And yet, in its way, it is a good heart for an *Amenokal* to have, if he is wise enough to choose counsellors who will teach his dumb heart to speak. My son, hear my advice. I have had three wives in my life. The first was chosen by my father, the last two I chose myself. And all three have spoken for my heart, when my head wanted to commit some folly. The Tamashek call me wise. They say I am a *Marabut*. They do not know how much of my wisdom I owe to the hearts of my wives...'

He leaned forward and gripped his son's hands. 'You have your father's heart, Ajor. That is why I want you to take a good wife. In a few days' time, the Princes of the Tamashek will come and they will swear to choose you as *Amenokal* when I am dead. But when you are Amenokal, and the day of your succession is not far off, you must have a wife who will reign with you. For it is possible to carry out the law to the letter, and still do injustice...'

'You will be Amenokal for many years to come,' protested Red Moon forcibly. 'I need your experience and your advice. As for a wife...'

'I have found one for you, and I shall send her gifts...' said Intallah benevolently.

'No,' said Ajor, and reddened.

'You say you need my advice, and yet as soon as I offer it, you reject it.'

Intallah withdrew his hands and they dropped lifelessly on his knees. His eyelids were half-closed, and Ajor saw that the conversation was a great strain.

'Forgive me, Father,' he said. 'My heart is full of a girl...'

'Who is she?' asked Intallah.

'Her name is Tiu'elen and she is the daughter of the Marabut, my teacher. She is very beautiful.'

'Ah,' replied the Amenokal, 'your blood says she is very beautiful. But what does your head say, my son?'

'I do not understand, Father.'

'Has not your head told you that your wife must come from the tents of a noble family? Have you forgotten that we are the offspring of the first Cherif of Timbuktu, descended from the family of the Prophet, praised be His name? You say this girl is beautiful. That is little enough. Beauty fades.' He lifted one hand like a tired flag. 'Beware of beauty, my son, if her heart is not warm.'

'She has a heart, Father,' said Red Moon eagerly. 'But it is timid and young and does not know itself yet. I do not know her mind. She has only spoken a few words to me. I cannot tell what she thinks of me...'

'That I can find out presently,' said Intallah coolly. 'But she is not of noble stock. Her father is a Marabut, it is true, but he belongs to the vassals and not to the nobility. The woman I have chosen for you belongs to the Idnan clan. After ours, the Kel Effele, it is the richest and most important tribe, and she is the Prince's daughter. You should take her as your first wife. You can have the Marabut's daughter as your second wife, as the Koran allows.'

'Never,' said Ajor. 'Tiu'elen or no one.'

There was a long pause. One could hear the flies humming and the clear voice of little Takammart.

'I shall think it over,' said Intallah. 'But do not forget that an *Amenokal* is not the freest among men, but the one most tied. And his power depends on those very ties and obligations.'

'I shall wait,' said Ajor. 'You must rest now, Father. We have spoken long...'

'Not long enough, my son. We have only spoken of personal matters. We have not yet mentioned the Tamashek and the Beylik. And now I want you to call Tuhaya back. For he is an experienced politician.'

'Very well,' said Ajor. 'If you wish it.'

As the three men sat together, Tadast, Ajor's stepmother, entered the tent. In spite of her corpulence, she was not clumsy. She placed a dish of charcoal on the ground and put on a little can of water to boil. Then she brought a tray with glasses, one of which was filled with green tea. There was also a sugar-loaf and a small hammer made of iron and mounted with copper.

She knelt down and blew on the embers to make the water boil faster. At the same time, she made a sign to Ajor that she wanted to stay and listen to the conversation.

But Ajor behaved as if he had not understood her gesture, and said, 'You can leave everything here. I will make the tea myself. We have important matters to discuss.'

She left the tent in eloquent silence.

Intallah said, 'You must have heard that the Tamashek may no longer use the Well of Asselar, and that twenty-one of our men have been killed there.'

'Yes, I have heard so,' said Ajor.

'But the Oued of Asselar has always been used by our shepherds, my son. There are nearly thirty waterholes in the *oued*. They have all been dug by our people.'

'The Kounta have also dug waterholes there,' said Tuhaya.

'That is true,' said Intallah. 'There is water enough for everyone. You could ride there with a hundred camels and there would be sufficient water for them all.'

Ajor threw the tea into the bubbling water.

The Amenokal continued: 'I do not need to tell you that Asselar is indispensable for us Tamashek. There is no water which acts so powerfully on the bowels, and there is none which makes the cattle and camels so strong. It is from the waters of Asselar and the fresh pastures there that our cattle get their firm flesh and the camels their well-set humps.'

'That is so,' agreed Tuhaya. 'And it is also true that for many centuries we have had our rights at Asselar.'

The tea had drawn. Ajor poured it into the glasses and passed them round. Then he broke up the sugar for the second and third glasses. Ajor looked up at Tuhaya. The latter returned his gaze politely and gave him a forced smile, so that his teeth protruded over his lower lip and emphasized his resemblance to a beast of prey.

'We need a *Marabut*,' said Intallah, 'to pray to Allah for the restoration of the well.'

Ajor put his glass down impatiently. 'Are our swords blunt or our right arms paralysed? Have we no camels to ride? We should remember our strength and drive the Kounta away!'

Intallah said, 'In these words too, do I see myself. That is how I would have spoken forty years ago. But then there was no Beylik in the land, or at least, his power did not stretch to Kidal. Our men were not slow to draw their swords when the Kounta disputed their rights, but they were outnumbered and killed.' He sighed. 'Do you know, my son, that many of the Tamashek have reproached me? They say, "Why has the Amenokal not called us to arms, to fight the thieving Kounta? The Amenokal takes our sheep and cattle but he does not lend us his sword." That is what they are saying, I know full well. I know my people. But they forget that I can do nothing without provoking the Beylik against us. He has promised to investigate the affair. It is taking a long time. It has already taken four weeks.'

'I rode to the Beylik on your father's behalf and told him all our troubles,' said Tuhaya. 'He gave me a ready ear...'

'It must have been his left ear, Tuhaya,' mocked Ajor. 'The right one was listening to the Kounta.'

Tuhaya replied unabashed, 'It is just as you say, Ajor. There is only one Beylik for both the Kounta and the Tamashek and it takes a long time to discover the truth.'

'And what is the truth?' asked Ajor.

'The truth is this,' said Tuhaya, weighing his words carefully. 'Our shepherds began to quarrel. The dispute began with a runaway ass and ended with a fight about the water holes...'

'Ah!' interrupted Ajor, 'and that is what you told the Beylik? That we started the quarrel?'

'He knew it already,' said Tuhaya.

'Then you have betrayed our cause by admitting as a fact something which has still to be proved! And how can it be proved? It is impossible. All our witnesses have been slain. Am I not right?'

'You are too impetuous, my son. You are as hot-blooded as a stallion fighting for its mate. You must learn that in any struggle, the truth must prevail in the end, not lies.'

'But in this case it is the lie which has prevailed so far. The Kounta have stolen something which did not belong to them.'

'Intallah's son,' said Tuhaya softly, 'believe me, I put our case to the Beylik as eloquently as the Amenokal would have done had he ridden to Kidal himself. But for the moment, there is nothing we can do but wait. I know the Beylik. As long as you are negotiating seriously, he will listen to you. But if you try to force his hand, he will force you.' He drained his glass and put it down in front of him on the ground.

He thought, this youngest son of Intallah's is like a tree with rich foliage and many thorns. But the camels will eat the leaves and rub off the thorns between their teeth. It took me much time and effort to hunt down Agassum, who would not share his spoils with me. But I got him at last. It was hard work to bring Abu Bakr to his death. But I succeeded, *hamdullillah*. And it will not be easy to tame this colt, but...

'It is as Tuhaya says,' said the Prince. 'But it might be a good thing if he would ride again to Kidal and talk to the Beylik, so that our cause is not lost through forgetfulness and neglect.'

'Yes, Father, send Tuhaya to Kidal. That is a good idea,' said Ajor with enthusiasm. 'But it would be a wise move to send me on a mission round all the camps and tents of the Tamashek. I must explain to our people why we are not going to war. If this is not done, they will lose their faith in the Amenokal, and they may even rebel.'

'I shall follow your advice, Ajor,' Intallah replied, 'and now we must go outside and say our prayers. The sun will soon be setting.'

Tuhaya supported the old man. It was a great effort for him to stand. Ajor saw that his father had gone terribly thin. The bones stood out at his wrists, and his legs were like two withered sticks.

Carpets had been spread out for the men. The women and children stood in the background. Intallah recited the verses of the prayers, and the others repeated them after him. They bowed towards Mecca, and threw themselves to the ground to show their humility. They prayed loud and long. According to the Koran, a community of prayer has much more efficacy than that of one man alone.

Then Intallah returned to his tent, leaning on Tuhaya and his son.

As Ajor came out again, his stepmother Tadast beckoned to him.

'Ajor Chageran,' she said, 'I have heard your voice in council.'

'You were eavesdropping!'

'No,' she said, 'you were shouting. What you said was good. I could tell that you were opposing Tuhaya.'

'I fear that he has betrayed our cause.'

'You are right,' said Tadast.

'But now the next step has been decided. Tuhaya is to ride to Kidal again. I myself will seek out the men of the Tamashek tribes and speak to them.'

'Good,' said Tadast, with lively approval. 'And you must stir them up against Tuhaya, so that your father sends him away...'

'You do not bear your name amiss,' laughed Ajor. 'Does not *Tadast* mean 'mosquito'?'

'In truth,' she said, 'my name shows me where my duty lies. If men are too weak to fight for their rights, I must goad them so that they prefer death by the sword to the sting of my tongue.'

'You will not sting me,' answered Ajor complacently. 'If you try, I shall draw your sting. But you will do what I ask.'

He had drawn himself up to his full height, so that she had to look up to him.

'You have learnt a lot, Ajor,' she said. 'You have learnt how to handle women.'

'I wish that were true,' he said. 'Now listen. I shall say no word against Tuhaya in the tents of strangers, for I do not know who are his friends and who are his enemies. But I shall command the Tamashek to bury their old feuds with each other and to unite against the Kounta. And I shall make the Beylik restore Asselar to us. Everything must be made ready for action when the tornadoes break and his aeroplanes cannot take off and the trucks cannot get through. I want you, Tadast, to talk to the women at the wells. You must tell them to prepare their husbands and sons to obey my orders. It must be like a fire spreading from blade to blade when the fields are parched, whipped by the wind until a sheet of flame flares red against the sky.'

'You will be a great man among the Tamashek,' she said admiringly. 'I shall do your bidding.'

That evening, for the first time, black rain clouds loomed up over the *oued*. But not a drop fell. It was still too soon. A heavy sultriness lingered into the night. The animals snarled restlessly and the men groaned in their sleep.

Next morning, Tuhaya set off on one of the Amenokal's camels to speak to the Beylik in Kidal, in the south-east. But Red Moon rode westward, to visit the tents of the tribes. He took his fastest camel and enough provisions for a month.

As they parted, Intallah said, 'I feel much better since you returned. I have placed my cares on your back. There they sit like a rider, tugging at the bridle. But show them that you can throw them off...'

Then he added, 'When you come back from your journey, I shall be able to tell you what I think of the girl you mentioned. *Bismillah*, my son.'

CHAPTER ELEVEN

The Princes in Council

THE PRINCES OF THE TAMASHEK gathered together at Intallah's camp. All the clans had sent their most distinguished leaders. The last to arrive were the Princes of the Ibottenaten and the Iforgumessen. Their tents lay to the north and east of Tamesna where their great herds of camels found fodder year in, year out, among the dunes. It took them seventeen days to reach Intallah's tent. And although they were the poorest, they were received the most cordially and entertained for a week.

They were strenuous days for the Amenokal. But his son's return had done him good and Tadast stood by his side. Perhaps it was due to her that the men from the Tamesna Desert were received with such unstinted hospitality.

There was much exchange of talk, but most of it was blown away on the wind. Some of the Princes prided themselves on their conversation, and still found nothing worth saying.

Intallah, Prince of the Kel Effele and the Amenokal of all the Tamashek clans in the Iforas Mountains, held his court on the third day. He sat in the circle of the men, supported by numerous cushions, only slightly raised from the ground.

The guests were silent. They did not want to miss a word.

Intallah scrutinized their faces one by one. There were the haggard features of Bi Saada, the Idnan prince who in his youth had hunted lions single-handed, armed only with his sword. He still carried a scar from those days on his right shoulder.

There was Ramzata with his bald round head and thick lips, always ready for a joke. There sat the Prince of the Iforgumessen whose noble descent was as distinguished as that of the Amenokal.

120

Some were lean with wrinkled, greyhound faces. They loved nothing better than long caravan journeys. Others were thick set and splendidly clothed, and one could tell at a glance that they were men of substance. They were as different as fresh grass and withered bents, as soft fur and dried leather. But they had two things in common. They spoke the same language, and they loved the same land. They hated the town and the fixed walls of a house, and their chief delight in life was to gallop full speed over the velvet sand on the swiftest camel they possessed.

Intallah began to speak.

'When a father leaves his tent, he does not entrust it to the weakest or the least capable of his sons. He hands it over to the strongest and wisest.'

'That is so,' murmured the Princes and nodded.

'My wives have borne me many sons,' Intallah went on, 'and I love them all. But only one can keep watch over the camp and be responsible for my herds.

'I am old and soon I shall no longer sleep in my tent and listen to the noise of the camels at night. I must take steps to see that after I am gone, my cattle are led to the well every day.'

'Yes, indeed,' chorused the Princes. And Bi Saada said, 'That is how a wise man orders his affairs. Truly you are a *Marabut*, Intallah.'

Intallah said, 'Some years ago, I gathered my sons about me and put this question to them, 'What leaves the most magnificent trail in its wake?"

The men looked at each other. They liked riddles and would have enjoyed trying to solve this one themselves. But they sat silent out of respect for Intallah.

'I had one son,' Intallah continued, 'who answered, "It is the trail of the gazelle. The gazelle's track is unique." Another son replied, "The spoor of the moufflon, the wild mountain sheep. There is nothing to compare with it." '

Bi Saada would have liked to say, It is that of the lioness about to spring. But he was too courteous to interrupt.

Intallah said, 'A third son thought it must be the track of a guinea fowl. It is so decorative and faultless.'

The Prince of Iforgumessen could not restrain himself any longer. 'Intallah,' he cried, 'did no one mention the track of the young camel in the red sand of the dunes?'

Intallah ignored him and said, 'Yet another son believed that the track of the ostrich was the finest, because it was so rare.'

The men shook their heads at this answer.

'But one of my sons,' said Intallah, 'gave me this answer. "Father," he said "the most glorious trail I know is the trail of the great tornado. The tornado's trail means water, it means pasture, it means life itself." '

'Ah!' cried the Princes. 'That was the cleverest answer, the best of all!'

Intallah said, 'That was the answer given by my son Ajor Chageran.'

Then they cried, 'He is worthy to guard your tents and breed your herds. In truth, it is so!'

Intallah said, 'He shall be *Amenokal* when I enter the gates of Paradise.'

They replied, 'Some of us are older men and our rank is as exalted as your own. But we want your son Red Moon to be *Amenokal* when you leave this earth.'

Intallah said, 'Swear it by the sacred Koran and by the beard of the Prophet, praised be His name. Swear that you will keep your oath and that nothing will alter this decision. Swear that my son will be *Amenokal*, come what may.'

Then they all swore the oath.

Tadast brought glasses of fresh tea and the servants offered tobacco all round. A sheep was roasted on a spit. The smell of mutton mounted to their nostrils and loosened their tongues. Only Intallah lay back among the cushions and refused even tobacco. But in his heart, he was satisfied.

While this was happening in Intallah's camp, Red Moon was riding from tent to tent, from *oued* to *oued*, from well to well. Wherever he stopped, he was certain of a warm welcome. He was plied with glasses of tea many times each day and he had to answer many questions. Men and women begged him to tarry. But his time was limited. Often he rode all through the night in order to meet some shepherds at a distant water-hole.

The girls admired his slim build and his uncommon spirit, but the former more than the latter. And they often forgot to hide their faces in their headcloths and gazed at him unveiled. But he did not look at them. He spoke only to the men and the youths. He was possessed by the determination to wipe out the defeat at Asselar. By turns he charmed his hearers and then provoked them until their passions were fanned to white heat and they wanted to ride to war with him there and then, intoxicated with the wine of their own words.

Never in his speeches did he mention the clans by name. 'We, the Tamashek,' he repeated again and again. And if people asked, 'Are the Ibottenaten with us?' or 'How can we ride side by side with the Kel Telabit, with whom we have an ancient feud?' he answered sharply. 'These are names I have never heard. But if you ask me if all the Tamashek are with me, then I will tell you, "Yes, all of them. They will come from Tin Ramir and from Tin Zaouaten, from Kidal and from Aguelhoc, from the Oued of Sadidän and from the Well of Sandeman. They will come from the rising sun and the setting sun." '

'When is it to be?' they asked, breathless with excitement. The mere idea of such a campaign fired their imagination.

Red Moon replied, 'When the first tornado whips the land, do not delay a single day, but make for my father's camp. You must ride your swiftest camels and sharpen your swords until they are as keen as daggers. You must bring your spears and wear your finest robes. But leave your shields at home. We do not need them...'

They said, 'We could come before that. We can leave our herds to the women and the girls and the old men.'

Red Moon shook his head. 'No one must come sooner and none must come later. Wait for the tornado. When the clouds tower like black mountains in the sky, come! When the rain flails the countryside, come! When the lightning flashes, come!'

Some hesitated. 'But then the *oueds* will be flooded. It will be difficult to get the camels through.'

Red Moon retorted bitingly, 'Anyone who does not know how to ride had better stay at home and eat pap.'

They laughed and he had won.

Where he could not visit every tent, the men rode out to meet him. They stopped him on the way to hear the words from his own lips. He reminded them, 'Do not betray our plans to the Kounta, nor to the Beylik's men.'

They said, 'We will be silent as the black rocks in the Adrar of the Iforas and as mute as the sand that covers the graves of the dead.'

The smiths who had pitched their tents by the water-holes gave their bellows no rest by day or night, forging anew the iron for the swords. The wind carried the ringing of the hammer into the silence of the *oueds*. Red saddles were repaired and the women wove plaited girdles from black goat's hair.

Red Moon wore a sky blue robe and a white veil and he rode a black camel. His red saddle had come from Agadès and his bright woollen saddle-cloth from Timimum. A silver amulet hung on his breast.

Everyone who saw him wanted to equal him in raiment, or at least to approach its splendour. Long hoarded treasures were brought into the light from the big brown and blue-painted saddle bags. Cloths were dyed rich purple and given a high gloss by beating with a piece of iron, and were handed over as veils for their sons. Leather amulets were ordered from the *Marabuts* as a protection against wounds, and had to be painted red and yellow by the smiths' daughters.

Boys rode through the *oueds* looking for wood for the shafts of lances, for not all were rich enough to afford iron shafts. And the men talked night and day of nothing but which camel they would ride for the gathering of the clans.

The hatred against the Moorish Kounta mounted to boiling point and the name 'Asselar!' was the battle-cry for all the Tamashek.

Red Moon rode from west to north and from north to east and with his words, he forged the unity of the tribe. Many of them knew that he had been designated the future *Amenokal*, and he was received with honours that were usually reserved for his father. To show their respect, the men galloped at full tilt towards his retinue, their camels foaming at the bit, and pulled up their mounts just short of a collision with Ajor's camel. Anyone with a gun fired bullets into the air which whistled dangerously over his head. The women placed their palms over their mouths and uttered piercing war cries. And the children called out, 'Stop, stop!' and wanted to touch his hand as he rode by. The *Marabuts* spoke favourable oracles and prayed for the blessing of Allah. Only the slaves stood in the background in dumb admiration. For they had no part in the expedition. They were mere household possessions and belonged to the tent, like mortars and mats, and they had to look after the cattle when their masters were away.

It had grown very hot and the time of the tornadoes was imminent. Over the sandy outcrops of the Iforas Mountains in the north, and over the granite rocks of the stony deserts of the south, whirls of dust, some pinkish red and some bright orange, danced their unpredictable dances. The air shimmered over the *reg* and in many wells the water failed. Dead calves were torn to pieces by hyenas and jackals, and lay here and there among the arid wastes. These young animals were not strong enough to withstand the long, hot, waterless days. Men and beasts yearned for the big rains, and searched the sky for signs.

Red Moon had nearly finished his journey and he guided his camel along the trail that led to his father's tent. During the last few days his task had been easy. He had reached the territory where the women had been primed by Tadast. The name Asselar was in everyone's mouth, and the campaign against the Kounta a foregone conclusion.

'Tadast has spoken to us,' they said to him. 'You have only to say the word. When will it be?'

'Come when the first tornado sets in,' he replied. 'And hold your tongues in front of the Beylik's men.'

'Whom do you mean?' they asked.

'I name no names,' he said. 'You know better than I.'

They said, 'The only man who visits the Beylik is Tuhaya.'

Red Moon answered, 'You must know. Guard your tongues.'

When he was still two days' ride from Intallah's camp, he charged a distinguished man of the Kel Effele to bear a message to the Amenokal of the Kounta in a place called Bourem.

'First you will say to the Amenokal that Intallah and Red Moon send greetings. They would like to talk over many things with the Princes of the Kounta which cannot be said by a messenger. But Intallah is sick and he cannot ride to Bourem. Therefore, we ask the Kounta to send to us a delegation of men of standing who can speak for the whole tribe. It would be best if the Amenokal came himself, but we do not want to suggest that he undertakes such a long journey.'

Red Moon thought for a while, then added, 'If they are afraid to travel through our land, tell them that Intallah guarantees them a safe conduct and unhindered return.

'If they answer, "Yes, we will come, but we must wait until the tornadoes are over," you will reply that Intallah has not long to live and it is not certain that his successor will be able to speak with the same weight for all the tribes in the Adrar of the Iforas. Therefore it is vital that their ambassadors come right away without delay.

'Do you understand?'

The Kel Effele said, 'I have noted every word. You can depend on me.'

Red Moon considered a little longer. 'I have one thing more to say. Make it clear to the Amenokal of the Kounta that he must send rich men with many herds, men of high rank. Not young men who only possess one camel. They are too impetuous and ready to take risks. But do not repeat that to the Kounta.'

The man saddled his camel and galloped off towards Bourem. He could not be back in less than two weeks. That gave Ajor a breathing space.

On his return, he discovered that Tuhaya had come back from Kidal on the previous day.

Tuhaya came to meet him before he had seen his father and said, 'I congratulate you, Intallah's son. There has been no dissension over your nomination as *Amenokal*. That is a good omen.'

Red Moon thanked him courteously and asked, 'What news do you bring from the Beylik?'

Tuhaya screwed up his eyes and made a wry mouth as if the sun dazzled him or he had taken a bite from a bitter fruit.

'It is harder than you think. The Beylik proposes to separate the Kounta and the Tamashek, so that no dispute can break out between them in future. He wants to hand over Asselar to the Kounta and make the Valley of Tilemsi the frontier. That would mean that the Tamashek must not cross the dividing line with their herds...'

Red Moon said nothing but his displeasure was clear from his expression.

'Hear me out,' said Tuhaya quickly. 'I answered the Beylik, "If you do that there will be great unrest. No one can say what the Tamashek will do." Then the Beylik sent you this message, you must keep this plan to yourself. He will take no action until he has been to see you in your tent and discussed it with you. That will be after the rains...'

'That is what I thought,' said Ajor, and there was bitterness in his voice. 'In order to spare the Beylik any embarrassment, we must forgo our claim on Asselar. He will send his soldiers into the Valley of Tilemsi and stop us from crossing the boundary.'

'You are disappointed,' said Tuhaya, 'but I said a great deal and if I had not gone – I tell you this in confidence – the Beylik would have imposed some punishment on the Tamashek because they started the quarrel at the well.

'I stopped him from doing that. But I do not wish to boast of it. Still, I beg you, do not start any trouble. A rumour has come to my ears that you talked a great deal in the tents of our people. I assume that you have been advising them not to disturb the peace, as we agreed.'

Ajor said, 'I must thank you very much for all you have done. I cannot dispense with your advice during this crisis. So it is important that you do not leave Intallah's tent for the next few difficult weeks. I have not managed to convince everyone that we should not go to war...'

Tuhaya swallowed these lies with relish. Praise and flattery were as important for him as millet and rice for hunger, and water for thirst.

But to his father, Ajor said, 'I have heard that a delegation from the Kounta is coming here to speak with you. I beg you to receive them kindly. But leave the talking to me.'

Intallah said, 'That is good news, my son. But I fear that you are hasty in speech and I have learned from Tuhaya that the Beylik is on the side of the Kounta. So they are not likely to be conciliatory. If there is strife, they will ask the Beylik for help. And that will be a bad thing for us.'

Ajor pacified him. 'I shall speak to the Kounta as softly as I spoke to the tribes of the Tamashek on my journey.'

Intallah was reassured. 'I shall not live long,' he said solemnly. 'I feel it. And therefore it does not matter which of us speaks. You are the *Amenokal*. You will have to bear the consequences of your words. Sit down by my side, my son. I have something to say to you.'

Red Moon sat down, his face slightly flushed. He guessed that this time his father was not going to talk politics.

'I have some news for you. It seems that the girl you spoke to me about is not too unsuitable for you. The two men whom I sent to my friend the Marabut have given me a good report. They think that she would be a fitting wife for an *Amenokal*. But they also said that there are girls from nobler tents and that beauty is no substitute for birth...'

'For me, there is only Tiu'elen,' replied Red Moon stubbornly.

'For you, my son... But possibly you are not the only man interested in this girl...'

'Why do you think that, Father?'

'She did not enquire about you and sent you no word of greeting. Also her mother does not seem to have any notion of a union between our families. And there is something else, too. Nearly every day young men, and old ones too for that matter, come to see High Summer and to bring her gifts...'

'No. That cannot be,' Ajor objected. And the red in his cheeks was so bright that Intallah noticed it.

'A Tamashek must never show his emotions,' he said in his cracked voice. 'It is as I say, my son. My trusted envoys tell me that all these visits have come about because of a song which is sung at every campfire.'

'Oh, that confounded song!' said Red Moon. 'The lad who made it up is a serf who has not even a camel to call his own.'

'Who is he?' asked Intallah.

'Mid-e-Mid ag Agassum,' said Ajor disparagingly. 'A silly boy, a conceited dripper of honeyed words. He only sang the song so that he could lick the sides of the millet pot. Afterwards he fell into Abu Bakr's hands and no one has heard anything of him since...'

'You are excited, my son,' smiled Intallah, with all the insight of an older man. 'It is not known if the girl has favoured one suitor more than another. And so I shall send presents with a wooer to the Marabut and ask him to discuss the bride-price. I shall arrange it tomorrow, inchallah.'

'No,' said Red Moon, 'not before the end of the big rains, not before the last tornado.'

'But why? A moment ago you were afraid that this girl might pick another man and now you want to postpone the wooing. You need not marry her immediately. You can wait until after my death...'

'Father, please do not speak so...' said Red Moon. 'I have other reasons.'

'I am listening,' said Intallah.

'I do not want to woo her until I have won a name for myself among the Tamashek. High Summer must know that she is marrying a man whom everyone respects...'

Intallah shook his head in bewilderment. 'And that, you think, will be after the rains?'

'*Inchallah*,' said Ajor embarrassed. 'Do not question me further.'

'You are going your own way early in life,' muttered the old man.

'Only this once, Father.'

'The cub is already wiser than the experienced lion,' said Intallah angrily. 'But that is the way of the world. Go now. I am wearier than you think.'

And Ajor left him.

Takammart ran out from a tent and pulled at his robe. 'Ajor,' said the child, 'I am playing at being High Summer.'

'Is that a new game?' he asked in surprise. 'Where did you hear that name?'

'It comes in a song we sing,' chattered the little girl, who, like all Tamashek children went about completely naked. She hummed:

> Tell me, O shepherds, do you know Tiu'elen?

'So that is your new game, is it?' And he had to laugh.

'Yes, Ajor. Will you paint my eyelids with antimony like High Summer?'

'All right,' he said. 'Just a little. Go and get some make-up from your mother.'

The child came back with a stick of antimony. Ajor knelt in front of her and with the dark blue pencil he painted her eyelids. And he even put a touch of it on her lips.

CHAPTER TWELVE

The Tornado

T HE KOUNTA DELEGATION arrived as the heat reached its zenith. The very air seemed to boil. You could not touch the rocks without blistering your hands. The livestock lay motionless all day in the meagre shadow of the thorn trees and only ate at night. The shepherds had driven their flocks to the few wells which had not run dry. Day by day they lowered bucket after bucket to bring the muddy brown water to the surface. Sometimes they had to wait three days for their turn, and even then there was not enough water for everybody. Cattle, sheep and young camels and donkeys collapsed within sight of the water-holes and had no strength to get to their feet again. The vultures were too sated to rise and fly away when a man passed by. And the ravens picked only the choicest delicacies, eyes, liver and intestines from animals not yet dead.

The children, too, suffered terribly from the heat. And milk had to be drunk early in the morning straight after milking, for it turned sour in half an hour.

The sky was covered, and yet the light was dazzling, for the clouds intercepted the rays of the sun and diffused them so that there was no shade.

Intallah had sent his friends to receive the Kounta delegation in a fitting manner. It consisted of seven men, among them a brother of their Amenokal.

If the Tamashek preferred to go about veiled to the eyes, the Kounta always went bareheaded to show the magnificence of their long black hair. They were more elegant than the Tamashek, with fine boned limbs and narrow heads. Their eyes were oval, their noses delicately curved. Fine down sprinkled their cheeks and many wore beautiful earrings of silver or stone.

The Amenokal received them in front of the straw tent which had been specially erected for them. The greetings were profuse and lengthy, and they would have been even more elaborate, if Intallah had not excused himself on account of his age and infirmity. He requested them all to be seated on the rugs spread out in the shady tent.

They drank tea and busily chewed the tobacco which was passed round freely. They discussed camels, and pasture, the shortage of food and the cost of living. They deplored the low prices they got for their sheep and also the high prices demanded for brides in various districts. But no one mentioned Asselar. Tuhaya reported the latest news from Kidal and Ajor Chageran was cordially congratulated by the Kounta on his unanimous election as the future *Amenokal*. But no one spoke of Asselar.

Ajor's messenger had done his work well. It was soon apparent from the conversation that the Kounta present were men of means. Some owned more than one hundred and fifty camels and over three hundred head of cattle, not to speak of sheep, goats and donkeys.

In the afternoon, huge dishes of rice and butter were placed before the naked feet of the guests and the slaves carried in roasted mutton, still hot from the fire.

The Kounta tore great hunks of meat from the ribs and legs and stuffed them into their mouths. Conversation was completely silenced. All one could hear was the loud smacking of lips and the cracking of small bones. Brown hands dipped into mountains of rice, which seemed to cave in of their own accord. Then fresh dishes were brought with mutton cooked a different way, boiled and cut into small pieces and so strongly spiced with red pepper that some of the guests found their eyes watering. Fresh butter was poured over the rice and big white onions tinged with red were added to it.

Intallah bade his guests not to offend him by leaving any food. They groaned and declared that they could not force down another morsel but still they managed to empty the dishes to the last grain of rice and they showed by their hearty belching that the food had been to their liking. A live sheep was brought in so that they could wipe the dripping fat from their hands on its fleece, and fresh tea with mint was prepared immediately, to soothe the grossly overstrained stomachs. Everyone's forehead ran with sweat and gummed their eyes.

Tadast passed round thorns of the *teborak* tree. They used them to pick their teeth and they spat out the bits on the carpets. This was a meal to seal friendships and to call the dying back to life. Intallah had fallen asleep, but he was very old and it offended no one. Ajor led the conversation in his place, and dazzled the guests with his excellent knowledge of Arabic.

It was nearly five o'clock before they betook themselves to their tents to sleep off the banquet. The air was as heavy as if the sky were a solid weight, pressing it down from above. Not a sound could be heard but the sawing of ants in the thatch, and the rustle of lizards as they snapped at flies so bloated with mutton sauce that they could hardly move.

Stillness reigned until just before twilight. Then a gusty wind sprang up. It blew from the south-south-west, driving clouds of pink grasshoppers before it. Tiny birds, clustered into round black swarms, haunted the derelict scene with uneasy, fluttering wings. The sickly grey pall hiding the sky, was whisked away by giant hands and plunged into invisible vats, to reappear with edges frayed, and dyed deep indigo. At the same time, clouds of red dust arose, only to be sucked aloft by fast-moving currents of air, and sent spinning along the towering clouds like witches' brooms let loose.

With a loud creak, dry twigs snapped off from the living plant, and went cartwheeling madly over stone and scree. Behind them crackled and splintered a whole army of whirling vegetation, which was hurtled against the thorn bushes, then pitchforked into the fray again, mutilated and shattered. Snakes lifted their hissing mouths expectantly against the wind, and peered from cover. Their ominous traces wound in and out of the sandy clumps of the *affasso* bushes.

But it was the crash of a rotten acacia tree which woke the camp from sleep. Camels bellowed cries of warning to their young. Sheep bowed their heads to the earth, whilst the goats bleated as they pressed round their leaders and young bucks jostled one another with their horns. The men lashed at the stubborn cattle with leather whips and sticks, to try to drive them to higher ground. A brown shape here and a white one there, broke loose from the moving stream of cows and tried to hide between the tents, only to be shooed back by the ear-splitting yells and upraised hands of the women.

Gazelles leapt high into the air, sailing across the wind like yachts in a stormy sea, frightening a girl who was driving her lambs to the shelter of an overhanging rock. Only the yellow-brown dogs, so thin that their ribs showed, took no notice of the tumult, but went on worrying the remains of the slaughtered sheep, and gnawing hopefully at the well-picked bones.

Kounta and Tamashek alike gazed with searching eyes at the jagged clouds veering this way and that, under and over at the whim of the ever-changing wind. Sand was thrown on the embers so that the tents would not catch fire. Newborn animals were roped to tree-trunks. Skins spread out to dry, were weighted down with stones.

Straight from the south, an ash grey wall loomed up, blurring earth and sky to one blanket of dust. The setting sun, suddenly penetrating it here and there, spattered it with flecks of rust. The wind was silent, as if it had paused for a moment to take a deep breath and summon the tornado from the depths of its bursting lungs and reeking throat.

The men cursed in their tents of straw, and pulled their veils close up to their eyes. Lightning flashed and thunder pealed through the warm dust which sprinkled the *oued*. In the livid half-light before night fell, the thorny branches of the trees stood poised like sinister grappling hooks, ready to bring the heavens themselves crashing down to earth.

Then the rain started. Countless guillotines sliced the baked soil, and hacked the sand, pulping the withered grass into mud.

Its stinging needles scourged the backs of the cattle and whipped against their closed eyelids. It smothered dunes and mountains in icy sheets and muffled the lightning behind dingy curtains.

Tiny rivulets trickled into the tents, digging little channels for themselves, oozing into puddles wherever they discovered a hollow, only to rise again to a new level, to dig new channels and find fresh hollows elsewhere. Rain dripped through the straw roofs on to the people below, seeping into their garments, so that dyes were loosened and skins were smeared with indigo.

Streams of mud flowed down into the valley, churning the floor of the *oued* into a soft dough, then overflowed until the whole breadth was filled and the deepest hollows flooded, and finally surged in a wild maelstrom into the night. Blocks of granite skipped like pebbles, and were hurled into fragments or rolled out flat. Trees rooted in the banks of the stream broke from their moorings, and were dashed into the flood, still laden with blossoms and nests.

And still it rained. Driven by the wind, the downpour pounded mercilessly against the walls of the straw tents, extinguishing the last sparks of the fires. Clothing clung to shuddering bodies. Colour ran from painted sandals. Not a single light gave comfort in the blackness, and the only evidence of living bodies close by was the steaming of their clothes. Mute, chilled to the marrow, the people squatted uncomfortably, longing for daylight. There was not a dry patch left for a man to lie down and sleep.

After two hours, the downpour subsided to a soft drizzle. Its force was broken. But no one dared to go out of doors, for the water still sucked and gurgled and they could feel the icy wind which made them shiver.

They spent the rest of the night as best they could, perched on saddles and boxes, until the sun rose at last in a ball of orange flame, looking down over the deluge. The main stream had gone down. A brown torrent foamed in the deepest cutting of the *oued*. Shattered branches stared, half buried in wet sand. Two calves marooned on an island, stood there, mooing. Iridescent

135

drops shimmered everywhere, trembling from twigs, bejewelling hair and beard, and the hems of flowing blue robes.

With the light came warmth. It embraced the newly created earth and took back in quivering vapour and steamy mist what the ground had not absorbed.

Flames worried the wet wood. Thick white smoke hovered over the ground and crept, warm and heartening into clammy garments. Men and women held their hands to the blaze, laughed for no reason at all, and waited in pleasant expectation for the kettle to boil. Soon there would be tea.

Intallah had been wrapped in a blanket that, by some miracle, had remained dry. His whole body shivered and he coughed terribly.

'It will be over presently,' he said. But Ajor and Tadast looked at him, worried.

Then Ajor turned to the Kounta and said, 'The season of fruitfulness is here. When the mist has lifted, we shall see fresh grass sprouting from the earth. We too should make a fresh start and bury our old strife.'

The most exalted of the Kounta, the brother of the Amenokal, replied, 'That is why we are here. But you must not forget that once the tree has been cut down, it will not take root again. We wish to talk peace. But we will not discuss Asselar.'

'If we do not discuss Asselar, there can be no peace,' replied Ajor firmly and gazed casually at the grey cloud waving over the *oued*. 'We Tamashek only want justice.'

'Yes,' said Intallah, laboriously finding breath between two bouts of coughing. 'Justice is the seed of peace and peace is the root of well-being.'

'We were not the ones to break the peace,' retorted one of the Kounta. 'Your herdsmen started the quarrel. They have paid dearly for it. But to prevent any further quarrel breaking out with fresh bloodshed, we are prepared to ask the Beylik not to inflict any penalty on you if we can keep Asselar. We do not ask compensation for the assault. We will be satisfied if we can drive our herds without hindrance through the Valley of Tilemsi, and we guarantee that none of your tents will be so much as touched.'

The Amenokal's brother from Bourem added, 'That is so. We want to leave things as they stand and to swear peace.'

Ajor laughed aloud. 'So the brigands want to keep their plunder! They tell their victims that they have been doing them a favour!'

'We must not quarrel, friends,' Tuhaya intervened. 'Intallah's son has spoken as young men do. Now let experience have the word. Make us a proposition that will satisfy everyone.'

The Kounta answered, 'Our proposal is to swear a treaty of peace. That is the most we can do. Perhaps you do not know, Tuhaya, that the Beylik is on our side. We are already going further than we need if we ask the Beylik not to punish the Tamashek for the attack.'

Tuhaya nodded to Ajor to confirm these words. But Ajor, forcing himself to speak calmly, replied slowly, 'If that is your last word, it is war. We do not want that.'

'We are not afraid of war,' said the Kounta. 'We have never been afraid of fighting.'

'Then war you shall have,' threatened Red Moon, pursing his lips.

'My son,' said Intallah, 'you forget that we want to settle this as friends. Surely the Kounta must see that we need our share of Asselar. Once they concede that, we can conclude a treaty of peace and bind it with oaths.'

The Kounta conferred in whispers among themselves, and shook their heads. 'Asselar will never be yours again.'

'I have promised you safe conduct.' Ajor's voice rose to a shout. 'That promise holds. But woe betide your herds, your camels, your cattle and your tents! And now, turn round! Look over there!'

They spun round. Out of the mist which still covered the *oued* came grey shadows galloping towards the camp. Veils waved in the breeze. Spears glistened and shone. Camels snorted. Faces grew clearer and were seen to be wet with mist and dew. Iron clashed on iron, and leather creaked against leather.

'Ajor, what is this you have done?' said Tuhaya.

Ajor replied, 'You have not seen anything yet. This is only the beginning. Today will see the *oued* brimming over with our men.'

Intallah stared at the spectacle and no one knew what he was thinking. The Kounta drew close to each other, their mouths set, their hands on their sword hilts.

The first arrivals had reached the fire. They slid from their camels, saluted the Amenokal with a light touch of the fingertips, then greeted Ajor. They cast threatening glances at the little group of the Kounta and ignored Tuhaya who had drawn his veil over mouth and nose.

Red Moon said, 'Pitch your tents and hold yourselves in readiness.'

'We will go,' said the Kounta. 'We have nothing further to stay for.'

'No,' said Ajor. 'You will go when it pleases me. Neither sooner nor later.'

The Tamashek arrived in small bands and long caravans. There were half-grown lads who rode young camels hardly broken in, and dignified men, bristling with weapons. There were some who carried rifles and others who possessed only a dagger. But as the mist lifted and the sun burnt down on pools and swamps, there seemed no end to the tribesmen who swarmed to the Amenokal's camp from every side. The babble of voices, the bellowing of the camels, the snapping of twigs to feed the fires mingled together into one threatening chorus.

It was now midday, and still they streamed in from the plains, Idnan and Kel Telabit, Kel Effele and Tarat-Mellet.

Ajor said, 'Tomorrow the Ibottenaten will be here and the next day the Iforgumessen. And we shall ride forth. But not to Asselar. We are going to ride on Bourem.'

The Kounta stood in stunned silence. They bent their heads and cast furtive glances at the ever-filling camp of warriors. There was no doubt about it. Red Moon had summoned all the tribes of the Tamashek to avenge the dead. But there remained one last hope for the Kounta. That was the Beylik. He would not tolerate an armed aggression on their tents and their herds. He would march in with his soldiers, his strong weapons, his cannon and his trucks.

It seemed as if Red Moon had read their thoughts.

'Tuhaya,' he said, 'I have an important commission for you.'

'You have summoned the Tamashek to their utter annihilation,' said Tuhaya. 'The Beylik...'

'The Beylik,' interrupted Ajor calmly, 'the Beylik is on my side.'

'That is not true,' said Tuhaya loudly and clenched his prominent teeth. 'If you believe that, you are deceiving yourself.'

'Listen, Tuhaya. Take your swiftest camel and ride to Kidal and speak to the Beylik.'

Tuhaya stared at him nonplussed.

'Tell him that first thing tomorrow morning, we shall declare war against the Kounta for the right to Asselar.'

'I do not understand you, son of Intallah. You make all your preparations for the battle in the greatest secrecy and now you propose to tell the Beylik himself when you are going to attack. He will learn what you are doing soon enough and he will destroy you and your men like so many mad dogs.'

'Hold your tongue,' said Red Moon, 'and obey. You will tell the Beylik that I, Ajor Chageran, am going to wage a war for Asselar that will lay waste the whole land as far as the River Niger. I shall fill in the wells and slaughter the shepherds in the plains. I shall set fire to the tents of the Kounta, until the land from here to Bourem is one huge blaze.'

'My son!' exclaimed Intallah.

'Let me speak, Father,' said Ajor in a voice which trembled with the excitement he could barely contain. 'Tell the Beylik that if he gives me his word that Asselar will be restored to the Tamashek, if he gives me his word that the families of the murdered shepherds will receive adequate compensation, then I shall disperse my troops and send them back to their tents. But I insist on a paper with everything in writing. Tell him that, Tuhaya. And if you do not obtain the right answer, do not dare to return to my tent! One thing more, Tuhaya. Just in case the Beylik has overlooked it. Tell him that the tornado has left all the tracks impassable for vehicles.

Do not forget that. He will want to think things over. And now, I shall discharge my promise and give our enemies safe conduct to the Valley of Tilemsi.'

He turned to the Tamashek standing near him. 'Mount your camels,' he said. 'We are off to Bourem!'

The Kounta saw that Red Moon would keep his word. They saw, too, that he wanted war and had prepared for it. And if war came, it would be a miracle if their herds and their possessions escaped destruction. They had been outwitted by this young man who had hardly been a name to them hitherto.

Ajor approached his father. 'I dare do it, Father,' he said, 'there is no choice. I cannot say to our people, "Renounce Asselar".'

Intallah's eyes were closed. 'Tuhaya says that the Beylik, the Beylik, my son...' The old man coughed and pressed his withered hand to his breast.

'Once the Beylik sees that I am more likely to make trouble than the Kounta, he will yield to my demands. The Beylik wants peace. It was only to ensure peace that he was prepared to give way to the Kounta. That is why I have to stop him.'

'And the Princes? Where are the Princes?' asked Intallah. 'Are they not with you too?'

'I did not tell them my plans,' replied Red Moon. 'They would not have followed me. They are too frightened of the Beylik. That is why I have spoken only to the people. The people are not afraid of the Beylik.'

'You have made enemies of the Princes, I fear.'

'If I win, they will all be my friends. If I fail, even their friendship will avail me nothing.'

Intallah did not answer. He breathed laboriously. Tadast brought him some hot milk. He swallowed it in cautious sips.

'Tell me, my son,' he whispered suddenly. 'Tell me the truth. Why are you gambling like this? Is it for justice? Or is it ambition? The truth, my son!'

Ajor bent down to his father. 'If there is no ambition to do justice, it can thrust no roots, it can never flower. Father, forgive me for not letting you know what I was doing.'

Intallah pushed him away with a movement of the hand. 'Allah will stand by you. He loves the bold. I understand why you are doing this. But that you did not give me your trust, that will I not forgive! No, my son, I cannot forgive that. Go!'

Ajor stood up and pointed to the figure of Tuhaya who was riding away. 'That is why, Father. He stood too near to your mouth...'

'Go,' muttered Intallah. 'I am your father... your father...'

Red Moon went up to the Kounta. 'We are leaving now. Mount your camels.'

And without further ceremony, he jumped on to his own stallion, called the Tamashek to follow him and led them off in the direction of Bourem in the South.

Across the plains, the howls of the camels rose to high heaven as man after man crossed his legs in front of his saddle and dug his feet into the animal's neck.

Thousands of hoofs beat over the sand, which was hidden by a waving sea of nodding heads and fluttering veils, of saddle crosses and bright blankets. On each man's left, the red leather sheath of the sword glowed like a torch. Loose in the right hand lay lance and reins. New arrivals rode up to them from the distance and fell into line. They surrounded the little group of the Kounta as flood waters urge round a clump of driftwood.

When evening came, they made a halt. The Amenokal's brother came up to him and asked, 'What are your demands if we give up Asselar?'

'Twenty camels for each murdered man.'

'That is too much,' was the answer.

'Very well. I will accept twelve if we can agree it here and now.'

'That is not possible. We must consult the Amenokal in Bourem.'

'You are his brother,' said Ajor. 'Tomorrow when the sun rises, you will ride on ahead and tell him that I am coming. If he wants war, he shall have it in five days' time. If he wants peace, let him send you back with the camels as compensation for my men.'

The Kounta went away, troubled.

'And say to him that he must tell the Beylik formally that he has given back the water holes of Asselar to the Tamashek,' Ajor shouted after him.

By midday on the following day, the count of the Tamashek riding under the command of Intallah's son had risen to one thousand two hundred, and the Tamesna clans had not yet arrived. They were still on the way.

In the afternoon, a small black dot appeared in the sky. It flew in from the southern lowlands, approaching rapidly. Then it circled over the cavalcade for quite some time.

Ajor said, 'Take no notice of the aeroplane. Do not watch it. Proceed calmly.'

The aeroplane flew off in the direction from which it had come and returned next afternoon as they neared the Valley of Tilemsi. Once more it circled over the Tamashek, this time so low that they could see the pilot in the cockpit.

But nothing happened and the machine flew back to Kidal with its angry hum.

A little white camel with a brand mark of the Kounta tribe on its neck was grazing unattended. Ajor had it seized and led before the Kounta delegation.

'Is this yours?' he asked.

'Yes,' they said. 'It bears one of the tribe's brandmarks.'

'Good,' said Ajor and ordered his men to kill it.

They slit its throat and it bled to death. The Kounta were made to watch.

Ajor said, 'That was only the first. The same will happen to all your camels. The Beylik's help will come too late. You have only three days left. Ride on ahead. If no one comes back with offers of peace, you will all meet the fate of this foal.'

They forced their camels into a gallop and granted them no rest until they reached Bourem.

On the third day's march, they were joined by the Ibottenaten and the Iforgumessen. There were now fourteen hundred men and as many camels. In times of drought, it would not have been possible for such a great company to remain together. No well could yield water for such a gathering. But immediately after the tornado, there was water in every *oued* and no one went thirsty.

By now, the Tamashek had entered Kounta territory. Wherever they went, there were signs that camp had been hastily struck, and cattle driven away. Abandoned tent poles lay haphazard in the sand.

Towards evening, the aeroplane appeared again, looped low over the tribesmen, and dropped a signal. It read, 'Stay where you are and wait for the messenger.'

The letter was from the Beylik and bore his signature. But Ajor told no one what was in it and forbade the man who translated it for him to let the others know. So they rode on and took no notice of the order.

The messenger arrived on the fourth day. It was Tuhaya. He was exhausted after his hard riding, and agitated too. His eyes had dark circles round them.

'*Salam aleikum*, Ajor Chageran.'

'*Essalam aleik*. What do you bring?'

'I have a letter from the Beylik for you.'

'Is it yes or no?'

'It is yes,' said Tuhaya, 'but believe me, I have never had to talk so hard in all my life.'

'I had rather you went on talking for a fortnight than lose Asselar,' replied Ajor. 'Translate the letter for me.'

Tuhaya read,

> 'With the proviso that the Amenokal of the Kounta agrees this decision, and that Intallah withdraws his troops unconditionally, the former water holes of the Tamashek in the Oued of Asselar are hereby restored to them forthwith.
>
> 'Ajor Chageran ag Intallah is solemnly warned that he must withdraw his men to the Valley of Tilemsi immediately. The soldiers of the Beylik are standing by.'

Ajor said, 'I shall withdraw when I have had an answer from Bourem. The Beylik has only thirty soldiers in Kidal. They cannot hurt me, and before he can get reinforcements, I shall have gained my objective.'

Tuhaya warned him, 'Do not try the Beylik's patience any further. He is furious with you.'

'What do I care for his anger,' replied Red Moon proudly, 'as long as I win back Asselar?'

On the fifth morning, they saw a long caravan approaching, led by the Amenokal's brother. He brought two hundred and fifty-two camels and a letter in Arabic. The letter offered peace.

Ajor read the letter aloud, and he had difficulty in adding a word of his own, so great was the cheering. At last he was allowed to speak.

'Take the camels to the widows of the murdered men,' he said, 'and ride with me to Asselar. We must go and take possession of our rights in the sight of everyone.'

Not all the assembled company rode to Asselar among the dunes of Timetrin. The older ones drove away the camels which had been paid as compensation and then returned to their own tents. They were mainly the younger men who followed Ajor.

Tuhaya, too, stayed by Ajor's side. He realized all too clearly that if he wanted to remain a power behind the throne, he had better keep close to this rising star from now on.

CHAPTER THIRTEEN

Intallah and Red Moon

RED MOON and his warriors remained among the dunes of Timetrin for several weeks. They watered their camels at the water holes of Asselar, and sent them out to graze, for the broad meadows were now fresh and green, and covered the land for miles like a carpet.

Meanwhile the news of the campaign led by the Amenokal designate had spread from mouth to mouth in the Iforas Mountains. Red Moon's name was on everyone's lips and in the tents and round the campfires his victory over the Kounta was the one topic of conversation. And Ajor's cleverness, his courage and his tenacity grew with every telling. People quite overlooked the fact that Intallah's son had had more than his share of luck too.

It was the women who praised him most. They made up songs about him and spoke with contempt of the men who had not participated in the great calvalcade.

Among these must be numbered all the tribal Princes. Ajor Chageran's preparations had not been wholly concealed from them, but they had feigned deafness and had preferred to wait and see what would happen. It had seemed to them sheer folly to jeopardize their good relations with the Beylik for the sake of this impetuous young man.

Ramzata ag Elrhassan, the Prince of the Kel Telabit, tried to throw scorn on the whole affair by calling it 'The Battle of the White Camel', because it had been the only casualty.

But in the weeks that followed, it was brought home to them that Red Moon had not only defeated the Kounta, but had also dealt their prestige a severe blow. In the eyes of their peoples, they had lost face.

They managed to hide themselves behind Intallah and when Red Moon came back to his father's tents, he was coldly received.

The Amenokal seemed to have recovered from his weakness. His shoulders drooped still, it is true, but he could stand on his own two feet, and often waited before his tent, gazing in the direction from which his son must return.

Ajor dismissed his men, for in the season after the great tornado every man was needed to drive the cattle into the salt pastures. The drought was over and now came the season of golden abundance. There were people who made themselves ill with too much milk, too much butter and too much fresh cheese...

Intallah wasted no words when Red Moon entered his tent. About Asselar, he only said, 'I am glad that the *oued* is free once more. You have stayed away a long time, my son.'

'I had to show the Kounta that Asselar is ours again. That is why.'

Ajor had broadened in build since he went away. His face looked more mature and his speech was more controlled and deliberate.

'You have not won many friends among the Princes,' continued the Intallah. 'They keep asking me if they chose you to be *Amenokal*, only for you to go over their heads.'

Ajor retorted, 'They do me an injustice. The welfare of the people comes before that of the Princes. I did not call them out to march with me because they would not have obeyed. They preferred to listen to the Beylik.'

'I thought you were wiser than you seem to be,' said Intallah reproachfully. 'For the sake of a small gain, you have incurred a great disadvantage. You have thrown away the saddle from the camel you ride...'

'I do not understand you,' said Red Moon, surprised.

'You will understand well enough, when you are older. You have shown the Tamashek that they can do without their Princes. But you are a Prince too, my son. You will be Prince of the Kel Effele when I die. The men who marched with you have learnt to despise their chieftains. They may learn to despise you too. Once the camel can find water without its master, it will not return to the old well.'

He sighed, for he read in his son's face that he did not share his apprehensions.

'Ajor Chageran,' he said, 'you have destroyed the time-honoured order of things among the Tamashek...'

'Nothing I have done was intended to hurt the Princes, Father.'

'My son,' said Intallah emphatically, 'when the Beylik came to us and said, 'All slaves must be freed', that was the first blow against us. We nearly came to grief over that. The negroes ran away, stole our cattle, left us to do all the hard work. Now you have dealt the tribe a second blow. Prompted by you, the people of all the clans have taken up arms and gone to fight the Kounta without their Princes and they have been victorious...'

'Under my leadership, Father.'

'They will forget that by and by. But they will never forget that it was done without the ancient aristocracy of the Iforas clans, never. You have touched a boulder, and it has started to rock. You cannot foresee when or where it will fall. And you do not know if it might not drag you into the abyss with it, too.'

'What do you want me to do?' asked Red Moon.

'I want you to placate the Princes. Share among them the camels you won as spoils of war.'

'I cannot do that,' replied Red Moon. 'Nor would it be right to do so. The booty belongs to the womenfolk of those who lost their lives at Asselar.'

'Booty belongs to the Princes,' said Intallah. 'That has always been the custom. If they think it fitting, the Princes will share it with the people. Do you want to alter our customs, my son?'

'*Bismillah*,' replied Ajor. 'I shall alter many things. I shall take a daughter of the vassals for my wife, not one of the nobles. And I shall do more. I want to create a new glory for our people in the name of the Prophet. And even that is not enough. As I lingered among the dunes of Asselar, I pondered day and night how I could weld the people, the Tamashek, into a great nation once more. You said just now that the Princes are the saddle on which I ride. But if the saddle turns awkward, I can ride the mare without a saddle, or I can get me a new saddle...'

'This business with the Kounta has gone to your head,' said Intallah. 'It is time you turned your mind to other things. I shall press on with the arrangements for your wedding. Perhaps you will show more sense when you have a wife in your tent.'

But in his heart he thought, if this son of mine continues as he has started, he will either become greater than ever I was, or he will perish...

He also thought, I am too old to show him the way. I have no strength left and my mind tires easily. Allah is great. His will be done...

He called Tuhaya to him and said, 'I do not think that my son regards you as his friend. He is very obstinate and wants to seek out his own path in life. But I shall help you to gain his confidence.'

'I have little hope that he will listen to my advice on anything,' grumbled Tuhaya.

'If you do as I say, you will be his friend. Woo him a wife.'

'Oh no!' replied Tuhaya. 'That is a dangerous game. If he is satisfied with the wooing, all may be well. But if he is not satisfied and quarrels with the woman, he will never forget my part in the business. And I shall regret it all my life.'

A smile played over the wrinkles and folds of Intallah's face.

'Red Moon knows the girl already, and he wants to marry her. You have only to do the wooing. He will be very grateful.'

'Who is it?' asked Tuhaya inquisitively.

'The daughter of the Marabut with whom he studied. She is called High Summer, and rumour has it that she is very beautiful.'

'She does not belong to the tents of the nobles, Amenokal. There will be strife, I tell you. Such a wedding will cause bad blood between you and the nobles. They will ask, "Are not our daughters good enough for the descendant of the Cherif of Timbuktu?" They will say, "It is not seemly for the Amenokal to be advised by a daughter of the vassals". Tuhaya looked down as he continued, 'You know that our womenfolk have more influence over our heads and hearts than we admit. They hear our secret dreams, and press us to do this and not to do that...'

He did not dare look the Amenokal in the face as he said these words. For Intallah had listened to the advice of his wives all his life and in spite of his age he was guided by the young Tadast in many ways.

Intallah sighed. 'Red Moon has set his heart on this young girl. It is not for us to worry about the outcome. That lies in the hand of Allah, praised be his name. Still, if you do not wish to carry out the wooing, I shall have to find someone else to do it.'

'If you ask me, I shall do it, although I have a premonition that this marriage will bring bad luck, either for your son or for me. But I shall do your bidding. When shall I start?'

'Go back to your own tent now and tend your herds,' replied Intallah. 'The moon must change twice yet before the rainy season is safely over. That will be the time. I shall give you presents for the Marabut and you will speak to him in my name about the price he demands for his daughter.'

'Good,' said Tuhaya. 'It will be done as you say. But what shall I do if they do not accept the wooing?'

'I should like to see the man who would refuse the Amenokal's wooing,' was Intallah's rejoinder.

'I was not thinking of the father, Intallah. I was thinking of High Summer.'

'Before her marriage, a woman has no tongue,' said the Prince sharply. 'A girl has no more say than a mare which is exchanged for another. I have spoken enough. Go and tend your herds, and come back when the cattle are fat with fresh grass.'

And Tuhaya went away.

As the rainy season came to an end, the Tamashek returned from the salt pastures to their usual feeding grounds. Instead of grass, the camels ate twigs, and leaves from the trees. Their humps were firm and tight, and their coats shone like silk. The zebu cattle had developed the powerful hump characteristic of their breed and their skin was taut, without a fold or wrinkle. The tents of copper-coloured leather were brought out and mended and replaced the grass huts. The nights began to get cooler and by day the wind blew steady and warm from the north-east.

One day Tuhaya entered the Amenokal's camp to discuss the presents for the Marabut with Intallah and Tadast.

Tadast said, 'One sheep is enough, for the girl is not of noble stock.'

Intallah disagreed. 'The vassals may give one another sheep as presents. But you forget that my son is not a serf. We must give a young unbroken camel.'

Tuhaya nodded to each in turn, and said, 'A sheep seems to me too little and a camel too much. Give me two strong calves.'

'Yes,' said Intallah. 'That will do. Now, how many beasts will the Marabut demand for his daughter? The bride-price in those parts is quite considerable, and every year people expect more for their daughters. And as I am the richest man, they will expect the maximum from me.'

'Intallah,' said Tadast with animation, 'you must pay a good price, but you must not pay as much as you gave for me. This girl has nothing but a pretty face. I am afraid that she may even be thin. Do you still remember how many camels you sent my father, Intallah?'

'I remember exactly,' replied the old man. 'There were seven fine camels, not more than four years old, and twenty black goats, a new robe and a silver bracelet for your mother, and silver tweezers for you.'

Tadast laughed, pleased. 'I still have them. Everytime I take a thorn out of my foot, I think of the day I received them.'

'I still feel that this wooing is a mistake,' Tuhaya said, 'but I shall carry it out as if it were a wife for my own son.'

'If you return bringing good news, I shall give you presents, a new tunic and a bracelet,' promised Intallah.

'But you must definitely not offer more than Intallah gave for me,' Tadast reiterated, and looked at her fingernails which were painted red with henna. They were very long, for Tadast never did any work.

Tuhaya took his camel and two sturdy calves, tobacco and tea, dates and rice, as well as a freshly pitched water-skin and he set off for the North. The way was long, and the two calves limited the distance he could travel each day. He would not be back before the end of the year, which was still three months away.

In spite of his misgivings, he was glad that he had not refused to go. This was the only way open to him to win the full confidence of the future Amenokal, and thus remain the influential man he had become in Intallah's shadow.

Tuhaya loved power. He would not hesitate to use any method, straight or crooked, long or short to achieve his aim. In the course of his life, he had become a rich man, and he now employed many herdsmen to guard his livestock. But no one knew exactly how he had got his wealth, for he came of poor parents. He had many enemies and there were not a few among the Tamashek who envied him. But as he had become the friend of the Amenokal, and even more inexplicably, had undoubted access to the Beylik, no one dared to oppose him openly. The only ones who had risked it, Agassum and Abu Bakr, had paid with their lives. There was only one man left who was in a position to do him harm, he thought, and that was Ajor Chageran. And now it was Red Moon who would be under an obligation to him.

CHAPTER FOURTEEN

The Great Ahal

MID-E-MID HAD GROWN strong and tall during the past year. Black down grew on his upper lip and its dark shadow covered his cheeks. He had spent the rainy season in the mountains, where there was ample water for his herds.

October came and went, and still Abu Bakr had not returned. So he decided to leave the animals in the care of the two negroes and ride out west to hear what was going on in the world.

Apart from Amadou and Dangi, he had not seen a single person for a long time, and he longed to hear other people's voices. Furthermore, the camp was very short of sugar, tea and tobacco. In particular, they needed salt. He took with him one of Abu Bakr's camels to barter for stores. But he was worried in case the animal were recognized by its former owner and he might call out the *goumiers* to arrest him. This thought was so alarming that he did not ride south, where he would be sure to meet the shepherds at the water hole of Tin Ramir, but he followed the track to Tin Za'uzaten. Perhaps the fool, Kalil, would have some news for him.

He had other things on his mind too. He longed to know how his mother was faring. Most of all, perhaps, he was anxious to know what had happened to Tiu'elen, for he had not forgotten what the old woman at Tin Ramir had told him.

This time, the way to Tin Za'uzaten seemed to him endless. Not only was he chafing with impatience, but he had the second camel roped to Inhelumé's saddle and it was not used to being led. It pulled and tugged and slowed them down all day.

As Mid-e-Mid came down from the plateau into the *oued*, he saw that there were no strangers there. He went down to the water-hole where the idiot was spreading thorny twigs over the opening. He was so absorbed in his task, that he only looked up when Mid-e-Mid made Inhelumé kneel to dismount.

'How are you, Kalil?' called Mid-e-Mid.

Kalil shaded his eyes with his hands and looked at him stupidly. Suddenly recognition dawned on his face. He stretched out both hands towards the newcomer. 'Mid-e-Mid ag Agassum!' he cried. 'Son of tears and laughter!'

He shook his head vigorously to show his pleasure. 'Kalil knows your camel. Yes, Kalil knows it well.'

'Which one?' asked Mid-e-Mid cautiously, for he thought he meant the one he intended to barter.

'This one,' said Kalil, pointing to Inhelumé.

'Ah, of course. You know it very well,' said Mid-e-Mid. 'But I have another camel here, Kalil. Look at this one.'

'I can see it,' said Kalil. 'It is strong and its hump is firm and fat.'

'I shall leave it here with you. If a caravan halts here, ask if they have tobacco and tea and sugar and salt, and offer them this strong camel in exchange. But only offer it to caravans coming from the North. Their beasts are weaklings. They will appreciate a good strong camel. Do you understand?'

'Kalil understands,' answered the fool. And to show him how well he understood, he slapped his low forehead and his prominent ears very hard with the flat of his hand.

Mid-e-Mid said, 'If you drive a good bargain, I shall give you a little of everything as a present.' He sat down in the sand and watched Kalil, who was squatting on his heels, looking for lice among his rags.

'Have you any news?' asked Mid-e-Mid after a long pause.

The fool shook his head.

Mid-e-Mid said, 'Have you heard of a girl called High Summer?'

'High Summer? Kalil knows.'

'What do you know of High Summer, Kalil?'

'Ayé... She is waiting for the moon.'

'For the Red Moon, Kalil?' asked Mid-e-Mid suspiciously.

'Red moon, white moon – it is all one.'

'Why is she waiting for the moon?'

The fool pulled a face. He opened his mouth and sang, 'La la la la, tumti-tumti-tum.'

'Is that all you know?' Mid-e-Mid was disappointed.

'Yes, Kalil knows.' He put his head on one side, placed his fists in front of his eyes and peeped through them. Then he held them in front of his mouth, his lips pouting, and he made a noise 'Uff-uff-uff,' as if he were blowing a trumpet.

'I can hear that you are making music,' said Mid-e-Mid patiently, 'but it is not sweet music, not the kind I like. I asked you about a girl, and you make this stupid music.'

Kalil took his hands from his mouth and hammered on his knee with his fist. Then he flung back his head and closed his eyes in rapture.

'Dum-e-dum-e-dumdi-dumdi-dum,' he whispered, drumming his knee harder than ever.

'Oh, now I understand. High Summer is making music. It is she who makes music.'

'When the moon comes... Kalil knows,' laughed the fool.

'By Allah, which moon?'

Kalil pointed to the sky where a pale moon gleamed in the morning sky. He crooked his left arm and stretched it away from his body and with his right hand he fiddled with an invisible bow on an invisible *amzad*, the one-stringed musical instrument of the Tamashek women. He pressed his ear against his arm, his bloodshot eyes screwed tight, as if he were listening entranced to inaudible notes. The wind blew over the *oued*, sprinkling the two men by the water-hole with a spray of fine sand.

'Oh! Now I know what you mean, Kalil... High Summer is holding an *ahal*.'

The fool seized on the word. '*Ahal, ahal*! When the moon comes. *Ahal, ahal, ahal, ahal*!'

'Are you sure that she is not waiting for Red Moon?'

'High summer waits for the moon, red moon, white moon, any moon,' he tittered. 'All the men will come, all of them. A great *ahal* when the moon comes.' And once more he fiddled with his arm, and swayed his body.

Mid-e-Mid thought, I must find out more. I must be there at the *ahal*. If Red Moon is there, if she is waiting for him... Yes, I must find out. I must know for sure.

He felt his heart pound. An *ahal* was a rare occurrence in the Adrar of the Iforas. Whenever one took place, men came from far and wide to listen to the women playing the *amzad*.

Young men came to the *ahal* to vie with one another in singing songs. And each tried to outdo the others in the richness of his robes, the adornment of his camel, and his skill in riding. The more a man shone, the greater the reward – a friendly look, a word of recognition, a round of applause. Sometimes the rivalry became serious and swords were drawn.

Occasionally, a man who distinguished himself at an *ahal* was encouraged to woo the hand of the girl who had held court. But this was comparatively rare and was, of course, the highest prize of all.

'Kalil,' said Mid-e-Mid, 'look after my camel. I am going on now. When I come back, I shall take the stores you get for it.'

The fool rose, and nodded. 'Mid-e-Mid,' he said, 'the moon has attacked the Kounta and overpowered them.'

'The moon! Always the moon,' replied Mid-e-Mid, nettled. 'Who can understand your nonsense?'

Kalil looked at him sadly, and let his arms droop. 'The moon shines in the South and spits cold fire. Where is the sun, Mid-e-Mid? Why does it not come to warm the North?'

'The sun in the North? What rubbish!' replied Mid-e-Mid and strode towards Inhelumé. Kalil followed him and just as he was going to mount, the idiot poked him in the chest with one finger. 'The sun is waiting in there, Mid-e-Mid. Let it out. I am freezing.'

And Kalil shivered as if he were really freezing with cold. He beat his body with his arms, held his hands as if over a fire, took deep breaths and hopped from foot to foot.

Mid-e-Mid sprang to his saddle and the beast reared.

'Give me the sun! ... Give me the sun!' implored the fool.

'Wrap yourself in a blanket if you are cold, Kalil,' replied Mid-e-Mid.

The fool held out his hands, pleading, 'The sun! Give me the sun!'

And there he stood with arms outstretched, long after Inhelumé had climbed the further bank of the *oued* and was already out of sight.

It was a long way to the Oued Tin Bojeriten. At midday, Mid-e-Mid rested in the shade of the thorn trees and in the evening he slept on the open *reg* or in a sandy hollow, or among the grasses at the foot of the black rocks.

He avoided the tents of the Tamashek which showed up flat and copper-coloured against the green of the camel pastures. He did not want to answer questions about the whence and whither and why of his journey.

When he reached Tin Bojeriten, he chose to remain in a side slip of the main flood bed until night fell. Then he hobbled Inhelumé and went on his way on foot.

He saw several riders who seemed to be making for the same tent. They were richly clothed and rode stately camels. One of them spoke to Mid-e-Mid.

'Are you going to the *ahal*?' he called out, without stopping.

'No,' said Mid-e-Mid. 'I wanted to see if I could get some tobacco anywhere. My pouch is empty.'

'There will be tobacco at the *ahal*. Men are coming from all directions. Someone will give you tobacco. Are your herds near by?'

Mid-e-Mid shook his head. 'They are some distance away. Tell me, whose *ahal* is it?'

'Don't you know?' The stranger was surprised. He was a young man, with his hair loosely twisted into plaits. 'Tonight is the full moon, and Tiu'elen has chosen this day for her *ahal*.'

'Tiu'elen?' asked Mid-e-Mid. But his heart thumped as the stranger pronounced the name.

156

'You must have been away from here a long time, if you do not know Tiu'elen,' said the man, more astonished still. 'She is the most beautiful girl in the land. She is the daughter of the Marabut. There are many suitors for her hand.'

'Has she decided for one of them?' asked Mid-e-Mid.

'I hope not,' said the rider. 'I should like to marry her myself. But of course, I am not the only one. Is my veil straight? I expect the hard riding has disarranged it.'

'It is quite straight,' replied Mid-e-Mid.

'Good. I should not like to be rejected on account of my appearance. People say that she sets great store by it. But I really am astounded that you have never heard of the girl. There is one song about her that everyone sings, "Tell me, O shepherds, have you seen Tiu'elen?" '

'Oh, yes. I seem to have heard the song,' said Mid-e-Mid. 'If she is really as lovely as the song says...'

'She is much more beautiful, I swear it. See for yourself. We are nearly there. I can see the fire burning near her father's tent. And now I must go. I do not want to arrive at walking pace. It is so much more impressive to arrive at a gallop.'

He flicked his camel over the crupper with his long leather whip, and the beast shot forward at a single bound, its head outlined against the night sky, and he reached the camp in a few minutes.

It took Mid-e-Mid a good quarter-hour to cover the same distance on foot. As he drew near, he found a great gathering of men sitting on the ground round the fire, forming a big half-circle. Others kept arriving. Tiu'elen's mother sat close to the fire with two women whom Mid-e-Mid did not know. High Summer was not to be seen.

As Mid-e-Mid was on foot, nobody took any notice of him. He had drawn his veil and he sat silent in the last row well to the side, so that he could overlook the whole company when the flames did not leap too high.

Mid-e-Mid did not remember ever having seen such a great *ahal*. Many of the men were known to him, only a few were

157

strange. Most of them were young men from the Kel Effele clan. But there were also some Tarat-Mellet among them. They spoke in loud voices to each other. Some of them boasted how well they could swing a sword. Others bragged about their camels and how much they had had to pay for their saddles.

They sat elbow to elbow and back against knee. They chewed tobacco, spat, chewed again, joked, wrangled, broke into song, then stopped, and they kept looking hopefully at the closed tent, where High Summer was said to be waiting.

As the moon rose over the distant mountains and spread its milky light over tent and fire and the blue garments of the men and women, Tiu'elen came out of her tent. Talking and laughter died away and all eyes turned to the girlish figure. She walked slowly towards her mother and sat down by her on the ground. The end of her wide, flowing robe was thrown loosely over her head, like a scarf.

In the flickering firelight, her face could be seen, now sharp and clear-cut, now restless and shadowy. One could make out high arched brows over night dark eyes, a soft, slightly open mouth which revealed the white of her teeth, and smooth hair combed back from her forehead, with the parting in the middle. When the night wind whipped the fire, her skin took on a pearly sheen and that ivory tint which the Tamashek prize above all other complexions.

Mid-e-Mid held his breath when he saw her. She was lovelier than he had remembered, more graceful, and yet more dignified too. Never before had he felt so keenly that of all the strapping young men around him, finely dressed and well-groomed, he was probably the poorest. He alone rode a borrowed camel and guarded someone else's herds. Only Telchenjert by his side, Abu Bakr's mighty sword, was his own. And suddenly he felt a wild desire to jump to his feet and challenge everyone to a duel, to show that in one way at least he could hold his own, and prove himself before High Summer. But the impulse died as quickly as it had been born, leaving him empty and depressed.

The Marabut's wife handed the *amzad* to her daughter. It was a big guitar-shaped instrument, sewn with light brown goatskin, and spanned with a single string of horsehair. The assembly was so quiet that one could hear the crackling of the fire, and the touch of the bow on the string as High Summer began to play. The bow caressed the string. The slim fingers did not err, and the notes soared true and tender into the darkness.

The men watched Tiu'elen, now her hands, now her face. Their heads were bowed, their mouths slightly open, as if they would have liked to taste the notes with their tongues, and touch them with their lips.

High Summer returned their glances without a trace of coyness. But she did not disclose by a single movement whom she recognized, whom she liked. Unruffled, almost as if she had been playing to statues, her eyes passed from head to head. The first two rows were clearly distinguishable in the moonlight, but those behind were blurred and dark. The listeners sat motionless. Only Tiu'elen's hands moved, only her hands and the dancing flames. Pinpoints of light from the fire were reflected in wide, staring eyes.

The music paused, then started again. A single note was repeated, then shimmered away into silence. No one stirred.

Then High Summer laid her *amzad* on her knee.

The spell was broken.

Someone laughed, faces beamed, voices surged. One man stood up and waved his arms, and then sat down again.

'More!' cried voices. 'Play us more, Tiu'elen!'

High Summer shook her head. 'I shall play again later. Now let me hear you sing,' she said in her light clear voice.

'What shall we sing?' they asked.

'Whatever you like,' she replied.

'I shall sing *Amenehaya*,' called one of the Tarat-Mellet, and he began to sing without any more ado. He had a powerful voice.

> Inalaran, lance-bearer, and the son of Intebram,
> Come when the cattle graze in salt pastures
> Come to the Well of In Tirgasal.

159

He sang four verses and he sang them well. But Mid-e-Mid thought, his voice is too hard. He sings because he knows how to. He does not sing because he must.

One young man with a strong aquiline nose called out, 'Let me sing the last verse, High Summer.'

The girl nodded. 'Yes, do, Mohammed ag Infirgan.'

And Mohammed sang. His voice was rough, and his pronunciation was not very clear, but he put his heart into the song.

> Even Magidi, the grey-haired Magidi,
> Dances his stallion in time to the drum-beats.
> At night, the warriors sing round the fire,
> Inalaran and Intebram's son,
> Singing the song of the men who are free,
> By the ancient Well of In Tirgasal.

He received loud applause and closed his eyes delightedly.

'Let me sing, High Summer!' 'No, let me!' They all wanted to show her what they could do. They were eager for recognition, for a word of approval, for a look of encouragement from her eyes.

'I know a new song,' said a thick-set man with broad, high cheekbones.

'If it is new, I should like to hear it,' decided Tiu'elen. 'Who wrote it?'

'I wrote it myself.' He was rather surprised at his own daring, and continued, 'It is not a masterpiece. But I made it up especially for you, High Summer.'

Tiu'elen laughed. 'I hope that you made a good job of it, Bocha. Sing it.'

And Bocha sang:

> Guess who is this maiden.
> Her hair is oiled with yellow butter,
> And reflects the sun and the moon.
> Her eye is as round as the circle
> When a pebble is thrown in the water.

> Her feet are like the hoofs of camels,
> And her fingers...

He got no further. A storm of laughter drowned the rest of the song.

'Feet like camels' hoofs!' they roared.

'Why don't you chop your tongue off and throw it in the fire?'

'Up on your own hoofs, Bocha, and back to your tent!'

High Summer had covered her face so as not to show her laughter. Bocha was so angry that he sprang to his feet to attack the nearest mocker. But the others disarmed him, and held him down and threatened to kill him if he did not hold his peace.

Tiu'elen started playing the *amzad* again to smooth over the incident. Talking and laughter were hushed.

When she had finished, a murmur of admiration rose to everyone's lips. Then the stranger with the plaits, whom Mid-e-Mid had met, said, 'High Summer, may I sing a prize song to a camel?'

He did not wait for her permission, but began to sing in a clear, almost striking voice, in praise of his mare, which had carried him to battle in the war against the Kounta.

Opinions were divided. Some found the song good. Others thought that it might have been sung better, and that the rhythm was poor. But Tiu'elen nodded her approval and smiled, and that was more reward than the singer had expected. He tore a silver bracelet from his wrist, and threw it to High Summer.

The girl examined it closely and placed it in her mother's lap, for she did not wish her acceptance of the gift to give rise to further quarrelling.

'Who will sing now?'

One man in the last row stood up. His face was veiled. As hardly anyone noticed him, High Summer had to ask for silence.

'Let the veiled one sing,' she said.

Everyone turned their heads, but they could only make out a slender black shadow, for the moon was behind the clouds, and the fire had sunk low.

The man said softly, but so clearly that everyone could hear, 'Someone else has just sung about a mare. I shall sing the praises of a stallion.'

'Go on,' they exclaimed, 'but sing loudly, so that we can all hear.'

Then Mid-e-Mid sang the Song of Inhelumé.

> I drank the white waters of Telabit
> Of Sandeman and In Abutut,
> But I found you not, Inhelumé.

There was an excited whispering. 'He is singing about Abu Bakr's camel!' For Inhelumé was famous throughout the land.

> I followed your track to Sadidän
> From tent to tent where the campfires smoke,
> But I found you not, Inhelumé.

Mid-e-Mid's voice was slightly muffled by his veil, but still it sounded so true and so sweet, that everyone was moved and could not take their eyes off him. High Summer thought that she had heard his voice once before. The timbre seemed familiar. But the song was a new one and it deceived her, so that she could not identify the singer.

> I breathed your name to the whirling wind,
> I whispered it to the singing sand,
> I asked them both, where have you gone?
> But I found you not, Inhelumé.
> Only Tallit, the Lady Moon,
> Hears the stamp of your hoof
> As you drive the mares
> Turbulently across the dunes, Inhelumé.

When he had finished, there was a deep silence. And no one dared to break it. Then the Marabut's wife handed the silver bracelet to her daughter, and High Summer threw it to the stranger, who caught it deftly and sat down without saying a word.

Only then did the storm of applause break loose. 'Ah!' they cried. 'Ah, singer! Who taught you that song? No one has sung like that so far!' They would not be quiet until he promised to sing them another song.

'Come to the fire, so that we can see you better,' said High Summer. 'Stand opposite me here.'

Mid-e-Mid went over to the fire. He did not drop his veil. And no one knew who he was, for he had shot up in height during the months of his absence, and was much taller than when he had set out to look for his mother's donkey. His shoulders had broadened and his voice had deepened.

Then he sang a second song, *The Moon of Irrarar*.

> The moon shines yellow on Irrarar
> But my heart is as black as stone,
> Black as the Well of Aït Nafan,
> And sad as the eyes of the wounded gazelle,
> For I am thinking of you.
>
> Bay at the moon, dogs! Jackals, whine!
> Sweeter to me is the howl of your anguish
> Than amzad and flute and lark song at morning,
> Than cattle lowing in the fields at sunset,
> For I am thinking of you.
>
> Let the stones fall dumb at the feet of the moon
> The yellow moon of Irrarar,
> Let sand and stars and wind arise.
> Never again will they see me smile
> Unless you return before day dies,
> For I can only think of you.

As he sang the last line, he pulled off his veil. And High Summer recognized Mid-e-Mid.

The men jumped to their feet and cried, 'It is Eliselus! He has come back!'

Forgetting all their dignity, they ran to greet him, putting their arms round his shoulders and shouting, 'Don't you remember me, Agassum's son? How often have you sat by my fire? And by ours too? And slept in my tent, drawn water from the well together, and watched the goats with my brother? Surely you remember me? And me? Quick, now!'

And they only let him go when High Summer came forward and touched his hands and said, 'I have waited a long time for you, Mid-e-Mid!'

'I have never stopped thinking of you,' he answered.

Tiu'elen looked round at the happy, excited faces, all sincere in the warmth of their welcome, for there was no singer in all the land to compare with Eliselus, and no one could be jealous of him. She said, 'Go now. The *ahal* is over. I thank you all for coming here.'

She took Mid-e-Mid's hand and led him to her mother.

Reluctantly the men went to find their camels. They would have liked to stay and listen to Mid-e-Mid. And on their long journeys to their tents through the moonlit night, they could talk of nothing but his happy homecoming and his incomparable songs.

The news of Mid-e-Mid's return spread like wildfire through the Adrar of the Iforas from Timea'uin to Kidal, from Tin Ramir to the Valley of Tilemsi. Everywhere there was great rejoicing. And *The Moon of Irrarar* and *The Song of Inhelumé* were passed from mouth to mouth.

CHAPTER FIFTEEN

The Wooing

THAT SAME NIGHT, Mid-e-Mid had to tell the long story of his capture by Abu Bakr, his flight from the *goumiers*, the meeting with Kalil the fool, and the time he had spent with Amadou and Dangi in the ravine. Tiu'elen and her mother hung on his very lips and only interrupted him to tell him what they knew of the death of Abu Bakr. For the first time, Mid-e-Mid was really convinced that the brigand was no longer alive.

'What do you know of my mother?' he asked.

'She is well,' said the Marabut's wife. 'She would never believe that you were dead.'

'My father is coming home tomorrow,' said High Summer. 'You must tell him everything. He was very upset when you disappeared. He was looking for a new pupil when Ajor Chageran returned to his father.'

'Oh!' said Mid-e-Mid. 'What do you hear of Red Moon?'

'He has become famous,' said High Summer, without a trace of emotion. 'He led a war against the Kounta and won back Asselar for the tribe. Look, here is the little flask of attar of roses which he gave me. I have never used it since you went away.'

At this, Mid-e-Mid flushed deeply.

'It is time to sleep,' said the Marabut's wife. 'I have spread a mat for you, Mid-e-Mid.'

'I shall not be able to sleep tonight,' said Mid-e-Mid.

But he lay down on the mat and drank a pitcher of milk which High Summer had brought him. 'There is still so much to tell you,' he said and held her hand.

'Tomorrow, Mid-e-Mid,' she said as she left him, and disappeared behind the walls of the tent.

When the Marabut's wife came out again a few minutes later to see to the fire for the night, Mid-e-Mid was fast asleep.

The Marabut returned early next day, for he had spent the night not far away. He was leading two young goats, and carrying a goats' milk cheese. They were presents for driving out a devil.

Three young camels had died one after the other in a certain stretch of pasture. The owner was sure that such deaths were unnatural. The meadow must be inhabited by a demon. So he called in the Marabut.

The Marabut followed the prescribed ritual. He recited certain prayers. Then a sheep had to be slaughtered and its blood was poured over the meadow. The flesh was divided among the tents of strangers.

'I hope that the devil will not come back,' said the Marabut. 'But some of them are very obstinate... But now, Mid-e-Mid, tell me about yourself.'

And Mid-e-Mid had to tell the story all over again. He rather enjoyed it, for he kept remembering things which he had forgotten the previous evening.

The Marabut asked him, 'Will you stay in the mountains and take possession of Abu Bakr's herds?'

'No,' said Mid-e-Mid. 'When I get back, I shall drive the animals to the shepherds at the wells and restore the ones that were stolen to their owners, as far as possible. But there are others that were stolen from distant places, far away from here. I can tell that by the brand marks. And there are many young animals which have never been branded.'

'Keep those, Mid-e-Mid,' nodded the Marabut. 'That will not offend the will of Allah.'

Mid-e-Mid said, 'But first of all, I must find out if I am still wanted by the *goumiers*. They fired at me in Samak. Perhaps they thought that I was Abu Bakr's accomplice. It is true that I have guarded his herds, but that was because I gave him my word... I have stolen nothing.'

The Marabut looked at him seriously. 'I have heard something about the affair. The *goumiers* who found Abu Bakr's body could not tell if he died of thirst or if he was murdered. They know that you were the last person to be seen with him. So they will want to know if you killed him.'

'If I killed him?' asked Mid-e-Mid.

'We do not say you did, Mid-e-Mid. But the Beylik would like to know for sure. He has made enquiries about you. My advice to you is this: do not carry Telchenjert, and do not ride on Inhelumé. They might give a false impression.'

'Telchenjert was a present. And I ride Inhelumé because Abu Bakr lent it to me until his return. As he is dead, I shall keep it. There is no finer camel in the land.'

The Marabut nodded. 'We believe you, Mid-e-Mid, but can you prove it to the Beylik? That is why I say to you, be careful with whom you associate and do not reveal yourself freely to all and sundry, until you are certain that the Beylik has nothing against you.'

'Yes,' said Mid-e-Mid. 'That is good advice. I shall follow it.'

Towards noon, the wife of the Marabut came up to them and said, 'I can see a stranger riding this way. Mid-e-Mid, go into the small tent where I have left the newborn lambs, and wait there until we know why he is coming to our tent.'

Mid-e-Mid did not wish to be in the way. He willingly took himself off to a small tent away from the main encampment, stretched out full length on a mat, and fell asleep.

The stranger rode a noble camel, and was richly dressed. He greeted the Marabut courteously, and asked where he could tether the two calves he had brought with him.

'My wife will take care of them and give them water,' replied the Marabut. 'Do not trouble about them further, but come into my tent.'

The stranger looked round, hesitating. 'Marabut,' he said at last, 'I have come to discuss business with you which is not for everyone's ears. Can we speak privately together?'

The Marabut said, 'There is no one in my tent. Please come in. My wife is preparing food, and my daughter is tending the sheep in the *oued*. We have no slaves to do these tasks for us.'

The stranger smiled at this and it was hard to say whether his expression was one of sympathy or contempt. He took stock of all the Marabut's possessions which were in the tent, and asked searching questions about his herds.

At length he said, 'I must tell you my name. I am Tuhaya. You have heard of me?'

'I have heard that you hunted down Abu Bakr, who did me grievous harm,' replied the Marabut.

'Yes. I hunted him to his death. Did you hear that?'

'I had heard that Abu Bakr is dead. But I did not know that you killed him.'

'I decided that he must die. And once I make up my mind, I always carry out my intention,' said Tuhaya.

The Marabut prepared tea. As he poured the water into the can, he asked, 'I heard that there was someone with Abu Bakr, a youth named Mid-e-Mid. Have you heard anything of him?'

'Mid-e-Mid ag Agassum? Yes, I know him. He is a cheeky young monkey who passes for a harmless shepherd. But I know for a fact that he made common cause with Abu Bakr. The Beylik will arrest him as soon as he shows his face. If his conscience were clear, he would never have gone into hiding. But that is not what I came here to talk about. I bring you greetings from Intallah.'

'I thank you,' said the Marabut. 'Is he well?'

'He is well one day and sick the next. All one can say is that he has not much longer to live. That is why my business with you must be dealt with speedily.'

'I am listening,' said the Marabut, and placed the can of water on the fire. 'It will take a little time before the water boils.'

'Intallah's son, Ajor Chageran, has been chosen by the Princes to be the next *Amenokal*, although he is the youngest of Intallah's sons.'

'He deserves it, Tuhaya. He was the most intelligent and scholarly pupil I ever had. He really is an exceptionally brilliant young man.'

He waxed enthusiastic and praised Ajor to the skies.

'I am glad to hear you say so,' replied Tuhaya, satisfied. 'Red Moon, so it appears, admires your daughter. And a few weeks ago, the Amenokal gave his consent to their marriage. Of course, it took me a long time to persuade Intallah that he ought not to oppose such a union. He wanted Red Moon to choose a wife from a noble family. But I am Ajor's friend, and at the same time, the Amenokal's trusted counsellor. And as I have heard much good of your daughter, I have taken it upon myself to carry out the wooing personally. What were you saying, Marabut?'

'Nothing, Tuhaya. I said nothing. This comes as a complete surprise to me.'

'Did not Red Moon hint at his affections when he was your pupil?'

'No. Neither he nor High Summer have said a word. They must have had a secret understanding. I am sure that my wife knows nothing...'

'That sounds just like Ajor Chageran. He keeps his plans to himself. I may tell you in confidence that Intallah was so half-hearted about this wooing at first, that he wanted to send you only one lean sheep. But Ajor insisted that it must be a strong calf. Then I praised your daughter's features so long – she must be very beautiful – that Intallah agreed to send two calves as a gift. They are the ones I brought with me just now.'

Tuhaya's eyes never left the Marabut's face. It did not escape him that the old man was deeply impressed by the generosity of the gift and that the honour which Ajor's choice bestowed on him was something beyond his wildest dreams.

Tiu'elen's father was universally respected, but he was neither distinguished by birth, nor rich in herds and camels, and he had no real prospect of ever becoming a wealthy man. Now he would become the Amenokal's father-in-law. That was much, much indeed, *hamdullillah*. That was Allah's reward for an abstemious life, for piety and for the strict observance of appointed fasts. *Hamdullillah*, Allah is great, Allah is great...

'If I accept your wooing, Tuhaya, will I not make Intallah my enemy, since he gave his consent so reluctantly?'

'You misunderstand me, Marabut. He was against the match at first. But day after day I put it to him that beauty weighs as much as high birth. And now he is most eager for the wedding to take place.'

'I do not underestimate your services in this matter, Tuhaya,' said the Marabut, 'and I do not know how to thank you adequately.'

'I do not ask for thanks, Marabut. My whole life has been devoted to performing acts of friendship towards other people. I have no regrets. Only twice have I reaped bitter ingratitude. Once from Mid-e-Mid's father, and once from Abu Bakr, whom I tried to save from the Beylik's wrath. But Allah loves the upright man and my enemies were slain, *hamdullillah*.'

The Marabut nodded at these words. It was the truth. Tuhaya had grown to be a great man among the Tamashek. The blessing of Allah rested on his undertakings for all the world to see. And a portion of this blessing would now extend over him and his daughter too. Blessed be the day Ajor entered his tent. Blessed be the day Tuhaya came. What unheard of happiness for Tiu'elen!

'I accept Intallah's wooing for his son,' he said in a firm voice.

'Good,' said Tuhaya. 'And now I am charged with enquiring the bride-price you demand for your daughter.'

The Marabut poured out the tea into the waiting glasses. He did it slowly, as if he needed time to think things over. It does not often happen that a man gives his daughter in marriage. And when she is to be the wife of the Amenokal, it needs more deliberation than ever.

'I must tell you, Tuhaya, that I have taken a lot of trouble with this daughter of mine. I have taught her myself. She knows *Tifinagh*, the writing of our people, and the writing of the Arabs too.'

'That is good,' said Tuhaya. 'That is more than most women can do, and she will not feel ashamed of her origin.'

'Yes, it is true,' said the Marabut with strong emphasis. 'She can be proud of everything I have taught her. She knows how to make beautiful leather work, and you should see the skins which she has tanned. I need not say how good she is with the young lambs and kids. Not one escapes her... And as for cooking – even my wife is not a better cook.'

'She will have servants to do the cooking. You forget that the wife of the Amenokal does no work. She is only there for her husband.'

'Yes, that is as well,' said the Marabut. 'If she does not need to work, she will remain beautiful. And she is very beautiful. Everyone says so. Believe me, Tuhaya, there is no shortage of suitors. When she holds an *ahal*, people come from far and wide to see her.'

'So I have been told. But now you must say what price you ask for her.'

The Marabut looked up and saw his wife approaching to greet the guest. He got up to stop her.

'I am discussing something very important,' he said. 'You must not come into the tent just now. Wait until I call you.'

'Is it some evil which threatens us?'

'No. It is good news. But wait until I call, and prepare some food meanwhile, the best we have. We have an exalted guest.'

She went away. He came back into the tent and prepared a third glass of tea.

'Have you thought it over?' asked Tuhaya.

The Marabut held the sugar loaf in one hand and with the bottom of the glass, he hammered it into pieces.

'A wedding is a heavy burden for the father of the bride. I must give her a brand new tent, and that is as dear as a thoroughbred camel, as you know. Then I must have a saddle made for her, which will cost two sheep, as well as tea, sugar and tobacco. I must give her a good camel from my herd, and many sheep and goats and donkeys, so that she does not come like a beggar maid to her husband. She needs sandals, and a new robe. And I must give her two water-skins of freshly tanned goatskin. As for leather saddlebags, why, the smiths will demand a calf for them alone. A lot of work goes into those bags. The leather must be shaved clean inside and out. It must be tooled and coloured. And you must not forget the leather fringes too. Yes, and the tent poles. Every pole must be properly carved. There are goat's hair ropes and blankets from Tuat. Oh! I do not know how I shall manage it all! I shall be a poor man after this wedding. And if Red Moon were not like a son to me, I should never agree to it, believe me, Tuhaya.'

Tuhaya had remained silent during this long speech. He swallowed his tea and rubbed his hands.

'You think that is a lot, Marabut. Think of Ajor. He has to give the wedding feast. Do you know that there will be several hundred guests? Then he has to give presents to the women who beat the drums, more presents to Tiu'elen, to her mother and to you. He must get new clothes and attar of roses and tobacco.'

'Yes, I know,' replied the Marabut. 'But I must give High Summer the copper tray for the tea, the glasses, the tea can and the kettle, the pestles and mortars, calabashes, pitchers, mats...'

'Red Moon must give you cattle and, properly speaking, he ought to give the wooer a present too. But I would not accept anything from him, for I have undertaken this journey solely out of friendship.'

'A plague on daughters!' grumbled the Marabut. 'They demand much more patience from parents than sons, and they cost a lot when they are given in marriage. And one never knows if they will not come back again, for if they do not bear children, they can be turned out by their husbands and then the father must take them back into his tent and resume the burden of their upkeep.'

'This is getting us nowhere,' Tuhaya interrupted. 'Tell me now, how many head of cattle do you want for Tiu'elen?'

The Marabut scratched his ear. 'Tell me first, what is Ajor prepared to give?'

'That is easy. Ajor offers you five young camels and ten goats. You know that the serfs seldom receive more than two camels.'

'That is no price for High Summer,' answered the Marabut. 'I cannot let her go for that. You must give me double.'

'That is quite out of the question. Not even if you were one of the aristocracy would you get double. You must be sensible and not ask for the moon.'

'If I give High Summer away as cheaply as that, I shall be a laughing stock among the Tamashek. But I will meet you halfway. Let it be eight camels and twenty goats, and a new robe for her mother and a sack of tobacco for me.'

'I can promise you the twenty goats. And I shall see to it personally that they are fine, black, long-haired beasts. But you will have to be satisfied with five camels. I shall have to discuss with Ajor the question of a new robe for your wife and the tobacco for you...'

'That is not enough,' repeated the Marabut. 'If there are to be only five camels, Ajor must give me some cattle too, four cows at least.'

'I can see that we shall never come to terms,' said Tuhaya. 'I shall have to go back to Intallah, and report that as far as I am concerned, the mission has failed. But you have been most unreasonable.' He rose and straightened his robes, and got ready to go.

'Stay,' said the Marabut, pulling him back into his place. 'We must not be hasty. I shall be satisfied with three cows...'

'I have no mandate to offer you any cows at all. But to prove that I am your friend, I shall talk Ajor into giving you two cows and a calf. Is it a deal, Marabut?'

'Five camels, twenty goats, two cows, a calf, a robe, a sack of tobacco – for Tiu'elen. It is a heavy blow, Tuhaya, for she is a very good daughter. But I want to see her happily married. I agree.'

They shook hands.

'*Hamdullillah*,' said the Marabut. 'She will be very happy.'

High Summer drove her lambs back to the camp. It was growing hot and the animals needed water.

'Where is Mid-e-Mid?' she asked her mother, who was sitting before the fire, stirring the millet.

'I think he is asleep in the little tent. But you can wake him now and take him some food. He cannot eat with your father. He has an important guest and wants to be alone with him.'

'Who is the visitor?' High Summer wanted to know.

'I do not know, my daughter. But your father says that he brings good news. Here is the dish. Take it to Mid-e-Mid now.'

Tiu'elen watered the lambs and then went into Mid-e-Mid with the dish of food. She found him still asleep. He had taken off his tunic and rolled it into a pillow for his head.

'Mid-e-Mid,' called High Summer softly.

But he did not wake. His hair stood up in spikes round his head. He had drawn up his knees and lay curled in a ball. His wide trousers billowed round his legs.

She put down the dish and shook him by the shoulder.

'Mid-e-Mid.'

He yawned and opened his eyes. When he saw who it was, he propped himself up on one elbow. 'I was just talking to you,' he said, 'and you agreed.'

'What did I agree? What was it?' She dropped near him on the mat so that her back rested against his knee.

Mid-e-Mid passed his hand over his hair, shyly.

'Oh! It is a long story, and really it was only a dream. I had better keep it to myself.'

'No, do tell me about it, Mid-e-Mid.' The cloth slipped from her head. A shaft of sunlight shone through the opening of the tent, and framed her smooth hair with a halo. Her big dark eyes were turned to his. Her hands lay open on her lap.

'I do not remember how it began. But I was riding on Inhelumé through the Oued Tin Bojeriten and you were on a young white camel by my side. And you looked at me... just as you looked at me last evening, when I unveiled my face.'

'Go on, Mid-e-Mid. Tell me more.'

The butter glistened on the surface of the broth and it steamed lightly. There was an appetizing smell, rather like that of fresh cheese.

'Oh! It is so hard to tell you, Tiu'elen! Let me eat first. Then I will try again.'

'Yes,' she said, 'eat.' She passed him the dish and turned away her head, for a woman must not watch a man eating.

He took a handful of food from the dish and ate. Butter dripped on to his brown chest. The complaining bleat of the lambs was muted in the midday stillness.

Once her mother called, 'High Summer!' But she did not hear her. She had ears only for the slight noise Mid-e-Mid made with his mouth as he ate. In a daydream, she felt the warmth of the tent, and the pressure of his knee in the small of her back.

The Marabut was talking to his wife near the fire.

He said, 'I have some good news and some bad news too. First I will tell you the bad. The Beylik is looking for Mid-e-Mid. It will be better for all of us if he can leave the camp without being seen.'

'Is that the truth?' asked his wife, alarmed.

'Yes, it is true. I do not want to get mixed up with his affairs. It is something to do with Abu Bakr's death. The Beylik thinks that Mid-e-Mid killed him and then robbed him...'

'I shall never believe that,' said the woman.

'I do not believe it, either. But he must leave the tent and go back to the rocks and wait there until the whole incident is forgotten. Otherwise, I am afraid he will end up in prison like his father. I must go back to our guest presently and eat with him. Meanwhile, you must get Mid-e-Mid away without being seen.'

'It is hard on the boy,' said the woman, 'and I cannot believe that he is guilty of such a crime.'

'All the same, you must do as I say,' said the Marabut. 'But now listen to the other news. You will be astonished. High Summer is to be married. I have just settled the whole thing.'

'What!' exclaimed the woman. 'And you never said a word to me about it!'

'It came as a complete surprise to me too. But it is all fixed. You will be delighted. The Amenokal himself has sent a wooer for Ajor. Ajor will be his father's successor, and High Summer will be the wife of the Amenokal elect... although we are only vassals, and have never belonged to the nobility.'

The woman wiped her face with her robe. 'Are you telling me the truth?'

'Of course I am – it is absolutely true. And we shall get five camels, twenty goats, two cows, a calf, a robe for you and a sack of tobacco for me. We should never have got that for our daughter if I had not been Ajor's teacher.'

'Oh!' sighed the woman. 'It is too much to take in all at once. I am very pleased. And yet, my heart is heavy. High Summer has never once spoken to me of Ajor. I did not know that there was an understanding between them.'

'Yes, they had kept it a secret. But you know that he gave you a flask of attar of roses for her. That should have made us think...'

'She never uses it,' said the woman thoughtfully.

'That shows how she treasures it. But listen. I shall tell you exactly what the messenger said and what I said to him. Then you will understand just how things have been arranged, and you can prepare High Summer in suitable fashion for the wedding.'

And he repeated in detail all that he and Tuhaya had discussed.

Meanwhile, Tuhaya had left the tent to stretch his legs. He walked round the encampment in a large circle and was just going back to the fire, when he heard two voices coming from the small tent. He stopped to hear what was being said. When he made out the words, he stood rooted to the spot and made no sound.

A young man's voice was saying:

'It was noon and we sought the shade. "Mid-e-Mid," you said, "there is a tree over there with plenty of shade. Let us rest there." I jumped to the ground and helped you down from your saddle. I brushed away the thorns and spread the blanket on the sand. We sat near one another, just as we are sitting now. Yes, Tiu'elen, just like this.'

A girl's voice replied, 'And then I prepared your food for you?'

'No. We did not bother with food. We only wanted to look at each other for ever and ever. And songs came tumbling into my head, one after another. But they did not pass my lips, for my tongue halted.'

'I cannot think of anything to say either, when I see you, Mid-e-Mid. Ever since the first time you came into our tent – Ajor was still with us then – ever since that day, I have thought about you. Oh! I do not know how to say it, but it is as if I can see you, even when you are not there. And the thought of you fills me, so that I do not know if I want to weep or to laugh...'

'We sat under the tree, and I wanted to take your hands. But mine were as lame as my tongue. It was you who touched my fingers. You said, "What are you thinking of, Mid-e-Mid?"'

'Then I could speak again. I said, "I am thinking of you, Tiu'elen. Day and night. Always." I said, "I have no herds. I have no tent. I am of lowly descent. I have nothing but my songs, and they are like the dust which the wind tosses and blows away."'

'What did I say?'

'You just looked at me and held my hands, High Summer. I felt the warmth of your hands and your eyes were as dark and as deep as the Well of Tin Azeraf...'

'You are a poet, Mid-e-Mid. What do you want with herds and tents? People love you and will always give you something to eat.'

'Yes, yes. But... still I could not help asking you...'

'What did you ask me, Mid-e-Mid? What was it? Tell me, quickly!'

'I said, "Will you be my wife, High Summer?"'

'And what did I answer?'

'I dare not repeat it. It was only a dream and it could never come true.'

'I said that I would, Mid-e-Mid. Of course I did.'

'How do you know? But you did say that – in a dream, High Summer, only in a dream.'

'I am saying it now, too. I am saying that I will be your wife. And we are both awake. Are you happy?'

'Happy? I cannot even begin to describe it. I am like the alemos when the rain revives it after a year of drought...'

Tuhaya glided away. When he was at a safe distance from the small tent, he hurried towards the fire.

Ignoring the woman, he said, 'I have something else to say to you, Marabut. Without delay. It is very important.'

The Marabut rose in surprise and accompanied his guest back to the tent.

'Have you changed your mind?' he asked anxiously.

'No. But perhaps we have cooked our gazelle before we have caught it.'

'What do you mean, Tuhaya?'

'It occurs to me that we have not asked your daughter if she consents.'

'But that is quite unnecessary. Of course she will consent. She will be happy to fulfil her secret wishes.'

'I am not so sure of that. I should like to hear it from her own mouth.'

'I shall call her immediately.'

'First speak to her alone and then tell me when she has answered you. It is not essential to ask a chit of a girl how she feels, but it often saves a great deal of unpleasantness afterwards.'

The Marabut was concerned at the sharp note in Tuhaya's voice, and he went at once to call his daughter as his guest left the tent.

'Yes, Father?' said Tiu'elen, and her cheeks were faintly flushed.

'I have something to say to you. Sit down.'

They sat down.

'A messenger has arrived, my daughter. He has come on your account and brings gifts for you.'

'For me?' she said, taken aback.

'Do you know who has sent them, my daughter?'

'No,' she said and shook her head. 'What are these gifts?'

'They are two strong calves, and the messenger has been sent by Ajor Chageran.'

She turned pale, for she knew the significance of the gifts.

'I see that you are moved, my daughter. And I have better news still for you. Ajor has been chosen to be the next *Amenokal*. And you will be the Amenokal's wife, my child.'

'No!' she exclaimed. She covered her face and lowered her head on her knee.

'My daughter,' said the Marabut. 'I can hardly believe it is true myself. He belongs to the greatest of the nobles, and we are only vassals and poor. But it is quite true all the same. I have already agreed with the wooer how many cows and camels Ajor will pay for you. You may well rejoice.'

'No,' she cried, throwing back her head-cloth and looking reproachfully at her father. 'I do not want him. I will not be his wife. Never, never, never!'

The Marabut could not believe his ears.

'The wife of the Amenokal, Tiu'elen! Do you understand what I am saying?'

'I beg you, Father, do not force me to take this man. I do not want to be his wife.'

'Child,' said the Marabut, 'Ajor is young and good-looking. He is very clever, and he has become famous by his victory over the Kounta. He is the chosen leader of all the Tamashek, and he loves you. Why else would he think of marrying you?'

'Please, Father, I ask you – send these presents back. There are plenty of other girls. He can easily find someone much more suitable to marry him...'

'Nonsense!' said the Marabut. 'Just say it is all right. I want to assure the messenger that you agree.'

'I shall never agree,' said High Summer stubbornly, and tears ran down her cheeks.

'You are most disobedient and forget your duty. I have already given my word and all the details have been settled. You cannot be released.'

She wept bitterly, but he went on, 'Think of the disgrace you will bring down on my head! Do you want me to break my word? Do you know that you are violating the law of the Koran which lays down the daughter's obedience to her father? I am afraid that one of the young men at the *ahal* has turned your head! But this I tell you. If I have to reject these presents, I shall lay my curse upon you and drive you from my tent!'

He stood over her, his fists clenched, his mouth set, and spat out the words between his teeth.

Tiu'elen put her hands over her ears and buried her face in her lap.

Her mother came running out of the tent. She had heard the Marabut's voice raised in anger.

'Such ingratitude!' he shouted in fury. 'She dares to oppose her father!'

The woman bent over High Summer and wrapped her wide robe about her shoulders.

'Leave us now,' she said quietly to her husband. 'You should have let me speak to her first.'

High Summer could only sob, and her robe grew wet with tears and the dye stained her face.

'My daughter,' said the woman, 'do not think badly of your father. He was so happy for your sake, to think that you had been chosen from among all the daughters of the Tamashek! You must see his point of view. He is a good man, and he believed that everything had been secretly arranged between you and Red Moon.'

But High Summer only wept.

Her mother said, 'Are you thinking of Mid-e-Mid, my daughter?'

The sobs grew louder.

'I thought as much when he sang for you yesterday. Why did you not tell me, my daughter?'

'I had never spoken to him properly until yesterday,' murmured High Summer, burying her face on her mother's shoulder.

'He has come too late, Tiu'elen. Allah has decreed it otherwise. You are very young, still not sixteen summers. You do not care if Mid-e-Mid has neither flocks nor a tent. Nor do you realize that he is too restless to stay faithful to a wife at home. His songs drive him from place to place. But a woman cannot live like that. A woman wants a man for herself alone. Believe me, my child, you would never be happy with Mid-e-Mid. He would go from tent to tent singing his songs, and the girls would all admire him, and he would not be faithful to you.'

'No!' exclaimed High Summer. 'He will never stop loving me!'

The woman put her hand lightly on Tiu'elen's shoulder and felt how the girl trembled.

'My child,' she continued, 'everywhere in the world, fathers look for decent men to marry their daughters, and they are happy if they find one who is not a scoundrel. Your father has found a man who is not only very fond of you. He is also the greatest and the most highly respected man among the whole tribe. Could he have done better for you?'

'No,' said High Summer. 'But I want to marry Mid-e-Mid.'

'You must look at it this way, my daughter. Marriages are nothing but bonds of friendship between families and clans. We, the women and the children we bear are the pledges of these friendships. But for us, the men would be at each other's throats. Allah knows that we do not marry for our pleasure. He knows that we suffer and that we sacrifice ourselves for the sake of peace between families and clans and tribes.

'As daughters, they barter us for camels and goats, and as mothers, they have time only for our children. And yet, they could never do without us. We are the salt in their food and the comfort of their eyes.

'My daughter, you must see that you are nothing without your family, your father and his brothers and my brothers. We are always behind you. We are your refuge if your husband beats you or abuses you, drives you from his tent or wants a divorce. Believe me, Tiu'elen, the husband is not important. It is the children and the family who count. Come, my child, do not let your mother go on talking so. Come on. Tell your father that you consent.'

High Summer sobbed afresh.

'Mid-e-Mid has gone away,' said her mother.

'Why?' said High Summer and raised her head.

'I had to send him away. The Beylik is looking for him... They say that he is responsible for Abu Bakr's death.'

'That is not true,' protested High Summer. 'It cannot be true.'

'I do not believe it either. But if he stays here, the *goumiers* would find him and they would throw him into prison like his father. A murder is a murder as far as the Beylik is concerned.'

'Mid-e-Mid has committed no crime,' said High Summer with glowing cheeks.

'That may be so, my daughter. But still the Beylik will hunt him down, as he hunted Abu Bakr. He will know neither peace of mind nor rest. And a wife would be a great handicap to him...'

'I promised him that I would marry him.'

'Choose him in your heart, High Summer, but marry the man your father has chosen. You know that a girl's word has no weight. It does not count even as much as a half-promise by a man. It says so in the Koran. But I will give you one piece of advice. If you want to do something for Mid-e-Mid, you can only do so as the wife of the Amenokal. Only he has the power to intercede with the Beylik for Mid-e-Mid. And Ajor will speak for him if you ask him to. Ask him, Tiu'elen. He will not refuse your request, for he loves you.'

'Do you really think so, Mother?' she asked, looking up.

'Yes, I do indeed. I know what men are like. They refuse nothing to a young wife. She can demand the fruit of Paradise. Do this for Mid-e-Mid, and you will be doing more for him than even his own mother could achieve.'

She wiped the girl's face with her hand and rubbed off the blue stain and smoothed her hair. 'I shall call your father. You need only nod your head. It will take some time before you are ready to leave here to join Ajor's family.'

And High Summer nodded, her resistance broken.

When the Marabut told his guest that he had his daughter's agreement, Tuhaya said, 'Now everything is settled and we know where we stand. There are some girls whose hearts must be broken first, but they make the best wives in the end. I shall tell Ajor that High Summer is being prepared for the wedding. Give her plenty of milk to drink, Marabut, so that she gets fat, and does not disgrace the Amenokal's family. For they all expect a beautiful, plump daughter-in-law.'

The Marabut accompanied him part of the way and was pleased with the day's work.

And Mid-e-Mid rode off towards Tin Za'uzaten in the firm belief that Tiu'elen would one day be his wife. And the threat of the Beylik troubled him as little as the flies buzzing round Inhelumé's tail. He sang all the way, and he gave the fool Kalil half of everything he had bartered for the camel.

CHAPTER SIXTEEN

The Women Quarrel

WEDDINGS ARE LIKE SONGS. It takes longer to compose them than to perform them. By the Well of In Tebdoq, where Intallah had pitched his tents, all the necessary arrangements for the wedding were put in motion.

From the tents of the Idnan, the Kel Telabit, the Tarat-Mellet and the Iforgumessen, came messengers asking what date had been fixed and announcing at the same time that the heads of the chief families would attend.

In the Oued of Tin Bojeriten, the Marabut set about his part of the preparations with alacrity. Almost every day, the smiths appeared at the Marabut's tent to show him a half-finished saddle or the beginnings of a saddlebag, skilfully worked, but they extorted advance payment in the shape of tobacco, dates, pepper or butter, milk, lambs or kids.

'They will make me poorer than I have ever been before,' groaned the Marabut. And it was no exaggeration. The new copper-red tent alone cost him twenty fat sheep and a kilogram of tea. He had to barter four goats for a pretty silver trinket-box. For the saddle, he had to give a five-year-old riding camel and yet another one had to be sacrificed for the coloured blankets bought from a caravan out of Tuat.

The nearer the day for departure came, the more the craftsmen pestered him. For an especially beautiful pattern on a saddlebag, he had to add butter and milk to the agreed price. Even the smallest and least pretentious articles had to be paid for – hobbles for the camels, green and red leather straps for the harness, leather fringes for the saddle girth, a new water-carrier of the finest brown goatskin, sandals and ear-rings, enamel dishes and tea cans of copper and tin.

In the end, he gave the smiths so many beasts in payment, that he and his wife ran the risk of going short of milk during the dry season. A few days before the departure, one black-skinned copper-smith arrived with a splendidly worked necklace for his daughter. As he had nothing left to pay with, he could only have it by promising to keep the man in butter and milk throughout the summer.

By the time Intallah's riders appeared to meet his future daughter-in-law and to conduct her and her father to In Tebdoq, the Marabut was so impoverished that he was glad to set off. He could hardly look at one of the black-faced artisans without physical revulsion. They reminded him all too painfully of how he had been fleeced.

High Summer seemed completely indifferent to the preparations going on around her. Only once did she betray any emotion. That was when her father showed her the camel he was giving her to ride, and which would remain her own property, even in her husband's tent. It was a tall, snow-white animal, with shining brown eyes and slim, almost graceful legs. She remembered that Mid-e-Mid had described such a camel, when he told her of their dream ride together.

She did not cry much these days. Her mother's words had made a deep impresion on her, and she was virtually convinced that her marriage was the only way of saving Mid-e-Mid from the Beylik's hands. She began to look forward to the coming festivities with something approaching enthusiasm and she no longer thought of Red Moon with the same distaste which she had felt during those first few weeks after Tuhaya's visit. Then she had lain awake night after night and had wept all day as she watched the lambs in the *oued*. Now she steeled herself to carry out her new tasks and to make all necessary sacrifices. She must hide her unhappiness in the depths of her heart. But the image of Mid-e-Mid was always present. It wandered with her wherever she went and she felt that she could still hear the tenderness of his voice as he softly sang *The Moon of Irrarar* for her.

Against her father she felt no grudge, for she saw what trouble he was taking to equip her splendidly for the wedding. At the end of January she took leave of her mother and set out southwards for the Well of In Tebdoq. She was accompanied by her father and four riders. There were four heavily laden baggage camels roped to her white mount, which had red blankets of sheep's wool folded beneath the saddle. She herself was dressed in new robes of dark purple. On her wrist gleamed bracelets of yellow gold, presents from Ajor Chageran and his father.

As the caravan moved slowly through the *oued*, men and women came up to them to wish High Summer good luck. And the men who had been invited to the wedding joined the cavalcade. This brought new cares on the Marabut's head, for of course, it was an understood thing that he had to feed these guests too. As the provisions had been calculated for a much smaller company, he had to incur fresh debts as he went, for courtesy forbade him to turn away the newcomers.

There were young men, too, who came just for a last glimpse of High Summer. Among them was Bocha, with his flat moon-like face and prominent cheekbones. He was the one who had made the unfortunate comparison of Tiu'elen's feet to camels' hoofs and had been laughed out of court. He rode at her side, silent and with downcast eyes. When she spoke to him, he replied in monosyllables, but suddenly, he pressed something into her hand, exclaimed, 'The blessing of Allah go with you always,' whipped his camel and dashed off at a wild gallop. It was a big, yellow leather amulet, decorated with tiny stones and intended to ward off the evil eye. She wanted to call after him, to thank him for his gift. But he had already disappeared behind the crest of a hill, leaving only a hazy cloud of white dust on the trail.

Young Mohammed ag Infirgan with the sharp aquiline nose and the merry eyes was another of those who came up to her and he told her that he hoped to be married soon himself. He wished her many sons and a venerable old age, and rode away waving and laughing.

By this time, Red Moon was getting impatient with the slow progress of the caravan. He sent his friends post-haste towards it, so that they could report if High Summer were in good health, and how many days longer the journey would take, how she looked and what she had said. He wanted to know how her camel was bearing up and if she wore his golden gifts. Had she mentioned his name, did she talk with the other men, or only with her father? Who helped her down from her camel? Who spread the rugs for her? In short, he asked all the sensible questions and all the ridiculous ones too. He tried to hide his agitation by assuming a solemn expression which betrayed him at once. And he kept asking his friends, 'Tell me the truth. Do you like her? Do you think she is beautiful? Very beautiful? Do you think we are well suited? Is she fit to be the wife of the Amenokal?'

And because they confirmed everything, he would not believe that they were giving him an honest opinion, and tried to find hidden meanings in their answers, and ambiguity in their words. And as time dragged by he drove himself and everyone in his company nearly to distraction.

The day the Marabut arrived at In Tebdoq, Red Moon could not be found. He had ridden off on his camel early that morning and he remained away until the evening. Intallah and Tadast received their future daughter-in-law with some reserve, for they did not want her to forget that she came from vassal stock.

Tadast came up to High Summer and whispered in a voice that was clear enough for everyone round her to hear, 'I thought you were supposed to be beautiful. Your arms are quite scraggy. You seem to have come from a hungry land.'

Intallah was cordial after his fashion. He enquired politely about their journey, conducted the Marabut to his tent, entrusted High Summer to his wife's servants, and ordered the slaves to erect Tiu'elen's tent.

Tiu'elen had been taken aback by Tadast's greeting. It had never occurred to her that she was acquiring not only a husband but a mother-in-law. And even if it had passed through her mind, she would not have realized the implications.

She had scarcely entered her tent and opened her baggage when Tadast appeared before her. She did not ask if she might come in. She sat down and started rummaging in Tiu'elen's belongings without saying a word. When she had finished, she asked, 'Is that all? Is that all you have to bring into my stepson's tent? Have you no jewellery? No clothes?'

High Summer could not speak. She just shook her head.

Tadast felt her arms and her body and said loudly: 'It is too late to feed you up properly before the wedding. But I shall send you milk three times a day to fatten you up a little. I insist that you drink every drop. I may not be present when my daughter-in-law takes food. But I shall give orders to the slaves to watch you. And I shall send you some clothes I no longer wear. They are not torn. I just do not need them. I have plenty of others.'

As High Summer still did not reply, she said, 'I am pleased to see that you know how to hold your tongue. Apart from Intallah and Ajor, there is only one mouth in this camp – and that is mine!' And she pointed to her own mouth to stress the point.

High Summer looked at her properly for the first time. Tadast's face, she had to admit, was both beautiful and intelligent, not yet touched by age, and not as outrageously fat as the rest of the body. But High Summer felt instinctively that she had to do something there and then if she were not to be hopelessly browbeaten for the rest of her life.

Without pausing to reflect, she lifted her hand and struck Tadast full in the mouth. All the misery she had suffered, all her suppressed rage and her blazing hatred of the woman before her went into that blow. It was so violent that it knocked Tadast over and she fell backwards and was too fat to get up.

'Now you know how many mouths speak here!' Tiu'elen cried out. 'Think twice before you send me your milk! I shall empty the calabash over the heads of your slaves! Think twice before you send me your old rags! I shall burn them in front of your tent! Think twice before you set foot in my tent again! And do not dare to make trouble between Ajor and me!'

Her voice shrilled. 'If you do, I shall scratch your face so that Intallah himself will not recognize you. Now – get out!' And she clutched Bocha's yellow amulet, for the look on Tadast's face was frightening. 'Get out!' she repeated and she pushed Tadast's leg to make her move faster.

Tadast crawled out of the tent, trembling with rage, but dumb as a fish. She veiled her face and ran to her tent as fast as her feet could carry her heavy body.

She sent no milk, and no old clothes. High Summer was greatly relieved and dismissed the incident from her mind.

At noon, Tuhaya was called into Tadast's tent. She had bandaged her mouth and spoke so indistinctly that the wily politician could hardly understand her.

'Tuhaya,' she said, 'that woman has treated me outrageously. She struck me, the wife of the Amenokal! She has insulted me, threatened me and trodden my presents in the dirt. She has forbidden me her tent and denied me the right to speak to my own stepson. Oh! If only I had stood my ground and stopped him from marrying a girl of such contemptibly low birth! If only Red Moon were here, so that he could punish her. He ought to have her beaten publicly and then send her back home with the dirty old Marabut. Tell me, Tuhaya, what shall I do? Shall I tell Intallah to forbid the marriage before it is too late? Or better still, shall I poison her? I know a poison which...'

'You are too excited, Tadast,' said Tuhaya. 'Where is that wisdom with which you conquer all our hearts? Why do you storm and rage instead of using your wits?'

In an instant she was calm, and even a man of Tuhaya's experience would hardly have believed that such a change of mood could take place so quickly.

'What do you advise me to do, Tuhaya? I shall have my revenge, but tell me how. Shall I speak to Ajor? I know that he will listen to me.'

'You cannot touch Ajor just now. He is in love with this girl, and will listen to reason as little as a bullock breaking loose from the pen. Nor would it be any use to talk to Intallah. He is old and loathes wrangling. He only wants to be left in peace. If you use violence and beat her or have her beaten, Ajor will be your enemy for life. In his present mood, it might provoke him to a deed of bloody madness.'

'But must I do nothing and swallow this insult? Is that what you recommend, Tuhaya?'

'You are the daughter of a wealthy prince, Tadast. Have you ever asked me for advice in vain? Have I ever let you down?'

'You are right. I trust you and I will listen to you.'

Tuhaya passed his tongue over his lips, and his prominent teeth looked sinister as he bared them.

'Wait until the wedding, Tadast. Humiliate her in her proudest hour. Shame her before all her guests, but in such a way that you will win Ajor to your side.'

'How can I do that?' She tore the bandage from her mouth and her upper lip showed faintly swollen.

'I shall tell you a secret that I alone know. With this secret you have her in the hollow of your hand. It is up to you to use your knowledge how and when you will, and expose her shamelessness to the world.'

'Tell me what you know, Tuhaya. You will never regret it.'

Tuhaya said, 'When I was in the Marabut's tent, I accidentally overheard a conversation between High Summer and Mid-e-Mid.'

'Who is Mid-e-Mid? I have never heard of him.'

'But you know the name Eliselus, do you not? It is the same person.'

'Oh! You mean the singer. What did they say? Tell me quickly.'

'They were together in the tent and I heard High Summer say, "I will be your wife, Mid-e-Mid," and he replied, "I am like the *alemos* when the rain revives after a year of drought..."'

'Do you mean that this... this vagabond is philandering with Ajor's wife? Good. That is much more than I dared to hope for.'

'Wait, Tadast. There is more to come. Although the Marabut had agreed to the marriage, Tiu'elen did her best to oppose her father with tears and sobs, and wanted to go with Mid-e-Mid. She was so upset that her mother had to talk to her and soothe her. I heard it all. Ajor does not know what he has let himself in for. For my part, I would never have sought out this Marabut's daughter. I was against it from the start. But no one listened to my advice. Youth is in the saddle here. The old people are only allowed to settle the bills afterwards...'

'You do not know what good your words have done me, Tuhaya. They are like healing balm on festering wounds,' said Tadast, getting up.

'There is one thing more, Tadast. This young man, Eliselus, as they call him, is wanted by the Beylik. It was he who murdered Abu Bakr and robbed him before I could reach him with my sword. I have held my tongue for a long time, but now there is no doubt that the Beylik is on his track and I cannot shield him any more. He is a lost man. Yet High Summer wanted to fling herself round his neck. She preferred his companionship to that of the future Amenokal. Need I say more?'

Tadast had risen. Her cheeks were flushed and her eyes sparkled.

'Never has a friend given better comfort than you, Tuhaya. I shall return her blow in such a way that she will feel the sting as long as she lives. I shall send you two negroes for your words. Tuhaya.'

'I do not need them, Tadast,' he said firmly. 'I value your friendship more than all the slaves in my tents.'

And he left Tadast feeling the satisfaction of a hunter who has set his trap so cunningly that his quarry cannot possibly escape.

It was night when Red Moon returned to the camp. The broad plain which lay between the mountains of the *oued* was dotted with campfires beneath the clustered stars. The singing and shouting of the men, the bellowing of the camels, the laughing of hyenas filled the darkness and only died away at daybreak when the cattle were driven in leisurely cavalcade to the well.

That night Ajor could not sleep. He tossed and turned restlessly, unable to close his eyes. He longed for the hour when High Summer would be led by his friends into his own tent. He could lead men confidently and play upon their feelings while he himself remained detached. Yet where his private affairs were concerned he was tormented by vague apprehensions, and dim forebodings.

Next day, the marriage convenant between Intallah and Tiu'elen's father was drawn up by a visiting Marabut and signed and sealed with prayers. Ajor was present physically, but his spirit was a day ahead in time.

CHAPTER SEVENTEEN

The Wedding

THE STARS LINGERED still, hesitating to give way before the blue-grey light of day. Beyond the camp jackals crouched like dogs, lying in wait for heedless lambs. Their pointed muzzles sniffed the wind. They were the first to see the yawning start of a new day, the tents pushed open, the mats rolled up. They heard the clicking noise 'Dak, dak,' which the girls and women make to call the goats, and they smelt the smoke of the wood-fires, as it curled in gauzy shreds over the *oued*.

There was an old stone wall not far away towards which numbers of men, all dressed in their ceremonial robes, were making their way. Their broad sandals crunched the hard, crusted sand. The edge of their robes touched the ground and the *cram-cram* heads embroidered them with their prickly yellow stars. The women, whose plain blue robes might have belonged to the Sisters of one great Order, stood back against the high ramparts of dressed stone. The men collected in the middle of a clearing and took off their sandals. With their bare toes they kicked aside the camel dung which littered the area.

Slim, silent and straight as a lance, Ajor stood apart, his face turned towards the mountains where a purple gleam announced the rising of the sun. As soon as the red rim of the fiery orb was visible above the grey, he lifted his arms, cleansed his face with sand, and recited the morning prayer. And behind him stood the ranks of the Tamashek, the men of his family, their friends and guests, the Princes with their retinues, the shepherds of the Ibottenaten and the Tarat-Mellet, the Kel Effele and the Iforgumessen. There they stood, nobles and vassals, and, well apart, the black slaves and the smiths whose skins were just as swarthy. Finally came the little cluster of women, modestly huddled together, and among the women, inconspicuous, yet the focus of curious glances, stood High Summer, her face veiled.

Ajor's call to prayer echoed long drawn over the plains and was repeated in chorus by the men. The murmur of voices grew to a resounding paean, as they called on Allah, and then died away to a whisper as the worshippers fell to the earth and touched the hard ground with their foreheads. The devout and the sceptic alike were carried away by the solemnity of the moment, and filled with a common feeling of purpose and dedication, while the golden ball of the sun rolled over the ridge of the mountains and swept aloft in a blaze of colour. *Allah akbar* – God is great. And nowhere is he greater than in the upland valleys of the wilderness.

The crowd wandered back to the tents in little groups. Tuhaya hardly left Ajor's side. Since the wooing, a kind of friendship had sprung up between the young Prince and this man of dubious loyalties. There was no affection in it, but a mutual recognition and respect. Ajor Chageran admired the older man's knowledge of people and his political astuteness, and Tuhaya saw the advantage of being on the right side of the future Amenokal of all the Tamashek in the Iforas Mountains.

But in character, what was subtlety in Ajor became a talent for intrigue in Tuhaya. One was clever, the other cunning. Ajor thought continually of the greatness of his people, Tuhaya merely of his own prestige. People admired the son of the Amenokal. The notorious cattle-dealer was feared and even hated by many. They made a curious pair.

The Princes stayed near Intallah and watched the two of them with ill-concealed suspicion. They considered that Red Moon's fame had spread too far and too fast for one so young. They believed that Tuhaya had secretly been a party to the war against the Kounta, and that his ride to the Beylik was merely a blind. They did not say so, but they regretted that they had let Intallah talk them into accepting Ajor as their leader. Someone more docile and less capable would have been more to their liking.

At first, they had intended to boycott the wedding. They had not forgotten that Ajor had pointedly ignored them over the march to the Valley of Tilemsi. But Intallah's personal request, and a hunch that this might provide an occasion for common action against Tuhaya – and incidentally strike a blow at Red Moon too – had decided them to come. And so among the wedding guests, there were tension, hostility and reserve.

To entertain the assembly, Ajor had offered a prize to the man who would chase the festive ox from the herd to the campfire and kill it.

The cattle were grazing on the north side of the Oued In Tebdoq. It was a tricky business to single out one beast from the herd. And it was trickier still to hunt it over the rocky barricade that bounded the *oued*.

At a sign from Red Moon, all the young shepherds who wished to compete mounted their camels and rode north with wild cries and circling whips. Spurred on by the applause of their friends they drove the nervous camels over the rocks across to the far side, right into the midst of the grazing herd. The cattle started moving in one compact mass, and tried to break out first left and then right. The men whipped them back. A monstrous cloud of dust arose. Riders collided and were thrown from their saddles. Cows tried to protect their fallen calves by standing out against the stampede and were in turn overwhelmed and trampled. Young bullocks, panic-stricken by the whips, charged each other, reared on their hind legs, and butted their way back again into the welter of carcases, hoofs and horns.

By the time the men had decided on one powerful, humpbacked steer and singled it out from the herd, the group of riders had thinned out considerably. Many had fallen. Others were marooned in the sea of maddened cattle, and their lives were in danger. But no one gave them a thought. At last, there were only seven men left, crouching low in their saddles. These seven started chasing the copper-brown steer towards the camp.

The terrified animal scrambled up the stony path faster than its pursuers, and turning suddenly, stood at bay against a block of granite. One young Tamashek tried to kill it with a well-aimed blow between the horns, but the bull charged and he was thrown from his saddle. His wounded camel dragged him down the hill, caught in the reins, but his cries were met with derisive laughter from the remaining six, who returned to the chase with renewed energy. They managed to divert the steer towards the camp, but it swerved again and retreated back to the rocks.

The third onslaught was more successful. The ox was driven into the camp, where it was received with excited cries and much clapping and cheering. But the rejoicing soon changed to screams of panic as the animal broke loose among pots and calabashes and tent poles, scattering sheep and goats to left and right, and galloping straight towards the group of women, who fled shrieking and yelling, and threw themselves into thorn bushes or flat on the ground. Then the steer pulled up abruptly, and seemed to be taking thought for a moment. One young Tarat-Mellet took advantage of this second. He jumped down from his camel, and struck the beast one mighty blow in the neck with his sword. The animal turned to its assailant, dumbly reared its head and then crumpled and fell. A great stream of blood gushed from the wound. The legs jerked, the tail flicked once or twice, and the ox was dead.

Ajor handed the Tarat-Mellet a new sword as a reward. 'May the enemies of the Tamashek perish like this steer,' he said. Then he called the servants to cut up the carcase and prepare the meat. Everyone was delighted with the hunt.

But there was one exception. By accident, Tuhaya happened to be standing close by when the shepherd struck the fatal blow and the blood had poured over him, soaking his garments. It was not that his robes were soiled, for he possessed several others. But he was convinced that it was a bad omen. For he was as superstitious as all the Tamashek and feared evil spirits on earth more than the Devil in Hell. 'Blood calls to blood,' he said darkly.

At noon, the *Tindé* started.

The Princes and the elders had grouped themselves well back, seated on a hillock, so that they would have a good view over the whole field. The women sat huddled together in one large group, with High Summer, veiled, in the middle. Near her were three girls with the drum, a wet calfskin stretched taut over a big calabash. They squatted in front of it and beat out the monotonous rhythm.

Dum-dum-dum-dum-dum-o-dum-o-dum-o-dum-dum-dum-dum-dum.

The young men in their finest blue robes rode up reining in their camels, so that their heads were held high up on a level with the cross of the saddle. They looked like proud ships gliding by, silhouetted against the boundless ocean of the blue sky.

Dum-dum-dum-dum-dum-o-dum-o-dum-o-dum-dum-dum-dum-dum...

The beat of the drum quickened and the camels went faster too. Black eyes and brown eyes glistened with excitement and uneasiness. Their underlips hung down. Flecks of green and yellow foam dripped to the ground. The riders sat bolt upright, impassive, like so many stuffed dolls. The reins lay loose and light in the left hand. Not by a single gesture or movement did they appear to control or guide. It looked for all the world as if the camels themselves had taken the initiative and conceived the idea of a mad, exotic dance round the women in the centre.

Faster and faster pounded the drum. The camels came so close to the crouching women that some of them closed their eyes. But the old men on the hill goaded the riders into ever more daring feats.

'When we were young,' they shouted, 'when we were young, we knew how to ride! The Iludjan! We want the Iludjan!'

It did not look as if Ajor, or for that matter, anyone else, took it upon himself to lead the Iludjan, the climax of the *Tindé*. The riders closed up into one long row and circled round the group in ever-narrowing spirals until the animals were practically touching, tail to head. The tempo of the staccato beats mounted and the women shrieked their blood-curdling cries, and the camels pricked their ears in terror.

'Faster!' cried the old men. 'Faster!'

But now, even they had no reason to complain. They looked on breathlessly, with mouths agape as the spirals narrowed and men and camels seemed to lean inwards as if a solid wall of centaurs were spinning round the central group, a living merry-go-round, whirling with unbelievable speed round the huddle of women in the middle.

And all the onlookers sprang to their feet and shouted, 'The Iludjan! The Iludjan!' and the drums thundered. The camels dipped their heads and suddenly there was a flash, as naked swords were brandished on high and melted into one glittering, gleaming ring of steel.

And yet, one light movement, accidental perhaps, was sufficient to bring the swirling, revolving mass to a halt. Tiu'elen's headcloth fell back, and for a moment, her face was revealed. And this moment was enough to stamp on Ajor's brain for ever the waxen pallor, the eyes shaded blue with antimony, the soft full mouth, the smoothly parted hair and the small determined chin. And it seemed to him that she had unveiled herself for him alone, under the cover of the whirlwind dance of the camels. He tore a silver chain from his neck and threw it into her lap. The cheering carried even to the ears of the Princes and rejoiced his heart. He thought that he saw an answering look of gratitude, and with one bound, he broke away from the Iludjan.

Many years later, when he had long become the paramount chieftain between the Ahaggar Mountains and the Great River, he confessed that never before or since had he experienced a moment of such utter happiness. And perhaps this admission brought High Summer nearer to him than all the presents and honours he might ever bestow upon her.

And now the Iludjan was over. The women and girls got up and went back to their tents, and the men led their camels into the *oued* to cool off after the fantastic circling of the *Tindé*.

In the late afternoon the wedding feast began, and went on into the night.

The guests fell upon the sacrificial ox, as well as sheep and calves, in such quantities that shortly before it grew dark, more animals had to be slaughtered. They ate rice with melted rancid butter, sharply spiced with red pepper, and calabashes and beakers were passed from hand to hand with a refreshing drink made of pressed dates, millet and water. There were not a few who gorged themselves until they were sick, reason enough to start filling their bellies all over again without restraint. They were smeared with fat and milk and meat, and did not rest until all the bones were gnawed bare and the dishes scraped clean. Accustomed as they were to hunger, to meagre, monotonous fare, it was a joy for once to feel the satisfaction of streaming abundance. Beards dripped, bodies were plastered with sweat and fat, and arms were greased to the elbow with butter by the time they had finished the banquet.

There was no one there who did not sing the praises of Intallah and Tadast, and who did not express his appreciation with lavish belches and eructations. It was a feast after the hearts of the Tamashek, magnificent, indescribable, and worthy of Allah in Paradise. *Hamdullillahi!* They picked their teeth with thorns, murmuring blessings on the young pair, wishing them many sons, and as many camels as the sands of Tanesruft; wishing them eternally green fields and overflowing wells, and underlining their good wishes by spitting exuberantly to all the four winds and uttering groans of gratitude and repeated sighs of '*Hamdullillahi!*'

It was as if the smell of freshly roasted mutton lured new crowds to the *oued*. Even when night fell uninvited guests, men, women and children edged nearer to the feast, hoping for a bone which still had a fragment of meat clinging to it, or a calabash which had not been licked quite clean.

As the wood fires flared into the night, the women, who had eaten apart from the men, came back to the main company. The climax of the celebrations was approaching.

In the red firelight, the men gathered around the jolly Ramzata ag Elrhassan, the fat Prince of the Kel Telabit. He was their foremost singer, even if he crowed like a cock. But he had a penetrating voice and he knew how to make himself heard. The women formed a group around Tadast, taking cover, as it were, under the protection of her sharp tongue.

Red Moon and High Summer had to sit side by side on a raised mound of trampled earth between the two groups. They were not allowed to look at each other nor to speak. Ajor was quite at ease, and found the conditions no strain. But Tiu'elen suffered. In spite of her veiling, she could feel the gaze of the assembly piercing her like arrow points. She feared a secret attack from Tadast, against which she would be unable to defend herself. She did not know who were her friends there, nor who her enemies. She felt that she had been sacrificed and abandoned, and for the first time, Red Moon's presence was some comfort to her in her distress. She could feel the warmth of his shoulder in the coolness of the night, and imperceptibly, she leaned against it. If only this were over, she thought. But I am doing it for Mid-e-Mid. And I shall speak to Ajor about him when we are alone. And she thought, what will Mid-e-Mid think of me when he hears that I am married? The prospect frightened her. She imagined that she could see his face among Intallah's guests. But there were only the nobles and Tuhaya, and, at the edge of the group, her father. She did not know anyone else there.

Ramzata started to sing a mocking song.

> A bullock strolled through the grass so green
> Searching for a mate.
> No heifer grazed in the grass so green
> So he comforted himself with a simple sheep
> In the grass so green... in the grass so green...

The men shook with laughter. They understood the allusion to Tiu'elen's humble origin. And the nobles clamoured boisterously for a repetition of the verse. Only Intallah frowned and the Marabut covered his eyes with his hand.

Tuhaya rose. 'Who will sing about the march on Tilemsi?' he asked, to prevent any more mocking songs about the bridal pair. He had already heard that some young men wanted to sing about the war with the Kounta.

Two men got up, but their songs were poor. People jeered at them.

But there were also admirers of Tiu'elen among the guests. They called for the song that had been heard for the first time in the Oued Tin Bojeriten, 'The moon shines yellow on Irrarar'. And everyone could tell that it was a song about High Summer by the way they sang.

Red Moon pressed his shoulder harder against Tiu'elen to convey his happiness. But High Summer did not respond. The song had reminded her only too vividly of the man who had composed it for her. She lowered her head.

Next moment, she heard a voice that she would have recognized in a thousand. When she had heard it before, it had been caressing and tender, but now it rang out bitter and incisive to her ear.

Mid-e-Mid had pushed his way through to the front. No one had noticed him before. His head was bare. High Summer could see deep lines round his mouth. His slanting eyes looked swollen. His expression was one of contempt. No, she thought, it cannot be. But it was his voice that cried, 'I shall sing!'

She thought that she would faint. Waves of blood surged to her head. She trembled. She did not hear the cry, 'It is Eliselus! Eliselus is here!' She was deaf and dumb, and turned pale, then red with shame. She bit back her tears, but could not stop a few of them falling. She wanted to speak, to ask him to leave the feast, not to torture her. She wanted to jump up and explain everything to him. But she had to remain silent on the mound of earth, helpless in full view of the assembled guests.

Looking straight at her, Mid-e-Mid began to sing.

> Bahu was my horse.
> Her eyes flashed fire, her muscles were steel.
> She tossed her mane
> Flying over the *reg*.

A murmur went round the listeners, for the name of the horse was unusual.

> Bahu means lies.
> Bahu was my horse.
> Each day at the well
> I drew her fresh water
> And stammered my passion into her ear.
>
> Bahu was my horse.
> Bright was the saddle
> Bright was the blanket
> Brighter still glistened her nostrils and eyes.
> Singing she carried me and my happiness.

They cried 'Eliselus!' They thought that the song was finished. But Mid-e-Mid waved his hand for silence and sang the last verse with his eyes closed.

> Bahu was my horse.
> But when the stallion called from the hills
> Only her tracks were left in the sand.
> The night wind carried their murmurs of love.
> Bahu was my horse.

'What a song!' Intallah muttered. 'This young man sings far better than anyone we have heard so far.'

Then applause rang out over the field and fetched the echo down from the hills. But High Summer's heart was wrung, for she knew who was meant by Bahu. There were two other people who knew as well. Tuhaya was one. Tadast was the other.

Tuhaya was already regretting his haste in telling Tadast of the conversation he had overheard. She would speak out now. But this was not the right time. Mid-e-Mid's song had won the hearts of all who heard it, and they would not let him get hurt. Tadast's words might wound Tiu'elen deeply, but Ajor's wrath would fall on him, Tuhaya.

In his concern, he stood up to go and restrain Tadast and made a sign to her to hold her peace. But she took no notice of him. She stood up and shouted at the top of her voice.

'Men of the Tamashek, do you want to know who is the liar? Do you want to know, Ajor Chageran?'

At her shrill voice, the noise stopped. Every face was turned towards her.

'Do you know who lay in Mid-e-Mid's arms and promised to be his wife? Do you want to know who received his answer – "I am like the *alemos* when the rain revives it after a year of drought!?" Do you know, Ajor, who was ready to enter your tent for the price of two calves?'

The silence was so deep that one could hear the fire crackling.

Tadast pointed to High Summer, who had laid her head on her knee and was sobbing pitifully. 'There! There is Bahu!'

Tuhaya saw that he could not stop things now. Red Moon might drive Tiu'elen away with abuse and disgrace. But he also saw that the newly won trust and friendship which Ajor had given him when the wooing was successful would inevitably be withdrawn. With all the guile for which he was notorious, he tried to turn Ajor's anger on to Mid-e-Mid.

'Tadast's mouth speaks the truth,' he cried out loud. 'As true as I am standing here, I heard those words when I was in the Marabut's camp to carry out the wooing. Men of the Tamashek, Mid-e-Mid has turned the girl's head. Mid-e-Mid is to blame!'

His skinny hand pointed to the singer and all eyes gazed at the dark face of Mid-e-Mid. And still deep silence reigned. But it was the silence that precedes the first lightning of the hurricane.

'Men of the Tamashek!' Tuhaya shouted. 'For Ajor Chageran's sake, I have held my peace so far. But now the jackal has broken into the flock. In the hearing of you all, he has besmirched Tiu'elen's honour. I should be to blame if I did not speak out now.'

His finger still pointed to Mid-e-Mid. His voice quavered, out of control. 'Men of the Tamashek! I hunted your enemy Abu Bakr into the desert, but it was the son of Agassum who came treacherously in the night and killed him with his own sword, and then robbed his corpse. Seize the murderer and hand him over to the Beylik!'

In the confused murmuring which followed, the Marabut's voice rose uncertainly, 'I do not believe you, Tuhaya. My daughter...'

But his words were drowned in the uproar which followed.

With one huge leap, Mid-e-Mid sprang at Tuhaya. He grasped Telchenjert in both hands, and the bronze hilt gleamed above his head.

'That is for my father!'

The sword struck Tuhaya's hands which he held above his head to protect himself. He sank to his knees.

'That is for Tiu'elen's honour!'

The second blow felled the man to the ground.

'And that is for your lying mouth!'

The hilt shattered Tuhaya's skull.

There were cries of horror, but as Mid-e-Mid pushed his way wildly between the rows of guests, no one made the slightest effort to stop him.

Only Tadast screamed, 'Ajor! Avenge Tuhaya's death! Send High Summer back to her father!'

But the singer mounted his camel unmolested, and rode off into the night.

The men thronged round the spot where Tuhaya's body lay. Tadast's voice shrieked above the noise, 'Cowards! Will no one follow the assassin?'

She tried to elbow her way through the crowd of men. But Ramzata pushed her back. 'You are more to blame than Mid-e-Mid. Go! Go to your tent, mischief-maker!'

There was a spontaneous hum of approval from the rest of the Princes. And one distinguished Ibottenate from Tadast's own family said, 'We do not want to get mixed up in this affair. Mid-e-Mid has broken the peace. But that is for Intallah's son to deal with. Not us.'

'Not for you!' fumed Tadast. 'An outlaw slays your friend Tuhaya and you do nothing?'

The men dissented. 'He was never our friend.'

And Ramzata said, 'A man who has no friends will find no avenger. If you have a quarrel with Tiu'elen, that is none of our business. If Mid-e-Mid has a grudge against Red Moon, that is none of our business either. He must look after his own honour...' He grasped Tadast by the shoulder, and turned her round to face the camp. 'Look there...'

They all turned round. They saw Red Moon bend down, take High Summer in his arms and carry her across to her tent. 'That is not the way a husband usually sends his wife back to her parents,' said Ramzata acidly.

Tadast turned pale. Her eyes stared as if she could not get her breath. Speechless, she hurried over to Intallah who was the only person still seated. 'Intallah,' she gasped, 'what are you going to do?'

Slowly the old man replied, 'I shall take counsel with my son.'

Then she knew that she had lost.

She told him to lean on her shoulder, but Intallah did not reply. He took his stick and with tired steps, shuffled towards his tent. He thought, this is for Red Moon to deal with. It is his wedding. And it is his wife. After a while, he thought, Tuhaya knew that he would die. He did not want to do the wooing. He guessed that it would mean his death.

The Princes came to his tent and sat round him.

He asked, 'What would you do in my place?'

They answered, 'Leave it to Red Moon, Amenokal. If he sends his wife away, that is all right. If he keeps her, that is all right too. But it hardly looks as if he is going to send her away...'

Intallah nodded. 'I think as you do. But what shall we do when the Beylik learns that a man was killed and sends his *goumiers* to us?'

Ramzata considered a moment. 'Tuhaya was responsible for Agassum's death. And Agassum's son killed Tuhaya. That was his good right. That is the right of the Tamashek. Why should we give up our rights and help the Beylik to arrest one of our own tribe?'

The other Princes were loud in their agreement. Intallah realized that Tuhaya had not a single friend among them. He was relieved that no one expected him to have the singer brought to justice. But still he argued, 'It could be that my son will want to punish the disturber of the peace...'

They replied, 'We cannot prevent him from doing that. But we will not help him in any way. May Allah grant him wisdom to do what is right.'

'Allah is great.' Intallah was satisfied with this verdict of the Princes. In his long life he had lived through much discord and strife. Now in his old age, he valued peace above all things. And if he went out of his way to avoid disputes, it was not from weakness, but a sign of wisdom, and in the firm belief that Allah alone determines the fate of humanity, and that men are but his tools.

He ordered the servants to make tea and to throw more wood on the fire.

'Tea will do us good,' said the Princes. And there was silence for a while, until someone said, 'It was a splendid feast.' And that was a hint that they preferred not to talk any more about Tuhaya's death.

But the other guests went on talking for a long time about nothing else. And all the discussions ended with, 'Let us wait and see what Ajor Chageran will do.'

And all that night, campfires burned in front of every tent, until the sun rose next morning.

CHAPTER EIGHTEEN

Night Watch

THE LEATHER WALLS of the tent had been lowered and thick mats pushed in front of the entrance. The air lay heavy in the tent. Time could only be measured in heartbeats.

Tiu'elen lay stretched out on a rug. Half-suppressed sobs were the only sounds in the darkness.

Red Moon held her hand.

'I do not believe a word Tadast said,' he told her. 'You must know that I do not believe her.'

He paused, expecting an answer. But no answer came. The hand between his fingers was cold and gave no response.

'Tadast was frightened of losing her influence. That is why she abused you... High Summer, say just one word to me. Say that she was lying... High Summer...'

Lightly he stroked the bones of Tiu'elen's hand and placed his fingers between hers. I should have guessed that Tadast was against our marriage and would try to drive her away, he thought to himself. Her name is more than appropriate – Tadast the stinging mosquito.

He touched High Summer's face. It was wet with tears and her lips quivered.

'Do you not trust me, High Summer?' he asked her gently.

Tiu'elen's voice was muffled. 'You are my husband,' she stammered.

'Yes,' he answered. 'That is true. But it is not enough. You must trust me. Speak to me.'

She clenched her hand. A beetle rustled and a mat creaked.

'Send me back to my father,' she sobbed. 'I cannot stay with you. Tadast spoke the truth.'

She beat the hard floor with her fists.

'The truth, Red Moon... and Mid-e-Mid spoke the truth too...'

With a groan she turned on her side and took her hand away. He felt his heart contract.

'It cannot be,' he murmured.

She whispered wildly, 'If you want me to speak the truth...'

He wiped the sweat from his forehead. 'Go on,' he muttered.

'I did not want to marry you, Red Moon.'

'But you accepted my parting gift when I left your father's tent,' he said. 'You put attar of roses in your hair. Do you not remember?'

'I only did it once. I did not want to offend you. Only once. The flask is still in my saddlebag. It is quite full...'

'But when I sent a wooer for you, you did not reject me.'

'Oh yes I did!' she replied vehemently. 'But I had to obey my father. A girl's feelings are worth nothing among the Tamashek. Her heart beats so lightly that no one troubles to listen to it.'

'I did not know,' he said, disturbed. 'Had you really promised to marry Mid-e-Mid?'

'Do you want the truth?'

He did not dare to answer. He felt that his heart would break with anguish.

She said, 'Since the day that Mid-e-Mid rode up to our tent, I have thought of no one else. He was as poor as I. But his songs were his gifts. How could I have thought of you as a husband, Red Moon?'

He took a deep breath. 'And now? What do you think now, High Summer?'

'Allah ordained that I should be your wife... But I beg you, send me back. I have dishonoured you...'

The silence in the tent was like a wall between them.

'I cannot hold you if you want to go,' he said at last. 'But I implore you now, stay with me...'

Tiu'elen sat upright. 'You want me to stay, Ajor?'

'Yes.' He held his breath. He heard his pulse throbbing.

'It is against all custom,' she whispered. 'After all that has happened...'

'I have already broken the custom by rejecting the daughters of the Princes. Do you think I am frightened of breaking tradition a second time, High Summer?'

'But if I stay, Red Moon, will you trust me? Will you trust a woman who is still thinking of another man?'

She waited for Ajor's answer as a person in dire distress waits for the arrival of help. Her hands lay on her knees, her lips were parted, and her heart beat fast like the beak of a small bird trying to tap its way out of the shell.

Red Moon thought for a long time. He knew that this was the moment of decision for them both. This was the hour in which it would be seen whether a man would snap like a brittle reed, or take new root in the fertile earth. Right and custom, time and place, all heaped the burden of decision on Ajor's shoulders, and it was for Tiu'elen to accept his judgment in all humility.

And in that hour and that night, a young man fought a great battle and won a mighty victory over himself. It was a conquest as outstanding and as painful as the one with which the girl had sacrificed herself to her father's wishes. And in that hour and that night, High Summer and Red Moon were worthy of each other.

'I trust you as I trust my own heart,' said Ajor. 'And I will prove it to you. Take my best camel and go and look for Mid-e-Mid. I offer him my friendship and I want him to sing at my fire again and at all the fires in the Iforas Mountains...'

Then her hands found his shoulders and she put her arms round his neck. And his face drew close to hers, which was still wet with tears.

'You must go to him, High Summer, and tell him that he is under my protection if the Beylik tries to arrest him. Tell him that he is welcome in my tents. And tell him that I am doing this for your sake, High Summer.'

She laid her head on his shoulder and wept. But they were tears of relief. And it was as if Red Moon had unlocked her heart, which had been bolted and barred since the day that Tuhaya had come to her father's tent.

Ajor put a blanket over her, and a cushion under her head. 'I am going now,' he said. 'I feel very happy. I shall sit by my fire and wait for the dawn, and for every new day until you come back to me...'

'*Inchallah*,' said High Summer, 'I am yours.'

A tent pole creaked. The leather folds flapped in the breeze. A pebble crunched under Ajor's sole.

The fire was a dim glow, covered with white ash.

Ajor knelt down and fanned the embers. Blue flames leapt up. He put some wood on. The branches crackled and bent in the heat. Sparks danced in the wind. He tasted the bittersweet smoke. A smile played on his lips.

I do not need the fire, he thought. I am warm within.

In the morning, Ajor's riding camel stood waiting before Tiu'elen's tent. A broad saddle of the type used by women had been placed in position and blue and yellow blankets hung below it. When High Summer came out of her tent, the negroes whispered, 'He must have said, "I do not want to see your face again," and he is sending her back to her father.'

They ran to Tadast to tell her the news that Ajor had decided on a divorce.

Tadast gave a harsh laugh. 'I had better see for myself,' she said.

She threw on a robe and went towards Tiu'elen's tent. Halfway she stopped. She saw Red Moon helping his young wife into the saddle and she saw too, that the camel was not the one that High Summer had brought with her as a dowry, but Ajor's finest mount.

The slaves could not understand why Tadast ordered them to be beaten.

But High Summer rode forth into the morning to find Mid-e-Mid.

The tears of the previous night had left their traces. Her face was pale and cold, her eyes were large and hollow and very clear. Her lips were tightly closed, but the hard lines of stubborn determination which had set about her mouth during recent weeks had melted into a tender seriousness.

She met a shepherd in the Oued of Irrarar, who told her that Mid-e-Mid had spent some hours by his fire before daybreak. Then he had ridden off towards the North.

She thanked him and set out over the plains studded with pale yellow *alemos*, with trees among them here and there, riding towards the black stone hills. A network of cattle tracks straggled over the mountains half covered in sand, and blue and white lizards disappeared at the sound of the camel's hoofs.

High Summer rode on as far as the twin peaks of Tin Badouren, where she planned to spend the night. A boy, driving home his cattle, stopped when he saw her. He greeted her politely and stood gazing inquisitively at her, his hands leaning on his staff, his left foot rubbing the back of his right knee.

'Tell me, have you seen Mid-e-Mid?' asked High Summer, feeling in her bag for some dates.

'He is at the water-hole of Tadjujamet, watering his camel,' said the boy.

'Is it really Mid-e-Mid?'

'Yes, it is,' said the boy positively. 'He is riding a stallion. It is called Inhelumé. I know it. It used to belong to a bandit.'

'That is right,' High Summer confirmed. 'Would you like some dates?'

Without changing his position, the boy held out his hand. High Summer gave him as many dates as his hand could hold. Then he held out the other hand, while he emptied the first ones into his scrip.

'How far is it to Tadjujamet?'

'On that camel,' he said, pointing to Tiu'elen's mount, 'it is two hours. But it will soon be dark. Will you find the way?'

High Summer hesitated.

'If you wait until I have taken the cattle home, I will come back and guide you there.'

'I will wait. But be quick.'

He nodded and ran off, for the herd had already set off along the familiar track without him.

As the sun was setting, an old man came back with the boy. He said, 'I could not believe what the boy told me.'

'Why, what did he tell you?'

'He said, "By the Mountains of Tin Badouren, there sits a woman. She is very beautiful. She is looking for Mid-e-Mid. I am going to show her the way to Tadjujamet." '

'Yes, I am looking for Mid-e-Mid,' she retorted curtly. 'Why is that so remarkable?'

The old man hesitated before replying. 'The boy thought that you might be Tiu'elen.'

'I am Tiu'elen. And now let me go with the boy. I have little time to waste.'

The old man looked at her, shocked. 'Are you not Ajor Chageran's wife?'

'Yes,' said High Summer. 'Of course I am.'

'And you are riding alone to find Agassum's son?'

She nodded.

'You should not do that,' said the old man. 'People will talk. They will gossip about you in the tents. I mean you well. Turn back. I can ride to Mid-e-Mid for you if you like, and give him a message.'

'I must do it myself,' said High Summer. 'No one can do it for me.'

'When a woman is young, her place is in the tent,' said the old man. 'But that is Ajor Chageran's affair...'

'Quite right! It is certainly none of your business,' said Tiu'elen tartly. 'Do not detain me any longer.'

'People will talk,' repeated the old man shaking his head.

'They are talking already,' she answered bitterly. 'What do the people in the tents know of a broken heart?'

But the old man did not understand her.

She climbed into the saddle and threw the reins to the boy. 'Lead the camel,' she called to him.

The old man muttered, 'Youth, youth... What are things coming to?'

And he stumped off, talking crossly to himself, regretting the long detour he had made just to satisfy his curiosity.

The night was warm. The boy ran barefoot and did not seem to feel the thorns and the sharp-edged stones. Once he stopped short and pulled the camel back a few paces.

'What are you doing?' asked High Summer.

'There is a snake on the path. I can hear it hissing.'

He lifted his cudgel and with one blow, broke the snake's back. Then he ran on.

The three water-holes of Tadjujamet lie in a rocky valley, which opens to the south. The boy pointed out Inhelumé's hoofmarks, for High Summer was too high in her saddle to make them out. 'Those are Inhelumé's tracks,' he said. 'His legs are hobbled. Mid-e-Mid must still be here.'

'I shall dismount,' said High Summer. 'Stay with the camel and wait for me.'

The animal knelt down without a sound. High Summer gave the boy some more dates and went on alone.

The sand was cool. The earth was strewn with camel droppings. She could feel them hard beneath the thin soles of her sandals. The first two water holes were covered with thorny twigs. The third was open. But there was no one there.

To the right of the rocks was a tall tree with bare branches. She ran towards it. There she found Mid-e-Mid stretched out on a blanket, his head resting on his saddle. He heard footsteps and jumped up.

'Who is there?' he called.

'It is only a girl,' she replied.

He recognized her voice.

'High Summer?' he asked incredulously.

'I followed you, Mid-e-Mid.'

'You might have spared yourself the journey. A promise can only be broken once.'

She stood before him, a slender shadow, her eyes dark in her ivory face.

'You must listen to me,' she pleaded.

'I have heard all I want to hear. Tadast has a very loud voice, and I am not deaf.'

'Oh, Mid-e-Mid, you do not know everything.'

'What is there still to learn? That the herds of the Amenokal are larger than mine? That a woman's word is like the smile of a scorpion before it stings? I know it all... I know it only too well. Go away, Tiu'elen.'

She said, 'I can weep no more. I have wept all the tears I had since the day that Tuhaya came to my father's tent...'

'Your tears mean nothing to me now. I can understand that it is better to marry the Amenokal than to be a poor man's wife.'

'Mid-e-Mid!' she cried.

But he went on implacably. 'But why did you lie to me? Why did you not tell me that Red Moon held your promise long before I came? And why did you hide the fact that Tuhaya was in your camp? Go away, Tiu'elen. Your words are like the wind blowing in one side of the tent and out at the other.'

She shivered.

He said, 'If you are cold, I will light a fire. Sit down on the blanket. But I will not sit with you.'

'Ajor has more patience than you,' she said. 'I do not need your fire. I only want you to listen to me.'

'Be quick, then.'

'It was my father's wish to make me Ajor's wife. I knew nothing about it when we talked. Believe me.'

'Go on,' he retorted. 'A few more lies are neither here nor there.'

She sobbed and pressed her hands to her breast. 'Then believe that it was the will of Allah. I swear to you that I did not know why Tuhaya had come to our tents. I did not even know he was there...'

'And why did you not tell your father what we had promised each other?'

'He would not listen to me. The voice of a girl carries no weight against that of her parents,' she answered.

He said nothing and she plucked up courage. 'Mid-e-Mid, until last night, I still belonged to you...'

'Oh! And yet you told Tuhaya the very words which I spoke to you alone.'

'No. He was eavesdropping and overheard us. And he told Tadast...'

'Perhaps,' he said. 'But it makes no difference. Why did you come here?'

She could not read his face, for no starlight fell between the boughs of the tree. But she sensed that his voice had softened a little.

'I am Ajor's wife,' she said, 'and he has not sent me home although he knows everything. He sent me to find you.'

'But why?' He was astonished.

'He does not want you to go into hiding. He asks you to be his friend for my sake. You can seek shelter in his tent, and he will help you against the Beylik.'

'I do not need him.'

'Then take his friendship,' she said. 'He gives it freely, without condition.'

'I shall think it over,' said Mid-e-Mid cautiously.

'But I have also come to ask something else of you. Come back to the tribe, the Tamashek. Come back and sing in our tents. Red Moon and I both ask you. Sing for us again. Allah was against our love. He will not oppose our friendship. I ask you, Mid-e-Mid.'

For a long time, Mid-e-Mid said nothing, but he looked into Tiu'elen's face and he saw how the night wind stirred her robes.

At last he blurted out, 'You must understand that it is a hard thing you are asking of me, but...'

'You will do it?'

'If you wish it,' he said softly. 'But give me time. I must have time. I need the free air of the mountains to think everything out. Perhaps it is for the best that things have turned out like this. Perhaps Allah wanted to tell me that it would be wrong to tie myself to a wife in a tent. Perhaps it is the will of Allah.'

'Take what time you need. But do come back. Be our friend, Mid-e-Mid.'

He said, 'I think that one day I may be able to sing again, now that you have come to me. I feel it. When my songs come back, I shall return to your tent, Tiu'elen. But give me time.'

'I am Ajor's wife,' she said, 'and I ride his finest camel. I shall give it to you, and you must give him Inhelumé in return.'

'You ask much, High Summer.'

She said, 'I have given much. But now let everyone see that we are friends. In all the clans they shall know that Mid-e-Mid rides Ajor's camel and that Ajor rides Inhelumé. That is the last thing I shall ask.'

Mid-e-Mid stepped out of the shadow of the tree and took her hand.

'Come,' he said. 'Let us find Inhelumé. He must be grazing here somewhere among the rocks.'

They went in silence side by side. The dry grass crackled beneath their feet and the warm wind lifted their hair. The stars shone with a soft blue light.

CHAPTER NINETEEN

A Song for Kalil

TIN ZA'UZATEN IS AN OUTPOST of life in the wastes of the Sahara Desert. It is the boundary between the Iforas Mountains and the Ahaggar Mountains, between the world of herdsmen and the world of caravans, between pasture and wilderness, at the crossroads of tracks and paths.

The *oued* was empty except for a swarm of grey birds twittering in the wet sand near the water hole. They flew into the air and swirled noisily into the tamarisk tree. There they settled, scolding.

'Ho there, Kalil!' called Mid-e-Mid. 'Where are you?'

The fool came out from under a tree. 'Mid-e-Mid ag Agassum! Kalil did not recognize you.' He pulled a face of apology.

'Have I changed?'

'That is so. You have a different camel.'

'So I have. I had forgotten about that.'

'Give me some tobacco,' said the fool.

Mid-e-Mid gave him a handful and dismounted. 'Water my camel, Kalil. It is thirsty.'

Kalil did as he was bid, but his eyes kept returning to Mid-e-Mid, whenever he could take them off the job in hand.

'It is not the camel,' he said at last.

'What do you mean, Kalil?'

' ...that makes you seem strange.'

'Well then, what is it? Are my clothes different? Or is it something else?'

The fool clicked his tongue and snapped his fingers.

'No – your heart is bigger.' He tapped his breast with his thumb. 'Bigger than your head.'

He laughed, pleased with himself. 'Kalil sees everything. Kalil knows everything.'

'Yes,' said Mid-e-Mid. 'You know many things. It is a pity that you cannot always say what you mean properly.'

'Oh,' said Kalil. 'Kalil can say everything. Your heart was sick. That is why it stretched. So!' He spread his arms out wide. 'Now it is big. If you tear it out of your breast, you will be as happy as a donkey at the well.'

'I was indeed an ass. But the water I drank was as bitter as the juice of the *tagilit* fruit.'

'What beautiful things you say, Mid-e-Mid,' crooned the fool. 'Beautiful, beautiful, beautiful. You are the *Marabut* for sad hearts, a bringer of happiness. You are an amulet...' He laughed aloud, and as he laughed, he wriggled first his left shoulder and then his right, as if he had an itch under his arms.

'Sing me a song. Just a little song...'

'I have no songs left,' said Mid-e-Mid. 'I cannot think of any.'

The fool took hold of his wrists and stepping backwards, he started pulling him towards the edge of the sand.

'Let me go,' said Mid-e-Mid impatiently. 'You have some crazy idea in your head.'

'Kalil will show you something... Just come. Come quickly. Very quickly.'

He let go of Mid-e-Mid's arms and ran on. Beneath the tamarisk tree he stopped. 'Come, Mid-e-Mid, Greatheart! Come!' He crooked his forefinger and beckoned.

Reluctantly Mid-e-Mid followed. 'Now what do you want? I can see nothing.'

He had reached the dense shade of the tree.

Kalil pointed to the ground. 'Lie there, Greatheart. Stretch yourself out, like a dead louse, like a calf skin spread out to dry.'

'Oh no!' said Mid-e-Mid. 'I see it now. You will do me some mischief. You are just a fool, and I should be one too if I let you play tricks on me. I must be off.'

217

Kalil looked at him lovingly, his prominent red-rimmed eyes widened, and one could see the dark blue pupils.

'Look up, Mid-e-Mid!'

Mid-e-Mid looked up into the green boughs. The small birds perched there were preening their feathers and pecking and chirping. He saw the hollow casing of brown earth which the ants build and stick to the bark to shield their sensitive bodies from the light. He saw the dark red resin oozing from the tree and he heard the humming of the bees, nesting in the hollow of the trunk. He smelt the pungent odour of the goats' droppings and between the highest branches he could see the blue sky and fleecy white clouds sailing past, as if they were in a hurry to reach a well before nightfall. He felt the softness of the dry sand, and he stretched himself out luxuriously to rest.

'Can you sing now, Greatheart?' whispered the fool. 'Can you sing for Kalil? A little song, just a little song for Kalil?'

Mid-e-Mid replied, 'Wait a while. Perhaps it will come soon.'

The fool sat down beside him, buried his hands in his lap and tried to control his heavy breathing.

Presently Mid-e-Mid said, 'Now listen, Kalil.'

The fool put his head on one side and listened.

And Mid-e-Mid sang.

> When the grass springs in the hills
> And the yellow *tamat* blossoms
> Sway in the wind to lure the bees.
>
> When the fleece of newborn lambs
> Glistens between the thorny shrubs,
>
> When the clear call of the shepherds
> And the neighing of white horses
> Echo from the rocky valleys,
>
> Who remembers the tornado
> Crashing thunder, blaze of lightning
> Gushing torrents, scourging raindrops?

> All are long ago forgotten,
> And the girls go riding, laughing,
> Riding on their mouse-grey donkeys,
> Laughing, riding to the well
> And cup the water in their hands.
>
> In the camp the camels dancing
> Spin a circle round the women.
> Sun! Oh, sun! Our life, our sister,
> Spin a circle round our hearts!

'Ayé!' cried the fool. 'How you sing, Mid-e-Mid!'

> Sun! Oh sun! Our life, our sister
> Spin a circle round our hearts.

And he began to sing the song in his shrill voice, now humming, now saying the words, hopping backwards and forwards and waving his arms, like a young vulture, hovering on the brink of its first flight from the eyrie.

Mid-e-Mid watched him with a smile and made his way back to his camel which was nibbling at the branches of the tamarisk tree.

'*Bismillah*, Kalil,' he called. 'I am glad that you are happy.'

'Ayé, *bismillah*. Bringer of happiness, Eliselus the Magician, *bismillah!*'

And he turned and danced like the crested crane when he woos his mate.

Mid-e-Mid mounted his camel and rode slowly through the *oued*. When he turned back, he could see the fool tirelessly hopping and jumping for joy, and he could hear his hoarse, ugly voice still singing,

> Sun! Oh sun! Our life, our sister
> Spin a circle round our hearts!

Look at that now, he thought. There is a poor wretched fool, tormented by evil spirits, yet I can move his heart. I can make him dance and jump for joy, and that simply by singing a song to him.

Hamdullillah, he thought. At least I am good for something, even if it is only to make fools happy or those in despair, the sad, the yearning or people in love. And he thought, what need have I of tent and herds if I can do all this? I have something better to do than milking goats and tending cows. I must make people happier, the girls at the well and the men in the tents, the fool in his helplessness and the Amenokal, the loneliest of men. And High Summer... she needs me too, just as I needed her to make me sing again... *hamdullillah*.

Mid-e-Mid rode to his tent and told Amadou and Dangi that they could go free. He gave them calves and a camel, and let them go where they wanted. He restored to their owners the cattle which Abu Bakr had stolen or he gave them away. He kept back only one pretty little grey donkey. That was for his mother.

He himself, however, resumed his wandering life again. He stayed a whole year in the North, where the mountains are black and purple and the plains are yellow with *alemos*. But his songs travelled far and wide from mouth to mouth and from tent to tent. They hummed round the campfires in the evening, while the millet cooked in its soot-blackened cauldron. They soared from the lips of sunburnt shepherds as they tarried with their flocks during the heat of the day in the meagre shade of the acacia trees. The women sang them as they pounded the brittle grey salt in wooden mortars, and it crumbled into fragments beneath the blows of their pestles.

Mid-e-Mid sang in the North. And the wind itself seemed to carry his songs into the green South, to the edge of the Valley of Tilemsi and into the Tamesna desert.

Red Moon exercised his protection over him when the Beylik tried to arrest him, for Tuhaya's death was not forgotten. High Summer called her first son Ahmed, and hung a lark's feather round his neck, so that he, too, should be a singer like Eliselus. And when the baby kicked and crowed on her lap, she said, 'He has the strength of his father, Ajor, and he has his forehead too. But he has Mid-e-Mid's beautiful voice.'

And because the women round her nodded, she believed it herself. Only Takammart said, 'He squawks like a cockerel, and has as many teeth as my father Intallah, and he has none at all.'

But people often say things they do not believe themselves, and so High Summer took not the slightest notice.

Afterword

No OTHER BOOK about the Sahara and its mysterious blue-veiled nomadic inhabitants captures the spirit of the place like this factual fable written in 1957. I first read the award winning Stella Humphries' fluent translation from the German soon after it was published in London by Methuen in 1960 and it sent me off to the heart of the Sahara, where I have travelled with the Tuareg many times since.

There are several histories and studies of these fascinating people, notably Jeremy Keenan's *The Tuareg* and the massive two volume study *The Pastoral Tuareg* by Johannes and Ida Nicolaisen, but none transports the reader into their lives as well as this touching children's love story.

Herbert Kaufmann travelled by camel a thousand miles through the central Sahara searching for prehistoric rock art, accompanied by two Tuareg. In those days most of the half million or so Tuareg still lived nomadic lives, the women tending the sheep and goats while the men made long journeys by camel to trade or to raid. The countries in which they lived, having been arbitrarily created by the colonial powers, were still under French rule. There was enough grazing to support their harsh lifestyle and although there was persistent friction as alien laws were imposed on them, life was generally good. Soon things were to change radically. The countries became independent and suddenly the Tuareg, the feared masters of the desert, who despised the black races of the south, found themselves outnumbered and outvoted by new masters. They rebelled. At the same time, a series of the worst droughts ever to be inflicted on that already parched region meant that most of their flocks died and most of the people had to flee to refugee camps. It was a terrible time, which lasted for over thirty years.

Now, however, things are at last a little better. Most Tuareg are
settled in the towns around the desert, but some have returned to
their traditional ways and if, like me, you are lucky enough to
travel with them, you will find a life being led very similar to that
described so beautifully in *Red Moon and High Summer*.

The story is a true one, based on real people and real events.
The same characters still travel with intense pride through the
land they love. The women are still searingly beautiful and the
men noble and honourable, invisible behind the veils they wear to
conceal all but their eyes. Kelakua, my oldest friend and
contemporary, with whom I have wandered the remotest regions
of the Aïr Mountains in Niger, has never let me see his mouth. It
is never exposed to women or those to whom he is not related.
But he is of the old school and many Tuareg men now go
unveiled.

Just as there were fifty years ago, there are still bandits roaming
the country, living off their wits and beyond the law. On a long
camel journey of forty days and forty nights, which I made
recently with Kelakua, we saw no signs whatever of the modern
world; just a handful of nomadic families with their goats and an
occasional fierce warrior, who would share our camp for a night
and then disappear like a wraith. On one of our last days, we
stopped to water our camels at a rare well near the western side of
the mountains. Beyond lay open desert for four hundred
kilometres stretching far away to the border of Mali and beyond
that to the foothills of the Iforas Mountains, where this book is
set. To our amazement, for the first time for nearly six weeks, we
heard the sound of a vehicle and in a cloud of dust a heavily
loaded Toyota Landcruiser roared up. Out jumped a figure who
could have been Abu Bakr. Swaggering and arrogant, he strode
towards us. He wore a blue boiler suit fastened with a wide
leather belt instead of the usual Tuareg robes, but his head was
wrapped in an indigo turban and veil. Kelakua and he greeted
each other cautiously, touching hands repeatedly and exchanging
the prolonged formal greetings. Suddenly, they embraced and
started laughing. I was introduced. 'This is Lussian' I was told.

'He is a famous rebel and smuggler. He has just been across to the Libyan border with a cargo of contraband and now he is returning to the Iforas. We are cousins, as my people came from there a long time ago.' Lussian grasped my hand and assured me that, as a friend of Kelakua's, I would always be welcome in the Iforas. Today it is a wild and unruly place, which has never accepted foreign domination. They live mostly from smuggling cigarettes and this illegal trade is, it seems, now one of the biggest operations of its sort in the world. Cheap tobacco is dumped by the big manufacturers on the coast of West Africa and then transported overland to Algeria and Libya. It is a dangerous but highly lucrative business.

Music, too, still plays a significant part in the Tuareg way of life. In fact, it is becoming much more important. It was always a means of sharing ideas and emotions between remote peoples, who only met rarely, and there were always famous singers like Mid-e-Mid, who not only sang beautifully but also had significant and sometimes rebellious messages to impart. Today, Tuareg music has flowered to incorporate modern rhythms and perceptions. It is being listened to and studied increasingly outside Africa and, as with reggae, part of the attraction is its rebellious content. For the Tuareg, this is immediate and highly relevant; for the new global fans, it makes the music exciting and alive. The *Tindé* described in *Red Moon and High Summer* has been a feature of the Tuareg calendar for centuries. It was an occasion to settle disputes, discuss politics – and to make music. For the last six years, at a remote oasis far out in the desert to the north-west of Timbuctoo, right next to the Iforas Mountains, an amazing international Festival in the Desert has been taking place. Some of the greatest modern African groups and an increasing number of international performers from Europe and America have made their way there. And, of course, the stars are the Tuareg hosts themselves. It is still very much their event, and the festivities include traditional singing, dancing, swordplay, camel races and exhibits of their colourful and elegant leather and silver work. The resultant recordings are getting rave reviews.

In this unexpected, but entirely logical, way their music is being heard far beyond their rocky hills and dried up wadis. The pure voices of Mid-e-Mid's successors are continuing his tradition on the very spot where he sang for High Summer. There is no better way to set the scene than to read this book.

Robin Hanbury-Tenison, 2006

The Tamashek People

Why not 'The Tuareg'?

The people in this story are generally called the Tuareg by Europeans. Scholars do not agree about the precise meaning of this Arabic word, but it is one with a slur attached to it, and probably means 'The Abandoned of God'. The proper name for this desert people is the Tamashek, and that is what they call themselves.

Who they are, and where they live

The Tamashek are unquestionably one of the white races, but their origins are not known. There are roughly five hundred thousand of them living in the mountainous regions of the Central Sahara, which is part of French West Africa. They are divided into several communities with differing customs and dialects, and the largest and most famous tribe is the Ulliminden who live by the River Niger. They are the fierce men of the blue veils who feature in so many stories of the Foreign Legion, although even they have been pacified by now.

The area in which this story takes place is the Iforas Mountains (Adrar des Iforas), an area roughly half the size of France with sixteen thousand inhabitants. The French have done much for the region by building roads and sinking wells and stopping the feuds and slave raids which were common. In recent years, oil has been struck, and this may prove of great importance in a country so poor in natural resources.

Terrain, climate and occupation

The territory is a rocky massif, with high plateaux, deep ravines, and broad *oueds*. The climate is hot and dry, with less than five inches of rain in an average year. In summer, the shade temperature may be over one hundred and ten degrees but the winter is much cooler, and the nights can be bitterly cold with icy winds.

There is no cultivation of crops, and the breeding of livestock is virtually the only industry. The animals feed on the natural vegetation, desert grasses, thorny shrubs, and several varieties of acacia tree. There is not enough water to breed horses, but there are cattle, sheep and goats, as well as the ubiquitous donkey. Pride of place, however, is given to camels, and they are indispensable to the Tamashek way of living. Because the attitude of the Tamashek to their pedigree camels is rather like that of Europeans to thoroughbred horses, we have called the male and female camels 'stallion' and 'mare' in this book, since there is no authoritative term in general use in English, and the alternatives, 'bull' and 'cow', did not sound appropriate.

Daily life

Being nomads, the Tamashek live in tents, which are made of leather, are copper-red in colour, squarish in shape, and supported by six or eight tent poles, elaborately carved. In the rainy season, they roll up the leather tents out of harm's way and live in barrel-shaped huts of straw and twigs. Apart from livestock, their possessions in terms of worldly goods are virtually non-existent.

The Tamashek only eat meat on feast days, and their chief food is milk, whether from camels, cows, sheep or goats. The staple cereals are millet and rice. They drink tea when they can, and it is always a little ceremony, as well as a means of quenching thirst. Coffee is far too dear for the majority, who rely on milk and water for the most part. Alcohol, even millet or maize beer, is unknown, and the only 'vice' is tobacco chewing, a habit common to men, women and children too.

Social organization

The social organization of the Tamashek is highly complex and varies from region to region. There are tribes which owe allegiance to a Prince or Chieftain, loose confederations of tribes under an *Amenokal* or King, and clans within the tribes. Woven into this is a caste system, broadly classified as 'nobles' and 'vassals'. In some areas, the castes are strictly hereditary. In others, intermarriage is not uncommon.

The nobles can best be compared with the Robber Barons of medieval Europe. War and pillage was their trade. They exercised 'protection' over their vassals from other marauding tribes, and for this they used to demand tribute. The French prohibited slave raids and abolished slavery, and the circumstances of the nobles deteriorated rapidly, unaccustomed as they were to doing their own work. It was difficult to change the attitude of centuries, that work was not only distasteful but dishonourable too, and those who failed to adapt themselves found themselves much poorer than their own vassals.

The serfs or vassals are almost exclusively herdsmen, and although they are physically indistinguishable from the nobility, they tend to keep themselves apart and to view the aristocracy with distrust. Now that the custom of tribute has practically lapsed, serfdom has gone with it, and the term 'vassal' is becoming a misnomer.

The artisans of the community are the so-called smiths. They are unique among black-skinned races in that they have almond eyes, well-cut features and straight noses. They seldom intermarry with the Tamashek, who despise them, despite their skills. No one knows their racial origin, and it is one of the ethnological puzzles of the region.

Although slavery has been abolished on paper, many of the negroes captured on slave raids in the old days have remained with their masters as so-called servants, content to work for a place in the tent and their keep. Their children inherit their status, and on the whole they are well treated and looked after when they are too old to work.

Religion, language and literature

The Tamashek are Mohammedans, although they are somewhat lax in their observance, and women enjoy much greater freedom and respect than they do in most other Moslem communities.

Their language is one of the Berber tongues, and literacy is more common among the women than the men. The Tamashek literature consists largely of songs and poems, and some of their most famous poets have been women. In the evenings, people sit round the campfires singing love songs, and ballads about heroic deeds and famous camels. These are genuine folksongs and verses are added as they are carried from mouth to mouth. One is reminded of the troubadours and ballad-mongers of the Middle Ages, and the ahal has some affinity with the medieval Courts of Love.

In 1903 the Abbé de Foucauld went to live among the Tamashek, and he it was who first recorded their language and collected their literature. His name is still remembered with gratitude for the benefits he brought, but in 1916 at a time of great political unrest, he was assassinated by a band of Tamashek who were never identified.

The characters in this story

There are still brigands like Abu Bakr, hiding out in the barely accessible mountains, and there are still girls like High Summer in the Adrar des Iforas. As for Mid-e-Mid, if you think he sounds very young for his role, the author assures us that he has made him much older than he was for the purpose of this story. When it was written, the real Mid-e-Mid was only twelve, yet his songs had made him as famous among his people as, say, the President is in the United States. Some of the songs in the book are his work, and have been taken down in the original on a tape-recorder.

Glossary

A note on pronunciation and spelling

The pronunciation of these words can only be indicated approximately as the Tifinagh alphabet does not correspond precisely with ours. The transliterations below are as near phonetic as possible. Where they vary from spellings used by other authorities, the difference may be due to dialect. The letter *g* is always hard; the letter *j* is pronounced like *y*; for example *Ajor* is pronounced *Ayor*.

Abatal	The Tamashek way of cooking the stomach and intestines of a slaughtered animal without using a cooking vessel or water.
Adjar	A common thorn tree with white and yellow blossoms and tough oval leaves.
Adrar	Mountain country.
Affasso	Desert grass, good camel fodder.
Ahal	A lively social gathering, where the eligible bachelors of the community attend, songs are sung and composed and the women play the *amzad*. Sometimes rivalry leads to quarrelling and duels.
Ajor	Moon or month. Ajor Chageran means Red Moon.
Aleik essalam	Peace be with you, the customary reply to the greeting *Salam aleikum*.
Allahu akbar	God is great.
Alemos	Desert grass, good camel fodder.
Amenehaya	The name of a popular song sung in the Iforas Mountains.

Amenokal	The leader of a loose confederation of Tamashek tribes, usually translated as King. It means literally 'The Owner of the Land'.
Amzad	Violin made of goatskin, with one single horsehair string.
Ayé	Look at that! Listen to that!
Balek	Watch out! Look out!
Beylik	The government; used in this book in the specific sense of the French colonial administration or Governor.
Bismillah	God be with you! In God's name!
Burnouse	a long hooded cloak worn by Arabs and Moors
Bussaadi	A dagger. Literally, 'I bring happiness' and hence, 'I send to Paradise!'
Cram-cram	A species of grass with tiny husks covered with barbed prickles which hook into the skin and are most difficult and painful to remove. Inside the husks are seeds which are ground into flour when other grain is scarce.
Djir-djir	Desert plant, rich in water, important camel fodder.
Elhamdullillah(i)	Thank God.
Eliselus	Mid-e-Mid's nickname. It is virtually untranslatable, but means roughly someone who is always merry, happy-go-lucky, 'blithe spirit'.
Goumier	Native born African soldier in the French army.
Had	Juicy green tufted grass, good camel fodder.
Hamdullillah	Thank God.
Iludjan	The dance of the camels, as described in the story.
Imochar	One of the tribes of the Ulliminden, notorious for their ruthless fighting.
Inchallah	Please God.
Inhelumé	The name of a famous camel. Literally, the ropes which secure packs to the camel's back.
Kounta	Important tribe of nomads, of Arab descent,

232

	who occupy the area near Bourem by the Niger. They breed cattle and camels.
Marabut	A holy man
Oued	The same as 'wadi' in North Africa. The dried-up bed of a river or watercourse, which is only filled after a tornado. Many are so broad that one cannot see the opposite bank.
Reg	Expanse of desert covered with hard sand and grit.
Salam aleikum	Peace be with you, the customary greeting of the Tamashek.
Suras	Verses or chapters from the Koran.
Tadast	A woman's name which also means mosquito.
Tagilit	A wild melon with juice more bitter than quinine.
Takammart	A woman's name which means literally 'Cheese from fresh milk.'
Talha	A thorny acacia tree.
Tallit	The moon, an alternative word to Ajor.
Tamat	A flowering acacia with a strong scent.
Teborak	A thorn tree with small bitter fruits.
Tifinagh	The script of the Tamashek language, mainly written from right to left, but can be reversed or even written in spirals! There are no vowels, eg, Tamashek would be Tmshk.
Tindé	Tamashek feast where there are tournaments, displays of riding and drum music.
Tiu'elen	A woman's name, which means literally the hottest time of the year, here translated as High Summer.
Ulliminden	Numerically the most important of the Tamashek confederations who live near the Niger. Formerly they were warlike and greatly feared.

The following names are some of the Tamashek tribes and clans mentioned in the story: *Ibottenaten*; *Idnan*; *Iforgumessen*; *Kel Ahenet*; *Kel Effele*; *Kel Telabit*; *Tarat-Mellet*.

ELAND

61 Exmouth Market, London EC1R 4QL
Tel: 020 7833 0762   Fax: 020 7833 4434
Email: info@travelbooks.co.uk

Eland was started in 1982 to revive great travel books that had fallen out of print. Although the list has diversified into biography and fiction, it is united by a quest to define the spirit of place. These are books for travellers, and for readers who aspire to explore the world but who are also content to travel in their own minds. Eland books open out our understanding of other cultures, interpret the unknown and reveal different environments as well as celebrating the humour and occasional horrors of travel.

All our books are printed on fine, pliable, cream-coloured paper. Most are still gathered in sections by our printer and sewn as well as glued, almost unheard of for a paperback book these days. This gives larger margins in the gutter, as well as making the books stronger.

We take immense trouble to select only the most readable books and therefore many readers collect the entire series. If you haven't liked an Eland title, please send it back to us saying why you disliked it and we will refund the purchase price.

You will find a very brief description of all our books on the following pages. Extracts from each and every one of them can be read on our website, at www.travelbooks.co.uk. If you would like a free copy of our catalogue, please telephone, email or write to us.

ELAND

'One of the very best travel lists' WILLIAM DALRYMPLE

Travels into the Interior of Africa
MUNGO PARK
The first – and still the best – European record of west-African exploration

Lighthouse
TONY PARKER
Britain's lighthouse keepers, in their own words

The People of Providence
TONY PARKER
A London housing estate and some of its inhabitants

Begums, Thugs & White Mughals
FANNY PARKES
William Dalrymple edits and introduces his favourite Indian travel book

The Last Time I Saw Paris
ELLIOT PAUL
One street, its loves and loathings, set against the passionate politics of inter-war Paris

Rites
VICTOR PERERA
A Jewish childhood in Guatemala

A Cure for Serpents
THE DUKE OF PIRAJNO
An Italian doctor and his bedouin patients, Libyan sheikhs and Tuareg mistress in the 1920s

Nunaga
DUNCAN PRYDE
Ten years among the Eskimos: love, hunting, fur-trading, heroic dog-treks

A Funny Old Quist
EVAN ROGERS
A gamekeeper's passionate evocation of a now vanished English rural lifestyle

Meetings with Remarkable Muslims
ED. ROGERSON & BARING
A collection of contemporary travel writing that celebrates cultural difference and the Islamic World

Marrakesh: through writers' eyes
ED. ROGERSON & LAVINGTON
A selection of the best travel writing on Marrakesh: a guidebook for the mind

Living Poor
MORITZ THOMSEN
An American's encounter with poverty in Ecuador

Hermit of Peking
HUGH TREVOR-ROPER
The hidden life of the scholar Sir Edmund Backhouse

The Law
ROGER VAILLAND
The harsh game of life played in the taverns of southern Italy

The Road to Nab End
WILLIAM WOODRUFF
The best-selling story of poverty and survival in a Lancashire mill town

The Village in the Jungle
LEONARD WOOLF
A dark novel of a native village struggling to survive in the jungle of Ceylon

Death's Other Kingdom
GAMEL WOOLSEY
The tragic arrival of civil war in an Andalucian village in 1936

The Ginger Tree
OSWALD WYND
A Scotswoman's love and survival in early-twentieth-century Japan